THE SECOND LIFE OF ARTHUR BLADE

RICHARD DRUMMER

Copyright © 2022 by Richard Drummer

Re-edited 4/2023

All rights reserved.

No part of this book may be reproduced in any form or by any electronic or mechanical means, including information storage and retrieval systems, without written permission from the author, except for the use of brief quotations in a book review.

This book is a work of fiction. Any references to historical events, real people, or real places are used fictitiously. Other names, characters, places, and events are the product of the author's imagination, and any resemblance to actual events or places or persons, living or dead, is entirely coincidental.

Cover artwork by Damonza

 Created with Vellum

*This book is dedicated to my daughters,
Deena, Devon, and Carly.
They continue to amaze me every day
and I couldn't be more proud.
Crazy Noodle, Knucklehead, and Screwball,
you are my heroes.*

ONE
THREAT LEVEL: RED

They know! How in the hell could they possibly know?

The driver drummed his fingers nervously on the wheel as he stared through the rearview mirror. A bead of sweat dripped down his nose and soaked into the cigarette that hung trembling from his lips.

A trio of inspectors had gathered around the shipping container, his shipping container. As he watched, another inspector and a security guard were flagged over to join them. This couldn't be happening! Everything had been arranged. That steel box should have sailed right through port customs, loaded onto his truck, and been halfway to its destination by now. He cursed under his breath as he thought about the son of a bitch who was paid a healthy sum to guarantee there would be no hangups.

The driver was thinking of calling in to explain the problem when yet another inspector arrived with a pair of cutters. He split the security seal, pulled the doors back, and all six men entered the container.

Panic-stricken, the driver looked around and decided to make a run for it while he still had the chance. His life was over if they caught him with this deadly cargo. He threw the cigarette butt out the window and reached for the gearshift when he heard laughter. The inspectors ambled out, chuckling and pointing back at the contents.

"My kids have no clue how much fun we used to have playing some of those pinball games," he overheard one of them say.

Another slapped him on the back. "Got some real classics in there. Some of my favorites. Great condition, too."

"Somebody has a lot of money for their game room. I'd love to have just one of those."

The lead inspector pulled the doors shut and crimped on a new seal. "Some people have all the fun," he said, waving over a lift truck.

Taking a relieved breath, the driver watched as the inspectors split up and headed away.

His container was hoisted high, and the lift operator motioned for him to pull under, then lowered the container onto the flatbed trailer. Once it was in place, the driver scrambled out and secured the retaining straps. All of these additional delays added another forty-five minutes and rush hour traffic to the two-hour trip.

Finally, he was waved ahead and drove toward the port check-out gate, the last hurdle. He handed his papers down to the guard, who gave them the briefest of glances before passing them back and waving him through.

The driver turned onto the highway, pulled out his phone, and thumbed a speed dial number.

"Da," the voice replied.

"I will be late. There was a delay at the port."

There was an uncomfortable silence before the man grunted and disconnected.

"Arrogant people," the driver mumbled, tossing the phone

to the passenger seat. Then again, this group was not known for their politeness.

"Don't ask questions, but don't get caught," his cousin had cautioned months ago when introducing him to the organization. "The money flows so long as you keep your mouth shut and just drive."

He'd stuck to the rules and enjoyed the large cash payouts. That was, until this shipment. Even his cousin had seemed unusually nervous when explaining the details and handing him a small plastic box with a red button. "Push this if you are stopped," he was told. The driver assumed the button would detonate explosives inside the container. He also had no doubt that the truck cab would go up with it. The money was good but not worth dying over, and he had no intention of getting caught or pushing the damned button.

Arthur Blade sat watching the video feed from a security camera overlooking the gates to Port Jersey Boulevard. Four container trucks approached, and he eyed the manifests for each. All were forgeries. That much was a given. But stopping the wrong one at this point would tip off the others and nudge them into defensive mode. Only scant details of their backup plan were known, but it was enough to avoid it at all costs.

Blade keyed the talk button on his handheld radio. "Logan, tell me what you see?"

Two agents worked on the ground with Blade, monitoring every truck as they crept toward the open road of I-78.

Garret Logan sat in a rusty pickup truck facing the intersection at Pulaski Lane. He clicked off multiple shots through a telephoto lens as the container trucks rolled toward him. "I don't see the mark on any of these," he answered. "Are we sure about this?"

"Stay put and keep watching," Blade advised. "Piper, can you get a better view?"

The second agent sat perched on a rooftop, controlling a drone hovering above the first truck, manipulating the tiny craft to photograph the rusty container's serial numbers. "I can't drop any lower without being seen." He had a thought and sent the drone over the cab of the second truck as he photographed the back of the first. "I'm sending images over now. Still not seeing our marker on this one. I'll go back and read the others again."

"Bloody hell!" Blade hissed. "Hold your positions until I get back to you." He pulled a phone from his jacket pocket and dialed the safe house. "It's Blade. Give me Folozchev."

A moment later, he was greeted by the deep, cigarette-strained Russian voice of Vladimir Folozchev. "Good morning, Mr. Blade. What for can I help you?"

"Vladimir, none of the shipping containers have the marking you told us about. Time is tight. I need you to tell me exactly what I'm looking for. Which box is it?"

Folozchev answered quickly. "This is information I am given. Is possible you are looking at wrong containers?"

"Only four boxes originated from Murmansk. If it's not one of these, then it wasn't on this ship. I need to know which one it is, and I need to know now."

"Well, is difficult to say. My source give only what I telling you. I have no more than this to share."

Blade ended the call and cupped one hand over his mouth, the fingers of the other drumming loudly on the Langley office desktop.

Reliable intel, my ass!

He was about to contact his field agents again but thought better of it and, instead, dialed the number for another safe house. A select few within the CIA knew this one. A familiar voice answered, "Blade, what do you need?"

"Let me speak with Uri."

A moment later, an older Russian responded in perfect English. "I hope this is not your idea of American hospitality, Mr. Blade."

Since his defection a year earlier, Uri Greggenkoff was treated as more of an enemy combatant than a valuable asset. Don Colson, the CIA director, suspected Greggenkoff of being a double agent and had set about to break him. Following the torturous questioning and inhumane living conditions, he was finally allowed basic comforts and adequate food. The company largely ignored the information he supplied, but Blade considered every word, comparing them to those from Folozchev. There were similarities but also glaring contradictions. The jury was still out on which of the two men was a plant sent by the SVR, the Russian equivalent of the CIA. Blade believed that one of them genuinely sought asylum in the US. Based on his own observations, he sensed they had gotten this one wrong. That conversation would have to wait for another day. For now, he listened attentively, weighing every word against what he understood to be true.

"There will be time to correct your situation," Blade consoled. "For now, I need you to tell me everything about this warhead shipment."

"I've told you all I know. Four containers, each with different manifests. Russian-made appliances in two of them. Used arcade games in the third. I don't know the contents of the fourth."

"Another source told us the container we're looking for would have the insignia of a maple leaf."

"Mr. Blade, does it sound logical to you that someone wishing to smuggle nuclear warheads into your country would mark the container in any way to distinguish it from the tens of thousands of others entering your port?"

"No," Blade admitted. "It never did. But we deemed the

information reliable. I need to know now if there is anything more that would help identify the container we're searching for."

Greggenkoff remained silent for a moment. "Mr. Blade," he said, "you and I have played a deadly game for most of our lives. And yet, both of us have survived to see this day. I am done and come to you seeking asylum in the very country I worked so hard to destroy. Tell me, will I ever be allowed to live your American dream?"

Blade dropped his head in frustration, hoping his instincts were right about Greggenkoff.

"Give me something, Uri. Tell me something we haven't already heard. Help me stop this. Do that, and you have my word that I will get you where you want to go."

"Let me think. There was a word they repeated. What is that word in English? Pin... ball? Yes, that's it, pinball! The warheads are in pinball machines."

"Swear to me, this is right, Uri. Both of our lives depend on it."

"I don't wish to see my future home destroyed by thermonuclear weapons. Save me one of these machines once you remove the bombs. I will put it in my new home in Minnesota as a reminder of our cooperation."

Blade had already ended the call and reached for the radio.

"Logan!"

"Here."

"Go back and pull the manifests. We're looking for a container of used pinball machines. There are warheads in at least two of them."

"Got it."

"Piper!"

"Right here."

"Get me good images of the serial numbers of the containers along with license plate numbers on the trailers.

Logan will let you know which one we're looking for as soon as we know."

"I'm on it."

Sam Piper maneuvered the drone as close as he dared to each trailer without it being noticed. "I've got clear shots of all four. They're splitting up on the interstates."

"Can you document which way each one is going?"

"I can try, but we're asking a lot of the batteries in this drone. I'll get back to you."

"Blade, it's Logan."

"Go ahead."

"We got lucky. A few of the inspectors remembered the pinball machines. We're looking for container 31484. The trailer has a Tennessee plate, 9266."

"Very good! Piper, did you copy that?"

"Got it, hold on. Okay, 31484 is westbound on I-78."

"Time to get some tails on that one," Blade said. "I'll get the B team rolling. Nice work, all of you. And Logan, give chase now and keep up until we can send backup."

Blade made some quick phone calls and then grabbed the radio. "Logan, have you got a visual?"

"Affirmative, the truck is turning south on 95."

"We suspected as much. He's likely headed for DC. Reinforcements are on the way. Pierson, do you have your assets in place?"

Agent Rudd Pierson joined the radio conversation with his heavy southern drawl. "We're about six miles north and coming in hot. You'll want to call the county mounties and tell them to stand down. I'm driving an old green pickup."

"Done," Blade acknowledged. "Tell me when you have eyes on our target."

Tense moments passed before Pierson radioed back in. "Target spotted, still about a half mile ahead in the middle lane. His estimated speed is five to ten over the limit."

"Maintain your distance for now," Blade instructed. "Henley and Cabrerra, what is your twenty?"

"Cabrerra here. I'm just coming up on Pierson. Henley is right behind me."

Blade envisioned the scenario and how to safely stop a thirty-ton truck full of nuclear warheads likely rigged with remote explosives. He recalled a similar take-down and directed his crew. "We're going to play this as we did in San Diego last year. Logan, maintain your position and offer assistance. Pierson, take the forward position and be ready to create the diversion. I need this driver to see a drunk hillbilly passing him. Cabrerra and Henley, port and starboard on the trailer, stand ready to disable it. Everyone got that?"

Each agent acknowledged and waited for the start command.

"Everybody follow Pierson's lead and coordinate with him. Pierson, you have the ball."

"Copy that, going in."

Pierson floored the pickup and weaved dangerously close to the container hauler, guzzling a beer as he passed the wary trucker. He pulled ahead and squeezed into the same lane just ahead of the truck. At the same time, Henley and Cabrerra took their positions on either side, lagging back near the tail of the container.

Pierson keyed his radio. "I'm directly in front of our target. Letting it fly in three, two, one—

He reached through the open back window and pulled on a rope holding down the tarp covering the pickup's payload. The black canvas tarp began flapping in the wind. He reached through again and pushed over an open crate. Pipe fittings and sections of black pipe rained out the back of the pickup and into the path of the oncoming container truck.

Pierson watched the driver's expression through the mirror as his face went from intensely focused to wide-eyed shock. The driver gripped the wheel as though bracing for impact. At that same moment, both Cabrerra and Henley took aim with silenced pistols on either side of the trailer, and each shot out a tire. The tires exploded with a thunderous boom, hurling steel belted rubber into the air like black shrapnel.

The container truck driver was making up for lost time when a drunken hick in a rusty pickup cut in front of him. He was thinking about passing when all hell let loose, and the road was suddenly littered with debris, hitting the pavement, then bouncing, and flying everywhere. A section of steel pipe flew up and crashed against the truck grill. The driver feared all this garbage could rip holes in the oil pan, the radiator, or the fuel tanks. He gripped the wheel tighter, looking for a clear passage to the shoulder. Then he heard the boom. The tires on both sides of the trailer burst into a fusillade of white smoke and flying rubber. It was all he could do to wrest control as it fishtailed back and forth. He worked his way to the shoulder and brought the rig to a halt, then hopped out of the cab, furious, ready to call ahead and let them know what happened. In all the confusion, he'd left the detonator on the front seat. He was about to go back and retrieve it when the driver of the pickup came stumbling toward him. *Drunk son of a bitch,* he thought. *Drunk, smelly son of a bitch!*

Pierson had watched the melee through his mirrors and pulled to the shoulder just ahead of his target. He took a big swig of beer and swirled it in his mouth, dumping a bit down his sleeveless denim shirt. He pulled on a CAT baseball cap and slid out, weaving and walking clumsily toward the container driver, who was already out of his cab inspecting the blown tires.

"Who is going to pay for this?" the driver screamed at him. "Look what your shit did to my truck!" He turned and pointed at the shredded tires, mumbling and waving his hands.

"Whoa, man, I'm sorry about that," Pierson said as he approached. "Damn tarp, just let go. Did my stuff do that to yer tires?"

The driver turned back to Pierson. He pointed, screaming and shoving his finger inches from Pierson's face. "You're going to pay for this! You better have insurance."

Pierson assessed the irate driver; no weapons, no remote detonators in his hands or on his belt. Just the cell phone, which could be used to activate a bomb. Acting faster than the driver could comprehend, Pierson grabbed his outstretched hand and bent his wrist up behind his back. The pain sent the man to his knees. Pierson snatched the cell phone and slipped it into his back pocket before pulling a pair of cuffs from his belt loop. He lifted the driver to his feet, cuffed one of his wrists, and attached the other loop around a steel bar on the trailer. Stepping away from the shocked driver, he dialed his phone. "Arthur, y'all can stand down. The target is secured."

Two
CHESS AT THE WHITE HOUSE

"That's a rather odd move, wouldn't you say? Even for you, old boy." President Walter Lux settled back in his chair and took a sip of bourbon, still examining the chess board. He set the glass on a ceramic coaster, careful not to allow the beads of condensation to drip onto the antique table in the East Sitting Hall. He'd discovered the soft yellow room with its massive fan window overlooking the treasury building was the most conducive to the quiet evening chess matches with his old college roommate.

Arthur Blade had placed his bishop in harm's way. Lux stared at his friend and the unexpected change-up in the man's usually strong defense. He tossed his previous gameplay aside and readjusted for the fortuitous error. His opponent had slipped up, and he could now envision a checkmate within five moves.

"I dare say you've stepped in it on that one," he said, gloating as he positioned a pawn so that Blade's bishop was doomed.

Blade looked up and cracked the slightest of grins. The

twinkle in his aged blue eyes made Lux think he was being conned.

"I remember that look, Arthur. I first noticed it when you came to tell me you were recruited by the CIA."

Blade nodded. "A week before graduation, as I recall. I went straight from our dorm room to a new career at Langley."

"Twenty years as a field agent, correct?"

"Twenty-one, but who's counting?" He shook his head. "So many operations in parts of the world where we had no business being. It was a dark time for the company."

"You oversaw many positive changes once you began directing the clandestine operations."

"The statistic I'm most proud of is the immediate decrease in lost assets. I saw to it that most of our people came home after their ops. My predecessors never appreciated the value of our field agents."

Blade moved an unimportant piece in the backfield, another sign that the game's fate had changed hands. Lux became more confident that his friend had erred and was struggling to build a new strategy.

"Has something distracted you?" he asked. "You rarely lose your edge like this." He moved another power piece into place, ensuring his victory, then leaned back. "This looks like a repeat of the title game, Arthur." He chuckled at the memory. "Of all the times to meet the love of your life, and you had to do it during the biggest chess match in your life. She's the reason you lost, you know. I remember the moment your eyes met." He grinned, shaking his head. "You were a goner."

Blade moved another worthless piece that would have no effect on Lux's win. "You're right," he conceded. "It was an odd moment for Ginny to enter my life. But losing the title match was inconsequential. Forty-two years together more than made up for that. I wouldn't have changed a thing."

The president nodded. "I was thrilled for the two of you. But—" Lux made a slow and deliberate move on the chessboard. "Then, as now, you let your guard down, and I was there to take advantage. By the way, your queen is toast."

Blade glanced at the board for another moment, his poker expression revealing nothing. His eyes raised to meet Lux's triumphant gleam. Without looking down, he moved his queen diagonally across the board to H8, right next to the black king.

Lux stared at his friend. "I cannot fathom why you did that." He took advantage of the gift and captured the white queen with his king.

Blade responded by sliding his rook from H1 and taking the black queen at A1. His unnoticed sacrificial trade of queens had caught the president off guard.

Control of the board now changed, and Lux found himself on the defensive. He backed a knight away from being captured, only to have Blade topple one of his pawns with a bishop. It also dawned on him about the brilliance behind Blade's sacrifice. The game would be over within three moves, and he was powerless to prevent it. Confidence gave way to disbelief. Lux's eyes darted across the board, taking in every piece, attempting to understand where he had failed. His jaw slackened as he knocked over his king in acknowledgment. "You sly dog. I didn't see that coming."

Blade smiled. "That was one of the lessons I learned the night of the tournament. Even defeat has its uses. In our case tonight, I allowed my opponent to bask in victory while working to assure his demise."

"And the other lesson?" Lux asked, folding his hands in his lap.

"Follow your heart. Ginny was the best thing that ever happened to me and a greater prize than any trophy."

"I'll give you that," Lux chuckled, leaning in. "But I did kick your ass quite soundly."

"That night was yours, Mr. President."

Blade pushed his chair back to leave.

"Are you sure I can't get the chef to fix you something before you go? You have eaten nothing the entire time you were here."

Blade shook his head. "I've had little appetite lately. No doubt, the stress of this last operation took more out of me than I thought. Thankfully, the nuclear warheads have been secured, and the threat no longer exists."

"That was excellent work by you and your team. But I'm surprised you haven't slowed down. You're seventy-two, Arthur. The CIA will keep taking from you long after there's nothing left."

"I would remind you, sir, that you are only one year younger, and the presidency has that same effect on old men. And speaking of which, this old man is going home."

Blade went to stand but dropped back into his chair. "That's odd," he said, his vision drifting out of focus. "I seem to have lost all energy." He pointed unsteadily at the president. "And there are two of you." His hand fell to his side, and all went black.

Arthur Blade awoke to unfamiliar surroundings. As the mind fog cleared, he recalled the last moments of the night before but nothing beyond. An empty gap occupied the space of those memories.

He looked around and took in every detail of the small room he was lying in; pastel walls, linoleum floors, and the distant scent of disinfectant. He was in a hospital. Tubes ran from his arm to multiple IV bags hanging from a pole, a small device was clamped on a finger, and a bundle of wires ran out from under his green smock. He put his hand to his face and felt an oxygen tube. *Much ado about nothing*, he assured himself. *Nothing more than a bit of over-exertion. Skipped one meal too many.* A fresh wave of dizziness forced him to rethink that conclusion.

He heard a rustling to his left and noticed someone sleeping in the chair beside him. Audrey Landers shifted slightly, and a book fell from her lap. Her brown eyes fluttered open and met Blade's.

"Arthur?" she said, standing. "Arthur, can you hear me?" Her concern exaggerated the worry lines on her face. If anything, Blade thought it made her even more beautiful. She wore her blonde hair tied back, but a long lock had come loose and hung down over one eye. Her floral printed dress had deep wrinkles like she'd slept in it.

"Hello, Audrey, I'm fine. Just suffering from a little post-mission duress, I suppose."

Audrey and Blade had dated briefly years after the death of his wife. Maybe it was still too soon after losing the love of his life. Maybe he would never look at another woman that way again. Despite that, they found a tight friendship in the place of romance and came to depend upon one another.

"Where are we?" he asked.

"Bethesda Naval Hospital. Do you remember what happened?"

"I'm afraid I don't. I was playing chess with Walter last night, beating him soundly, I might add, but then, nothing."

Audrey wrapped her hands around his. "Arthur, that wasn't last night. You've been here for two days. This is the first time you've been conscious."

"Well, that makes no sense at all." He looked again at her rumpled dress. "Have you been here the whole time?"

She nodded. "Walter called me as they were flying you here."

"Flew me here?"

"Aboard Marine One. You have friends in high places."

"I'm sorry to be such a nuisance, old girl. I'm sure this will pass, and I'll be fine. Do you know where my clothes are?" He attempted to raise himself up but fell back. "Well, that is an unwelcome sensation." His head sunk into the pillow as the room spun.

"Arthur, there has to be more to this than you think."

"I'd like to find out," he said. "Do you suppose I could speak with a doctor soon?"

"Would now be a good time?" A small entourage of white coats filled the doorway, a few of them not much older than kids. The eldest stepped forward and shook Blade's hand. He had a firm grip, a warm, southern drawl, and a shock of gray hair at the temples.

"Hello, Mr. Blade, I am Dr. Liggit, and these are some third-years who are studying your case." He motioned for the others to gather around the bed. "So tell me, how long have you been having these lapses of consciousness?"

"This is the first I'm aware of, I assure you," Blade answered.

Liggit pulled up a tablet and finger flicked through pages of data. "I have your lab reports. Most of your numbers look good for a man of seventy-two years of age."

"Most?"

"Yes, a few highs and lows. All expected, given your current situation. We also performed a PET CT and a few biopsies while you were in La-La Land. We're awaiting the pathology reports."

Blade sat up straighter. "Biopsies? On who's authority?"

The doctor flipped through his tablet. "POTUS signed all authorizations for treatment." Doctor Liggit scrolled back to the previous page. "The severity of this episode must not be taken lightly. My advice right now is to listen to what your body is telling you. The remaining test results should be in tomorrow. Until then, I suggest you eat everything in sight. Your body weight is low, as well as your triglycerides, red blood cell count, iron, magnesium, electrolytes, blah, blah, blah. About the only thing that's elevated is your white cell count, which is not good." He pointed toward the door, and his assistants headed out. "We'll talk tomorrow," he added. "Eat, Mr. Blade, eat!" Liggit smiled and gave a reassuring pat on Blade's shoulder, then blended into the cluster of white jackets.

"You do look a bit gaunt now that he mentioned it," Audrey said, giving Blade a critical once-over. "Are you sure this is the first time you've suffered these symptoms?"

"Just normal aches and pains. A few dizzy spells, but nothing on the scale of this."

"Then see it for what it is; a warning sign. Something is very wrong with you, Arthur, and I don't mind telling you that I'm worried."

Blade took her hand and kissed it. "Tomorrow will bring answers," he reassured.

"So, this is your new hideout."

Lou 'Azzy' Azzilonte stood leaning against the doorframe. Blade's brush-cut old friend was built like a brick and, at sixty-five years, was still the last guy to pick a fight with.

Audrey walked over, smiling, and hugged him. "Louis, it's so good to see you." Lou hated being called Louis by anyone but her.

"When you didn't show up at my retirement party, I figured something was up."

Blade winced. "How did I miss..." He shook his head. "Azzy, I'm so very sorry. I had every intention of being there."

"Don't sweat it, Arthur," Lou said, coming over and shaking Blade's hand. "You got a pass on that one."

"I hope you didn't make a special trip down here from Brooklyn just to see me."

"Would you have done the same for me?"

Blade gave him a sardonic stare. "Of course, I would."

"Well, there ya go."

"Why don't you two catch up while I find a cup of tea," Audrey said, heading for the door.

Blade flashed her a smile and turned back to Lou. "So, how did it go?"

Lou pulled the chair closer to the bed and sat. "I've never seen Paddy McMurphy's that full. To watch my picture go up on the wall above the bar beside some of the greatest officers to wear the uniform was an honor that I can't describe."

"I'm even more sorry I missed it. Congratulations. You probably had half the Long Island police department there. Losing their Chief of Detectives is a void that's hard to fill."

Lou chuckled. "They've known about my retirement for over a year and still haven't named my replacement."

"I know a great many people will miss you."

"Maybe some," Lou agreed, nodding. "But I didn't get to be Chief of D's by being everybody's best friend. You know that. I'll bet I had just as many detractors there as supporters."

"And not one of them would question your temerity or your ability to lead."

"I'd like to think so, Arthur. I've spent my career using the skill sets of every detective who served with me. Most would agree I always stepped back and let them do their jobs."

Blade nodded. "You had an eye for recognizing talent. The small size of your cold case file should attest to that."

"Have you given any more thought to retiring yourself?" Lou asked.

Blade shook his head. "With Ginny gone, I wouldn't have the first clue what to do with myself. I have no hobbies to speak of. Besides, the work is still rewarding enough, so why would I leave?"

Lou stared back. "What just happened to you should be a wake-up call. It may be time to think about walking away while there's still some life left in you. Believe me, you'll find plenty to do outside the company."

"Perhaps," Blade answered. "Speaking of which, how is the plan for your own watering hole coming along?"

"I put money down on a place in Key West that went belly-up. Let's just call it an extreme fixer-upper. I decided against the typical thatched hut canteen. Those are a dime a dozen down there. I'm going to take a bit of Brooklyn with me instead."

"A theme of sand and subways, is it, then?"

Lou laughed. "Yeah, something like that. Anyway, I have some special touches in mind. Hit or miss, it'll be unique, and it'll be mine."

"I hope to join you there and share a brew or two when you get situated. Provided, of course, you offer a varied selection. I have yet to find an American establishment that offered 'Courage Best by Youngs.'"

"Still looking for that one? I'll see about getting it on tap." Lou stood as Audrey reappeared in the doorway. "Be well, Arthur," he said, shaking his hand. "We'll talk soon."

"Goodbye, my friend," Blade called after him.

"Take care of him," Lou whispered to Audrey as he passed her at the door. "He looks like hell."

Audrey nodded, then took the seat beside the bed. "It was good to see him again. Speaking of old friends, Walter called asking how you were."

Blade struggled again to sit up. "That reminds me, I have calls to make. Covert operations go on with or without me."

"Walter assured me the CIA is on it. People have your back, Arthur. Let them do their jobs."

Blade nodded. "And you should take your own advice, dear girl. Go home and get some rest. I'm in a good place, and I'm not going anywhere."

Audrey flashed a look that he knew better than to challenge. "You eat everything they bring you. Do you understand me?"

"Yes, yes, I will do my best."

She stroked his cheek. "You are my best friend, Arthur Blade, and I expect you to be around for many more years. Remember that."

Blade blinked back the wetness and regretted not letting Audrey any deeper into his heart when he'd had the chance. True enough, there would never be another like Ginny. But he had been given a second chance, and he failed to act. He was fortunate that Audrey had remained in his life, even with the limitations he put upon their relationship. Now he wondered if there was any chance of allowing the flame to grow but quickly dismissed the thought as a selfish whim. Audrey was twelve years younger. She was healthy, vivacious, beautiful, and deserved to spend her remaining years with a man who possessed an equal spark and energy. A dark image of Audrey tending to his needs as he grew old and frail sealed the deal. He would not allow her to waste her remaining years chained to him. Gazing upon that warm, attractive face from a distance would have to be enough.

"What's going on in that busy brain of yours?" she asked. "You look as though you're cruising in the clouds."

Blade squeezed her hand. "That's exactly where I was." He let go and said, "Go home, please. I'll keep you informed about what the doctors say. Get some rest."

Audrey nodded and offered a brave smile. She turned and walked away, waving back as she disappeared out the door. Blade watched her go and felt a sudden emptiness as though all the air had been pulled out of the room with her.

Three
THE WORST OF NEWS

The following afternoon, Blade was wheeled to Dr. Liggit's office for the results of his biopsies. He'd regained enough stamina to walk short distances and entered the office with the aid of a cane. Liggit sat behind his desk, conferring with another doctor, and directed Blade to an open seat.

"Mr. Blade, this is Dr. Sabahi, the resident oncologist."

Blade shook the man's hand and looked warily back to Liggit. "I suppose this means you're about to tell me something I don't want to hear."

"The news is not good, Mr. Blade," Sabahi said with a heavy Indian accent. "Your high white blood cell count pointed the way. The PET CT and the biopsies confirmed our suspicions." He leaned forward, elbows on his knees, tenting his hands to his mouth. "There is never an easy way to say this, so please excuse my bluntness. You have pancreatic cancer, stage four. It has metastasized into your lymph nodes and lungs. If we'd caught this sooner, there may have been treatment options. Mr. Blade, I am sorry to inform you that you cannot survive this. No amount of chemotherapy or radiation will halt or significantly delay the inevitable." He took a deep breath and added, "You have about six months to live."

Blade stared back, expressionless, as a thousand thoughts flashed through his mind. His shoulders slumped, the only sign that he understood the bad news. "I see," he said.

Dr. Liggit continued. "Dr. Sabahi and I decided that being forthright was the best course of action."

Blade nodded. "Quite."

"Although he explained the futility of conventional treatments, there is one that we both agree upon."

"TRK inhibitors," Sabahi finished Liggit's thought. "The cancer has not yet reached your brain, but it will. A regimen of NTRK infusions may slow the spread."

"Why would I not just accept the inevitable and make my last days as comfortable as possible?"

Dr. Sabahi shook his head. "TRK inhibitors could stifle the creation of any brain gliomas as a preventive measure."

Dr. Liggit rose and perched on the corner of his desk. "your last days will be bad enough without cancer entering your brain. That, Mr. Blade, is a terrible way to go. Dr. Sabahi believes this therapy will have minimal adverse effects. It may also buy you some time to—get your affairs in order." The doctor set his hand on Blade's shoulder. "I'm truly sorry. I know you've dedicated your life to making this country safe. We will all mourn your loss."

Four
THE DONOR

Tommy reeked of deceit. Doreen smelled it all over him from across the room; the dime store perfume of a one-night stand and the scent of sex. A wiser man would have showered before coming home, but using his head and destroying the evidence of his trysts was probably expecting too much of her fiancée.

She sat hidden in the shadows in his favorite leather chair, watching as he pulled the door closed behind him. She marveled at his stealthy approach, avoiding every creaky spot on the floor. He'd had a lot of practice.

She thought for a moment of the other men she could have been with and how angry Tommy became whenever she so much as smiled at one of them. She mistook that possessiveness for true love, and they became inseparable during their senior year of high school. Five years later, he proposed on the night of his acceptance into the Navy SEAL program. Doreen had taken that to mean he was finally ready to be faithful.

She had watched in awe as Tommy progressed through his training, becoming a fine-tuned killing machine. On those rare evenings when he could leave the base, he told her of the torturous workouts and grueling tests of endurance. She marveled at what men put themselves through for the honor of acceptance into what was a very exclusive club. Every hostile nation respected and feared Navy SEALs. Tommy was already a fine specimen when he entered the program, but upon graduation, he reminded her more of a Greek God. Given his size and bulk, one would have expected his movements to be awkward and stiff, and yet his motions flowed panther-like with lightning-quick reflexes that never ceased to amaze her. She could only imagine the clandestine missions he'd been sent on and the fear any adversary would feel when pitted against this formidable dynamo of sculpted muscle. That was the part she couldn't wrap her mind around; how could he keep all that training in his head that made him a walking lethal weapon yet still not have a fucking lick of common sense?

Tommy was an amalgam of contradictions. Though she would never understand him, she had accepted the truth. No matter how many times she caught him red-handed, then listened as he lied through his teeth and swore his love and allegiance, he would never change. He was incapable of becoming a good, loving, monogamous husband to his future wife. Tommy was and always would be no more faithful than a henhouse cock.

She continued to watch from the cover of darkness as he cracked open the fridge and snatched a beer. He leaned back against the door and guzzled its contents.

What a piece of work!

Doreen admitted that she only had herself to blame. She'd been warned when they first began dating. Her mother used to say, "I hope he's great in bed 'cause he sure won't be good for even one stimulating conversation.'"

She was right, of course, but Doreen loved him still. Despite the faults that tore at their relationship, he owned her heart. They were destined to be together. Only Tommy couldn't get that through his thick skull. Maybe something else would. A bullet, perhaps. Before she could talk herself out of it, as she had on so many nights before, she closed one eye, took aim, and pulled the trigger.

His eyes crossed as the shot struck him in the forehead. Doreen could almost see his lights going out as his head jerked back. He stood for a moment longer before his knees buckled. Tommy fell back against the refrigerator and slid down to the linoleum floor, his eyes locked in a vacant stare.

"It didn't have to be like this, lover," she explained, walking over to his body. The lack of blood intrigued her. A direct head wound should have made a mess, right? But she had used her twenty-two target range pistol with standard ammo rather than one of Tommy's nine millimeters and hollow points. That had to be why. The mark on the center of his forehead looked more like a deep gouge than an entry wound, with just the slightest trickle of blood running down the length of his nose. The bullet must have grazed him and ricocheted off. Maybe going for a headshot at such a long distance wasn't such a great idea after all. She grinned, recalling the advice he always offered when aiming at a target. "You were right," she told him. "Aim small, miss big, right honey?" Even though the bullet hadn't penetrated the skull, his lifeless expression suggested he had already left the building. It was done.

She sat down on the floor beside him. "I'll join you soon, lover," she reassured. "Gonna be just you and me now." She nudged him with her shoulder, chuckling. "Remember our first date? You were so nervous that you couldn't pin a corsage to my dress. You weren't too much to look at back then. Took a few years for you to grow into your features. I stuck with you, though, didn't I? Yup, even when I caught you making out with Connie Freeman behind the home economics class. You always told me I was the only girl for you. I stayed true, and you know it." Her voice raised. "I gave you some of the best years of my life, and all you had to do was be a good, honest, loving man. But you couldn't do it, could ya, stud?" She elbowed him in the gut and noticed his hands twitch. That wasn't right! He should be halfway to meeting his maker by now. She felt his neck for a pulse. His heart was racing. She slapped his cheek a few times and noticed his pupils weren't fully dilated as she'd expected of someone on the brink of death. Her face turned sullen. "Goddamn it, Tommy, you can't even die right for me!" She took a deep breath, collected herself, and managed a smile. "Doesn't matter, baby. We go out together."

She took his hand in hers, gave it a kiss, and then nestled up against him, temple to temple. She gripped the pistol and held it against the side of her head. The single round would travel through her head and into his.

"Still love me? You better. We're going to be together for eternity. That means forever, dumb shit."

She pulled the trigger.

Five
Enter the Doctor

Arthur Blade sat in a secluded booth of a nondescript bar he shared the location of with no one. And yet he watched as a man carrying a small satchel entered, walked straight for him, then slid onto the opposite seat. The man folded his hands and gazed at him with a quizzical grin. His was a youthful face despite a full head of unkempt, gray hair. His custom-tailored charcoal suit was overdue for a trip to the dry cleaner.

"You're a hard man to reach, Mr. Blade."

"One might also assume that I don't wish to be found."

"Yes, I suppose that's—" The man thought better and changed tactics. "Mr. Blade, my name is Mark Rossenblume. Doctor— Mark Rossenblume. I've been in contact with the president, who suggested I might find you here."

"Leave it to Walter to know the whereabouts of his minions," Blade said, annoyed.

"Mr. Blade, I have something extraordinary to share with you."

"If this is about some experimental drug therapy to extend my life while making me wish for death, save your breath."

"Oh, no, sir, your condition is terminal. There is no hope of changing it."

"Then what has my esteemed friend sent you here to share with me?"

The doctor leaned forward. "Suppose I were to tell you there was a way, a remote chance with not the greatest of odds, mind you, but a chance, to live again?"

"To—live again." Blade leaned back and folded his arms. "I was about to offer you a drink, but you were just leaving. Whatever you're peddling is of no use to me." He reached for his beer with one hand while pointing toward the door. "You managed to find your way in here, doctor. Please do take this opportunity to go back the way you came."

"I know how this sounds.... "

"You have no idea how this sounds, or you wouldn't have even said it. You don't come in here and dangle hope to a man who has none."

"All I'm asking for is twenty minutes of your time. That's it. If I haven't managed to spark your interest, then I'll leave, and you'll never hear from me again."

"Twenty minutes, you say?"

"That's all. Twenty minutes in exchange for twenty, forty more years of life."

Blade settled into his seat. "Go ahead, then. Dazzle me. I owe that much to Walter for thinking of me."

"Mr. Blade, I have news of..."

"My name is Arthur."

The doctor smiled, took a breath, and began again. "Arthur, since the perfection of anti-rejection chemicals, most organ transplants these days are successful."

"That's great news, but my entire body is filled with cancer. What is it you're suggesting we transplant?"

"Sir, we've had limited success in partial cerebral exchanges."

"Cerebral, as in brain, as in— good god, man, you can't be suggesting... but you are, aren't you?"

"Call me Mark, and yes, to a point. A complete brain transplant will never happen in my lifetime. You cannot sever the spinal cord with any hope of reattaching the millions of connections. What we have learned, though, through trial and error, is that we can detach and replace both left and right cerebrums in their entirety. It is a lengthy and delicate series of operations that begins weeks before we make the first incision. In fact, there are no incisions made by us. There is not a doctor alive who could maneuver a scalpel between the cerebrums and the forebrain or cerebellum."

"Then how do you accomplish the impossible?"

The doctor's smile widened. "Magnetically charged nanobots remotely controlled by a five Tesla electromagnetic field."

"I pride myself on being somewhat tech-savvy, Mark, but that means nothing to me."

"I don't suppose it would. The basic theory behind this procedure was developed at about the same time as magnetic resonance imaging. Our technology uses an even more powerful magnetic field to control the direction and function of microscopic nanobots. By varying the field in infinitesimal degrees, we can direct these nanobots to move and cut between the cerebrums and the forebrain with nanometer accuracy."

Dr. Rossenblume flagged down a server and requested a glass of water.

"The astounding and most recent breakthrough," he continued, "is the hyper-healing technology. You can't just remove a damaged cerebrum and drop in a replacement. Tens of thousands of connections must be coaxed to reconnect."

Rossenblume slipped a large tablet from his satchel and began tapping. "That is the core and the brilliance of our procedure." He pulled up a 3-D image of a rotating brain and set it before Blade.

"Every bit of knowledge, every motion that we humans have ever learned, came as a result of our brains creating connections between the cerebrums and the forebrain. Our entire existence, our personalities, intellect, creativity, memories, everything that makes us uniquely individual and human, exists within the left and right cerebrums. Every motor function we learn, from walking, swinging a tennis racket, driving a car, directing a scalpel or a paintbrush, results from the brain creating specific neural pathways for each movement."

Rossenblume reached over and tapped the screen again. A new image appeared showing microscopic cross-sections of the brain.

"We've learned how these neural connections came to be formed. With that knowledge, we have created the perfect environment for the brain to repair itself and rebuild these severed connections."

Blade attempted to question what he was looking at but was so overwhelmed that he didn't know where to start. The doctor beat him to it.

"Stem cell doping is what we call it, for lack of a better term. The junctions between the cerebrum and forebrain are treated with a layer of adult stem cells in a specially modified solution of the naturally occurring neural chemicals, along with the donor's DNA. A high-octane brain repair concoction, if you will. The recipient, that would be you, spends the week prior to the procedure in a hyperbaric chamber of pure oxygen at four atmospheres. During that time, both the donor and recipient undergo a procedure called Induced Horizontal Gene Transfer. This also requires the resonant frequency of your body to be synchronized with that of your donor. Everyone's frequency is different, and this is a critical step in getting your brains in sync. Post-op requires three more weeks in the chamber, which speeds up the healing process exponentially. At this point, we've done all we can, and the brain does the rest."

Blade stared at the last images for a long moment before responding. "I'm assuming you've done this procedure many times already."

"The total count is three."

Blade shook his head. "This is nowhere near perfected, is it?"

"I would be remiss if I represented it as anything but experimental. Subject one was a failure. Subject two showed progress before dropping into a permanent seizure. Subject three has survived much longer than the first two, and we continue to adjust every step of the process based on what we see."

"One survivor, that's what you're offering me? A less than thirty-three percent chance, is that right?"

"Your odds would be better. I would put them at closer to thirty-nine percent."

Blade looked away, tapping the table with his fingers. "Why would I do this? To spend my last days as an experiment with lower odds than a coin toss?"

"Because I've seen your files. You don't have the time remaining that your doctors told you. The spread of your cancer is far more aggressive than estimated."

"You're telling me I don't have six months to live?"

"Sorry, no. Being honest, which is what you deserve, you have maybe two months on the long side, one on the short."

Blade cupped his hands over his mouth, blinking back the wetness in his eyes. "Mortality is a cruel mistress."

The doctor gave him a moment before continuing. "We've compiled gigabytes of data from each of our successes and our failures. We know what went wrong, and we've corrected the flaws."

"The ones you know about, you mean."

"True," the doctor admitted. "But we have proven that the procedure works. And while we don't know every aspect of the healing process, we are giving the patient everything necessary to survive. This doesn't save your life, Arthur. It offers another one. It can lead to options you never dreamed possible."

"I'm assuming the clock is ticking, correct?"

"Yes. In order for us to increase our chance of success, we must begin the pre-operative therapies as soon as possible."

"I see. And how much time are you giving me to make this decision?"

"Based on your rapid rate of deterioration, I would say twenty-four hours is the limit."

Blade lowered his head and blew out a breath. "You can't give me more than a day to think this through?"

"It's not me. Your cancer forces our hand. If you perish during the initial treatments, then nothing is gained."

"And your grand experiment would fail. That's a cold way to push your point, Mark."

"I apologize for the urgency. But with all due respect, I'm offering the gift of a new start. The only other choice is to allow the disease to finish what it started. It will kill you rather unmercifully. Or you can come with me for the chance at living a second life."

Blade acknowledged the doctor. His eyes wandered over to the bartender as he polished beer steins. Beyond him, the last rays of sunset shone through the picture window, silhouetting the steady stream of pedestrians on the street outside. As much as he thought he'd prepared to meet his death, the true finality now struck him with both barrels. Yes, he'd lived a full and rewarding life despite the loneliness. It would be so easy to walk away and let the damned disease finish what it started. But what if?

The setting sun reflected off a strip of the window blinds, illuminating Blade's face with a soft, warm glow. Within that moment, he caught a glimpse, a tiny snapshot of everything this world still offered. Life was precious, short, and worth clinging to, even if only to feel the next sunrise and all the promise that a new day offered. There was no decision to be made. He knew that now. He thought again of his beloved life partner, waiting for him on the other side to come join her.

"Not today, my darling," he told her, "not just yet."

His eyes returned to the doctor, wide and peaceful. "I'll buy you that drink now," he said.

Six
REBOOT

The image confused him. Blade was looking at an electric orange sunset. For a moment, he wondered why he couldn't feel the sea breeze or hear the calls of gulls. He blinked the image into better focus and realized it was a large wall painting and that he was lying in a bed.

His brain began processing all other input. Something obscured the periphery of his vision. Bandages, he surmised, gauze wrappings. His eyes scanned the small room from side to side. Not much else to see. A lone chair beneath the large picture. To the right, a door with a window covered by horizontal blinds. He tried turning his head to take in the rest but couldn't. He had no feeling in his neck or any of his limbs. It reminded him of a surgery years earlier when he'd received a spinal block. Only this was much worse. He had no feeling at all from the neck down. A flood of panic coursed through him.

The surgery!

Was it done? Had it failed and left him immobile? Maybe they hadn't done it at all, and he was right back where he started. He felt himself breathing faster, deeper, and though he couldn't feel the beats, he knew his heart was racing.

An alarm triggered in another room, followed by scurrying footsteps. The door burst open, and a nurse rushed to his bedside. She bent over him, shining a small flashlight into his eyes. "Can you hear me?" she asked. "Blink for me if you hear my voice."

Blade summoned all his energy into that one task. He slowly lowered, then raised his eyelids.

The nurse straightened, smiled, and silenced the heart rate alarm on the bedside monitor. "Welcome back, Mr. Blade," she said. "I've already called for the doctor. He's on the way. Do you feel anything at all?"

Blade managed two more slow blinks.

"It's okay," she consoled, "that's expected to pass."

Expected to pass? Blade was hoping for something more encouraging. But he now began filling in some blanks himself. He had obviously survived the procedure, which also meant he was now viewing this nurse through a new set of eyes. Someone else's eyes! The complexities of that statement alone made his brain feel as though it were on overload. Speaking of which, that wasn't even all him up there anymore, was it? He half expected to be sharing the cranium space with the ghosts of his donor. He closed his eyes, listening for internal voices. When none called back, he blinked a few times and tested his sight, rolling his new orbs back and forth, up and down, taking in everything in the room. He wasn't sure, but everything appeared more focused, colors more vivid, and he could zoom in on objects from foreground to background with amazing ease. How many years had it been since he'd been able to do that?

"You're doing just fine," the nurse reassured him. "All your vital signs are strong and positive."

His gaze followed her as she walked to the foot of the bed

and scribbled some notes on a clipboard. "The doctor will be in soon," she said, offering a smile. "Try to relax. You've made it through the hard part." He watched her leave the room as his eyelids grew heavy, and he was out before the door closed.

Blade awoke with a start as his body spasmed. He looked up to see the nurse now standing alongside Dr. Hanspratten. The doctor looked down with a satisfied smile. "Very good, Mr. Blade! Your motor reflexes are already responding to impulses from your brain. Ordinarily, it would require months or years to recover from the trauma you have gone through in our procedure. From here on, you will heal at a much faster rate. The process we incorporate accelerates the reconnection of neurons. The doctor patted Blade's leg. Be patient, Mr. Blade. I believe your progress will astound you. By the way, did you feel that?"

He did, but only as the most minimal of sensations. He blinked once for the doctor, who nodded his approval. The most pressing thing on Blade's mind at the moment, though, was being able to ask for a glass of water and hold it in his hand. He trusted the doctor at his word, but the return of simple muscle functions could not come soon enough. He was thankful to be so groggy, imagining the angst of being wide awake and unable to move a single limb. Hanspratten's words reassured him. The procedure was a success, and he vowed not to waste a single moment of this second life. The thought relaxed him back into a deep, restful sleep.

Seven
THE SUCCESSOR AWAITS

CIA Director Don Colson entered the sixth-floor conference room, where his lieutenants sat clustered around one end of the long table. His usual somber expression appeared especially drawn. It was clear that the director carried much more than the usual weight of the world on his mind.

"I'm going to start with the worst news, and it's going to go downhill from there," he said, pulling a stack of files from his valise and laying them on the table. "The president informed me that Arthur Blade has stage four cancer and has six months to live."

A low murmur rolled through the room as the men conferred amongst themselves.

Blade was the Director of Clandestine Service, the spymaster, and nearly every covert operation across his desk. Colson sipped coffee while waiting for everyone to digest what he'd just told them.

"This is the worst news to hit Langley in many years. Arthur has an encyclopedic knowledge of spycraft and an uncanny ability to monitor and direct our assets throughout the world. Let's just say it would take all of us, along with two supercomputers, to do the job he handles daily. Arthur is currently undergoing a procedure that offers some hope in slowing the onset of his symptoms. I know I speak for all of us when I say our thoughts and prayers are with him. If this procedure is successful, he will begin a lengthy debriefing within a week. If not...." Colson winced. "Well, let's not even go there."

Colson had already come up with a plan for dividing Blade's workload until he returned. "Bates, you and Tidwell will split the duties of Arthur's foreign assets. I'll supply a list of names and last known locations. From that list, you should be able to contact each and get a sitrep. I expect both of you to brief me on your initial findings by the week's end. The two of you decide who handles which agents. Just make damn sure we don't miss anyone."

"Winchell, you are to assume Arthur's role in the day-to-day affairs here at Langley. That includes a lot of paper pushing, but it needs to be done. You can coordinate between me and Blade's secretary to identify his open and active case files. From there, we can decide the order of importance of each. Be prepared. There are many."

Colson drummed his fingers, then added, "There are secondary issues that will have to be pushed into a holding pattern. One of the most pressing of these is the status of the defectors we have living in two of our safe houses. Uri Greggenkoff and Vladimir Folozchev both profess the desire to defect to this country. In return, both offer to share the details of their long careers with the Russian FSB and SVR."

He looked to Jerry Pritchard, Chief of Counterintelligence. "Jerry, I know you already have strong opinions on the subject. Put them on hold for another week. And go easy on the interrogations until then. Both of these spies seek asylum in our country. One is an asset. Intercepted messages tell us that much. The other is here to ensure we choose wrong and will then attempt to infiltrate the agency. Since the current status of both is stable, the issue will keep for now. We'll make our final decision after Blade beats his cancer."

Colson wiped his brow before continuing.

"Everything we do going forward is especially critical. Our esteemed elected officials on the hill will scrutinize every move we make to ensure we can deal with this internal catastrophe. Our primary priority is to keep our ship afloat. The second is to make goddamn sure these people don't see the leaks. If any of them have it in for the agency, now is when they will attack. Understand?"

All four nodded, scribbling quick notes.

"Good, then let's concentrate on what I've already given you. It's more than enough for now. Let nothing else fall through the cracks. Contact me or each other the moment you see an issue that is not being addressed or has the potential to get away from us. Got it?"

All three nodded.

"Good, we're done here."

Colson remained sitting, listening to the muffled comments as the room emptied. None of these men had any idea how difficult it would be to fill this one tactician's shoes. He had relied on Arthur Blade since becoming the director. When he arrived, Blade had already been in his position for ten years. The previous president and a group of senators elevated him to the directorship, then pushed hard to have Blade removed. Just being good at your job in Washington was never a guarantee of longevity. That was especially true of an organization that performed most of its work behind a veil of secrecy. He'd intended to comply with ousting Blade when he took the position. But once he understood the internal mechanisms of Langley and saw that Arthur Blade was the mastermind behind nearly every successful covert operation, Colson reconsidered and refused to let him go. He'd been right to trust his instincts all those years ago, and Blade continued to be the best choice for the job.

Colson stared at the stack of files yet to be shared with his team and let out a deep sigh. He'd never seen the company so vulnerable since he'd agreed to take the job. So much could go wrong, and it would be the smallest overlooked detail that brought the castle crashing down. Drop one ball, miss one deciphered message, and the critical intel of your field assets could be lost. Even worse, allow their situations and secrets to be compromised, and you risk their capture and torturous interrogations. Lost information was bad enough without losing lives. National security could hang in the balance. He said a silent prayer that they could glean enough information from Blade about his field agents and their assignments before cancer took him.

John Winchell paced behind his desk, walking a small oval path from wall to wall. His mid-level office offered little room to move about and no damned window. That was all about to change. Winchell would be moving into Arthur Blade's corner suite. All he had to do now was wait for the old gray bastard to assume room temperature.

Blade had been a thorn in his side and a hindrance to his own advancement within the agency for far too long. Not a day went by without crashing into obstacles imposed by him. The man was entrenched in every operation and had eyes and ears everywhere. No matter what precautions he took with his own operations, Blade somehow knew every detail before his plans were implemented. Langley was the kingdom of secrets, and yet Winchell couldn't keep a lid on a damn thing he did. Finally, he was near the end of the waiting game. Arthur Blade, the source of all his problems, the obstacle between him and a directorship, couldn't die soon enough.

Despite the uplifting news of Blade's illness, Winchell was still running damage control over the last situation that Blade had injected himself into.

"Why was he allowed to communicate with Vladimir Folozchev?" Winchell demanded. "That old Russian bastard is my asset. And how did he do it? I ordered the phone number to that safe house to be changed. What am I missing here?"

His right-hand agent sat silent, his eyes following as his boss paced the room.

"They changed the number, sir," the agent said in a heavy Korean accent. "The problem is, Arthur Blade still maintains access to most information going in and out and has dedicated people in every department. You don't deconstruct the network overnight that he built up over decades."

"Well, we damn well better start! The man is going to be pushing up daisies within months. It's a wonder he's still breathing. We need to know what he knows, Mako. Penetrate his inner circle. And for god's sake, find out who gave him access to *my* Russian defector!"

The office door opened, and Winchell's second assistant entered, slurping from a tall coffee cup.

"And where the hell have you been, Fossie? I told you both to be here on the hour. Even Mako made it on time."

Fossie took the other seat before Winchell's desk, unfazed, taking another sip. "You asked me to look into the warhead sting. I thought you would rather have me show up late than empty-handed."

"And?" Winchell held out his hands.

"You wanted access to Blade's phone records during the operation. Not gonna happen. That is impossible. No one has access, and I mean no one. Even a casual inquiry would send up red flags."

"Damn it, I am Folozchev's handler. No one should have access to him unless they go through me. Blade could never have caught that shipment without access to my Russian. He should have been forced to come directly to me, or the operation should have failed."

"But they stopped two Soviet warheads from being detonated in Washington, DC," Fossie pointed out. "How is that a bad thing?"

"That's not the point here, is it? Christ, Fossie! Pay attention. Everything in this building is about power. Both of you should know that by now. But there is no way I can replace Arthur Blade without the loyalty of my subordinates and access to every inside track of intel available to him. We need to know his secrets, and we need them now." Winchell thought for a moment. "You said you didn't come here empty-handed. I hope to hell that wasn't your idea of good information."

Fossie grinned. "I have more."

"Well, then out with it, man!"

"They used two different groups to coordinate the takedown. His inner team is the go-to for most of his operations. You won't get a crumb of info from any of them. The second team, though—" Fossie pulled out his phone and sent his boss a file. "Blade had a disgruntled agent on his team who's pissed about not receiving a promotion. He doesn't seem to know much, but he will sing for coin if you know what I mean. I just sent you his profile."

Winchell took his seat, flipped open his laptop, and studied the file. "This guy is a low-level hack!" he exclaimed, pointing at the screen.

"True," Fossie said, "but he still has a few friends inside what Blade calls his 'B' team."

Mako nodded in agreement. "You could offer this guy a spot on your transition team. He might pick the brains of his co-workers for the right incentive."

"That's what I was thinking," Fossie agreed. "This guy has no loyalty, and he measures his success in dollar signs."

Winchell grinned. "He could be very useful. I'll have the personnel department offer him a promotion. But be sure you don't let him anywhere near anything confidential. I wouldn't trust this guy as far as I could throw him. And speaking of my nemesis, where the hell is Blade? He's been MIA for days. Winchell told me he checked into some treatment center to try and battle his cancer. Fat chance! Still, I want to know where it is and if he's making any progress. We should be surveilling him twenty-four-seven. For all we know, he's spending his last days giving the Russians every secret they ask for. God, I would love to catch him in the act of passing secrets to the enemy before he croaks. Just some footage of him meeting with his handler would do it."

"Sir, you realize you're the only one in the entire CIA who believes Blade is a double agent, right?"

"Says you. And whose side are you on, anyway? Who gave you this job? I believe that was me. And that means you follow my directives. That is if you still like your job. You do like your job, don't you?"

Fossie set his coffee cup on a side table, crossed his arms, and stared back.

"Never underestimate my gut intuition on these things. I know Blade is playing both sides. One of his friends from MI-6 is selling secrets to the Russians and the Chinese as we speak. So is he."

"I suggest you have some evidence in your hand before running this theory up the chain of command," Fossie cautioned.

"No need for that. You think I'm the only one that believes this? Hmm? The director has had the same suspicions for years. He's just very cautious with whom he shares his theories. And please, don't offer any more advice. You're attempting to think way above your pay grade."

Winchell turned to Mako. "I would like a list of operatives that report to Blade. I also want to know whom he speaks to within the firm." He thought a moment, then added, "He was dating someone after his wife died. Find out who she is and if she's still in the picture. For all we know, she was the point of contact."

Mako scribbled a note and nodded.

"I'm going to share a little something with the two of you in the strictest confidence," Winchell said. "Folozchev keeps insisting there is a high-level double agent working among us. He doesn't come right out and name Blade, but that's who he's talking about. I want that name. Mako, go to the safe house and spend some quality one-on-one time with our defector. Don't hurt him too badly. No cuts or bruises on the face. But it's about time we put the fear of God into this son of a bitch. Let him know this is the day of reckoning. Either he puts up now, or we ship him back to the SVR."

Mako closed his hands into fists, cracking his knuckles. "I can do that," he said with a satisfied grin.

Eight
And Then He Was Gone

Arthur Blade had not served in the military, but the president insisted on a burial at Arlington National Cemetery. His years of service to the CIA and his country were sacrifice enough to allow him to rest with the nation's other fallen heroes.

"Arthur was my friend," the president eulogized. "I have never met a more brilliant or dedicated servant of the people. He gave his full measure in defense of this nation. For twenty-one years, he worked the front lines of the CIA. Once he transitioned to an office at Langley, it was natural for him to ensure the safety and support of those he had once served alongside. For another twenty-eight years, Arthur Blade fought the good fight as director of counterintelligence. We are safer now, thanks to his unselfish efforts. Today we mourn the passing of a patriot, a defender of the Constitution, a good man, and a wonderful friend. There will never be another like him." He looked at the flag-draped coffin and said, "Goodbye, Arthur."

Lou Azzilonti watched from the grave beside Audrey Landers. Neither had found the words to express their grief.

Blade's immediate team of Jim Piper and Garrett Logan stood by with their wives, all wincing with each loud crack of the twenty-one gun salute. Audrey was friends with Logan's wife, Jill, and the two shared a tearful exchange.

The president was handed the folded flag that covered Blade's casket, and he offered it to Audrey. She refused, saying President Lux knew him the best and the longest and should keep it. It was what Arthur would have wanted, she suggested.

Countless handshakes and hugs later, Lou escorted Audrey back to her car. Neither felt like attending a brunch being offered at a nearby restaurant, a favorite of Arthur's. The finality of the moment left them both longing for time alone with their thoughts. Lou offered one last embrace as she slid into her car and drove away, then walked the short distance to his SUV. He thought he had been prepared for the death of his friend. There had been little chance of beating back the disease, and both he and Arthur knew that. Still, the emptiness he now felt was crippling, tightening around his chest and squeezing the air from his lungs. He wiped away a tear as he opened the car door. It still didn't seem real and likely wouldn't for a long time to come. Good friends like Arthur only come around a few times in one's life. The thought made him realize that he didn't want to be alone, and he headed for a quiet watering hole he'd shared a few times with Arthur. He would toast his fallen friend before heading back into the city.

A secret service agent tapped the president's shoulder. "Sir, there is a Dr. Hanspratten here who would like a few words. He says you know him."

President Walter Lux recognized the name and motioned for his security detail to allow him through. "Doctor," he said, shaking his hand. "Good of you to come, thank you." He leaned in and added, "I wanted to thank you personally for all you did attempting to save Arthur's life. I wish it would have ended differently, but we understood from the beginning that it was a long shot."

The doctor nodded. "I'm sorry we haven't been able to speak sooner. The process is complicated, and his condition had to be constantly monitored. It left me little time to offer updates."

"I understand. Could you tell me how far along you were able to get with the treatments, and — did he suffer?"

Hanspratten offered a sly smile. "I think you misunderstood. Mr. President, the procedure was a complete success. Arthur Blade is very much alive."

Lux's knees nearly buckled. "How?" He looked at the dwindling cluster of mourners still standing graveside. "What is all this, then? And why am I just hearing this now?"

"Because we buried his name and his former body today. You would not recognize him now if he were standing right beside you. I expect he will be in touch once he's advanced a little further in his therapy. It is going to take some time. For now, speech, or any physical activity, is difficult. But I will tell you this. The new Arthur Blade stood and took his first steps this morning."

Nine
NOT ALL GOOD NEWS IS GOOD NEWS

John Winchell sat at his desk with head down, fuming, sulking, one hand squeezing his temples, the other wrapped around a stress relief ball. Its therapeutic effects were yet to be seen. He glared at his two lieutenants and snarled.

"Blade is not dead after all."

He remained still for another moment, then huffed as he pitched the ball across the room.

Mako raised a hand with lightning quickness and snatched it in midair.

"Son of a bitch!" Winchell yelled. "This can't be happening!"

Fossie leaned forward in his chair. "What are you talking about? We were at the man's funeral. What are we missing here?"

Winchell's jaw tightened as his hands curled into fists. "Colson just gave us the lowdown. Blade underwent an experimental procedure. His odds of survival were so low that they pronounced him dead, anyway. To the rest of the world, he will remain that way." Winchell released his fists and clasped his hands together. "This—procedure was some sort of experimental brain transplant, and now Blade, his gray matter anyway, lives on in some other poor stiff's body."

"You're shitting me," Fossie said, looking on in disbelief.

"No," Winchell's eyes narrowed. "I am not shitting you."

"I saw a movie like that once, only the new body still had a mind of its own and was always fighting against..."

"Fossie, for god's sake, you're not helping here! Don't you get it? If he survives, he becomes the most valuable asset in the agency. They won't just be debriefing him. They will take advantage of all that previous experience and use it in every future field op. The job will remain his for years to come while I'm relegated to living in his shadow."

Winchell reached into a drawer and pulled out a pack of cigarettes and a small fan, clicked it on, and lit up. "You know the real creepy part of this?" he asked, blowing out a lungful of smoke. "We wouldn't even recognize him if he was standing next to us in an elevator. Colson and the president both believe in keeping his new identity concealed like it's a state secret. We may never get a good look at the new Arthur Blade."

"So Blade is alive and well and surviving as a science project," Fossie said, shaking his head. "Why have we never heard this technology even existed? You would think the CIA would be the first to know. It's only been performed a handful of times, and the success rate is low. But someone decided he was worth saving. I would bet it was the president."

"So, what does that mean for you?" Mako asked.

"I will begin debriefing him as soon as he is up to it, which is still a few weeks off."

"Then don't look so glum," Fossie said. "He's not out of the woods yet. Hell, he might not even live till then. I'll bet a lot of things could go wrong and probably will."

"True enough," Winchell said, his stern expression softening. "Only one other patient survived more than a year. Bad things can still happen."

Fossie laughed. "Wouldn't it be nice if he tripped down the stairs and his brain flopped out?"

Winchell sneered. "Morbid, as usual, Fossie, but a rather cheerful thought. Having him back here in any form is not good for me or either of you. His job will never be mine so long as he can sit in that office. Let's hope he makes this easy for all of us and just dies after being debriefed."

Mako shook his head, jeering. "This all sounds like a lot of science fiction to me."

"Thank you for that deep analytical assessment," Winchell said. "Has it occurred to you that the idea of landing men on the moon was once science fiction?"

"The moon landings were fake."

Fossie chuckled. "That sounds like something Kim Jong Un would say. You sure you're from South Korea and not a little further north?"

Mako turned to him and sneered. "You're an asshole."

"*You're* an asshole!" Fossie shot back.

"Oh, for the love of peace, shut the fuck up already, both of you! We have serious issues to contend with and no time for a pissing match. Blade is an enormous problem, but not the only one we're facing right now. Jerry Pritchard is pushing for a decision to be made on our defector. Colson still wants to delay any decision until Blade can weigh in. Uri Greggenkoff has the inside track because Blade trusts him. He's wrong, and we need to prove it before Blade returns and mucks it up. And Folozchev is the only one who says Blade is working for both sides. I need something from him to prove Arthur Blade is a double agent. Mako, did Folozchev offer any information during your last visit?"

Mako shook his head. "The man keeps his secrets. I doubt

you would get anything more from him unless we used more aggressive means of persuasion."

"Well, that's just great," Winchell scowled, crushing his cigarette out in an ashtray in the drawer and lighting another. "We're offering this man a new life, and he's not even trying to help us. I wonder if he knows how close he is to being deported?"

"Maybe you're going about it the wrong way," Fossie said.

"Meaning what?"

"Meaning he offers information on his own terms. You get nothing out of him unless he wants to give it. Vladimir likes rewards. When he gets them, he offers a few crumbs. I say, give him something he wants and take the crumbs. Take every damned one. At least it keeps us moving in the right direction."

Winchell sat back in his chair, nodding. "Fair enough. I'll give that a try this afternoon. If that fails, then it's his own funeral. Did you get a list of Blade's associates?"

Fossie pushed send on his phone. "This is a file of everyone on both of his teams. He relies most heavily on Garret Logan and Jim Piper. I don't think you could crack either of them. His B team is comprised of a few floaters that are also used by Mansfield and Gilbertson. Again, most are loyal to a fault. The weak link is a guy named Duane Grady. His record is a little too clean if you know what I mean. If I had to guess, I'd bet his position in the agency was a political favor. Maybe Daddy got him the job. Anyway, Grady is the one we should be trying to bring over to our side. He might spill some secrets over a few beers."

Winchell nodded. "What are his guys doing without Blade in the meantime?"

"Anyone who knows anything is being tight-lipped. It sounds like they're reporting to Colson for the time being."

"Get what you can out of Grady," Winchell said. "Blade was seen with a woman numerous times. Anything on her?"

"Audrey Landers," Mako said. "They dated for a short time. I would not consider her important."

"Don't be so willing to discount a potential lead. She may be Blade's contact with the Russians or the Chinese. Check her out anyway."

Mako shook his head. "Waste of time. I have seen nothing to suggest Blade is a double agent. And if this woman is his contact, then she is the best I've ever seen. She sits alone when she dines out, walks a lot, and takes a pilates course. Her handler would have to be a server at the restaurant or one of the other women in her class."

"My gut tells me there is something there. Keep on it." Winchell snuffed out the last cigarette, ditched the fan, and wiped the ashes from his desktop. "And now I have to head out and visit with our defector."

"Be sure and arrive bearing gifts," Fossie suggested.

"You might be onto something there. I'll try it. In the meantime, I want you to do some digging into this clinic that did the procedure on Blade. Oh, and by the way, none of what we discussed about Blade, including his defiance of death, can be repeated. God forbid word gets out, and the leak gets traced back to this office. Do not let that happen. Understood?"

Both of his agents nodded.

"Get to it then," Winchell said, turning away. He watched them leave, then picked up the phone and dialed the safe house. His man, Mackie, answered. "Anything to report?" Winchell asked.

"Nada, quiet morning."

"Good, I'll be there within the hour."

Ten
THE TALE OF TWO DEFECTORS

John Winchell entered the safe house carrying a bag of bagels and four coffees. He handed two of the cups to the agents tasked with guarding Vladimir Folozchev and told them to take a break. He set the bag down, pulled out a coffee for himself, and placed the other one before Folozchev. The Russian looked up through heavy lidded bloodshot eyes and a cloud of cigarette smoke.

"What is occasion?" he asked. "You send tough guy to rough me up. Then you come make with nice. I think is called good cop, bad cop."

Winchell noticed a few blood droplets on the Russian's collar and a split lip. He'd told Mako to avoid leaving any marks on Folozchev's face. He'd done it anyway and still extracted no useful information.

Winchell faked a smile. "The occasion, Vladimir, is your wake-up call." He sat and pulled the lid off his cup, taking a big sip. "Ah, now, that's good. I don't know if it was worth the fifteen minutes I spent standing in line, but damn, they make good coffee!" He reached into the bag and pulled out a salted bagel. "I can't even eat these at home anymore. 'Too much sodium, all those carbs,'" he said, mocking his wife's health concerns. "You know what I say? You have to eat some of the bad stuff to offset the cardboard taste of the healthy shit." He tossed the bag across the table to Folozchev. "Have one. They're very good."

"Wife is right," he said, pushing the bag away. "Bad for blood pressure. Make you fat."

Winchell snorted. "So says the overweight, chain-smoking alcoholic." He leaned in and said, "Listen, I went to bat for you yesterday with the director. The problem is," he took another sip. "The problem is, you're not giving us shit. For three months, you've been in this safe house, taking up our time and tying up our resources. I told you when we started that the price of admission into this country was good, actionable intel."

He pushed away from the table and began pacing. "My director wants to cut you loose, and I don't mean into a nice apartment near DC. He recommends we put you on a flight to Ukraine and let you find your own way home. I'm inclined to agree with him. So here's what we're going to do. We're going to enjoy a nice private moment, just you and me, and you're going to give me something worth repeating to my superiors." He walked behind Folozchev and leaned in. "That, or we load you into the back of a C-30 transport, and you spend twelve hours freezing your ass off while thinking about how to explain to your superiors where you've been for the last ninety days. The next move is yours."

Folozchev snubbed out his cigarette in an overflowing ashtray and took a sip of coffee. "Is good," he nodded. "Better than in Moscow. But coffee is still best in Havana or Bogota."

"You worked in Columbia?" Winchell said.

"I have been everywhere."

"See, that's what I mean, Vladimir. You don't give specifics or anything that we can use. Should I call the airport and get your flight ready? Tell you what, you give me the identity of the high-level operative within the CIA. That will be your golden ticket to just about anything you could ask for."

Folozchev scoffed. "You forget I give you one. Arthur Blade."

Winchell shook his head, sneering. "Without a lick of proof. Back it up with facts, damn it. And give me another name."

"I am dead, man if I tell you."

"You have my personal assurance that you will be safe."

"Safe? Like safe when you send Korean goon to pound answers out me? This man, Mako, is sadist, yes? He like his job maybe too much. I think you tell him no punches to face, but he do anyway. Keep eye on this one. Do not trust."

"Thanks," Winchell said in a mocking tone. "Good to know. However, this is *not* the information I came here looking for. Time is tight, Vladimir. Either put up or get on the plane."

Folozchev's eyes followed Winchell as he paced around the table. "Go with easy one," he said. "Uri Greggenkoff is defector living in safe house. He is spy. Send him back to Moscow."

Winchell couldn't hide his shock at what this man knew. He decided this was where to begin if he wanted to keep Folozchev and deport Greggenkoff. "Time to earn your keep, Vladimir," he said. "Tell me everything you know about Uri Greggenkoff."

Folozchev crushed out a butt and lit another, inhaling a deep lung full and holding it a moment before blowing it out. "He is from old days at KGB. Then he go to FSB. He still works for FSB."

"We already knew that. But you're SVR. You guys are the computer hackers inside nearly every corporate mainframe around the world. Greggenkoff is FSB, so he's Russian national security and reports directly to Putin. We were told that none of your intel-gathering services shared information with each other. So how is it you know so much about him? And why do you insist he's a double agent? Did you work with Greggenkoff at some point? Give me one solid piece of evidence to prove what you're saying."

"Look at wife," Folozchev said. "He walk away and leave her home when he come to this country. If you defect, you take wife, no? If Uri defect then wife is taken to Black Dolphin Prison to pay for his crime."

The thought of the notorious Black Dolphin Political Prison made Winchell's muscles tense. Every known dissident locked within its walls never emerged again. He scribbled some notes. "I will look into this," he said, then watched as Folozchev sipped coffee and sucked the cigarette down to the filter.

"You tell me something," Folozchev asked. "Now that Blade is dead, you get promotion?"

"Another surprise. Where *do* you get your news, Vladimir?"

Folozchev shrugged. "I hear many things. Maybe your men talk. Maybe TV news. Big funeral, yes?"

Winchell nodded. "Yeah, big funeral, a little premature."

"Mean what?"

"You're supposed to be answering my questions, not the other way around." Winchell let out a sigh. "It means he's not dead."

Folozchev nodded, lighting another cigarette. "So no promotion. Bad for you, I think."

"Vladimir, how is it you know so much about Arthur Blade?"

"Your men, they talk about you."

Winchell's jaw tightened. Who was the big mouth on his team talking in front of a man who was supposed to be treated as an enemy combatant? No wonder they were losing at the counter-intelligence game. He would have to deal with them later. Right now, he had to keep his defector talking. "Tell me what you've heard."

"You want promotion. Arthur Blade is in way. Simple fix. Prove Arthur Blade is spy. Now he is not in way."

"It's not that simple."

Folozchev snorted and scratched his armpit. "I know problem go away, then come back. Blade is dead. Blade is not so dead."

Winchell blew out an exasperated breath. He felt like unloading the entire situation. Who else would understand his problem like someone in a similar position, albeit from the opposing side? He hated to admit it, but the crusty old Russian was the closest thing he had to a friend.

"Blade was dying of cancer. These doctors did a partial brain transplant. Blade now has a new body, a new face, and he lives to fight another day."

Folozchev nodded at this as though it was old news. "You have seen new Blade?"

"No, not yet."

"He will be different, yes, but not so much."

"Wait, how can you possibly know that? You've been locked in here for three months with no newspapers, no outside communication. And my men didn't know any of this, so they couldn't tell you."

Folozchev lit up again. Winchell was sure the man was knocking down four packs a day.

"New technology, but is old, also. Russian doctors experiment with same thing. They take one side of brain, implant to new host. Patient live few days." He shrugged. "They try again. Next patient live weeks. They try again. Now patients live years. Many problems." He closed his eyes, shaking his head while blowing smoke out his nose. "Bad way to go, but doctors keep trying." He looked up to Winchell. "Patient and donor must be very, um, what is word— same? Like twins, almost. Near same age, blood type, body size. All these things must be just so or new body reject new brain."

"You're telling me that the new Arthur Blade will look like the old? That he would still be an old man."

"Yes, yes, this I am told. Russian doctors say is only way procedure work."

"Well, that's all very interesting, but it doesn't help me now. I don't know when I will see the new Blade, if ever. They may keep his identity hidden from everyone. In that case, he'll work from the shadows and continue to be a pain in my ass until he meets his maker. Shit!" he exclaimed, dropping back into his chair.

Folozchev's droopy brows raised, giving Winchell a look that seemed to say, 'Do I have to explain everything?'

"You are in spy business," he said. "Think like spy."

"Excuse me?" Winchell said, incensed.

"Mr. Winchell, if Arthur Blade my problem, I find out about procedure, about health. I find who is doctor. Is only one? Here, maybe yes. If something happen to doctor, who is to treating Blade? Who is to give special medication, testing? No one, I think. No doctor, no Arthur Blade." Folozchev stared at Winchell as though waiting for the light to go on inside the man's head. A long cigarette ash fell onto the table. He took no notice.

Winchell's eyes narrowed. "Are you suggesting that I kill Arthur Blade's doctor?"

Folozchev waved his hand dismissively. "I say no such thing. I say what good spy do. Good spy go to doctor's office, get file on donor, take doctor out of picture. Maybe is good advice to you. Maybe not. You decide."

Folozchev took a big swig from his cup. "You right. Is

good coffee. I think nice steak dinner is good, also. Maybe you take me to nice restaurant for steak."

Winchell thought back to Fossie's words about offering rewards to the Russian. He had pegged Folozchev to a T, and Winchell was finally yielding some of those crumbs. At the same time, Folozchev was dangling a carrot of his own in front of Winchell, alluding to more secrets to be revealed in exchange for more preferential treatment. Okay, new rules, new game. But he still needed enough crumbs to resemble a slice of pie to take back to Colson and counterintelligence chief Pritchard. That was the only way he could justify spending any more time and resources.

"You still need to give me more than this before I can break protocol and take you off of the reservation."

The Russian reached into the bag and began devouring a bagel. He swallowed half of it at once and said, "You want something for boss? Okay. We exchange agents years back. You give us a few innocent Russians living in US. We give you your spy, Karl Owen. We catch him red-handed." Folozchev pointed to himself and said, "I do the interrogate. We turn Karl Owen. He work now for Commonwealth of Independent States. He is Russian spy. Uri Greggenkoff is handler. Karl Owen is very good spy. He send Greggenkoff many secrets. Greggenkoff tell me these things."

Winchell tapped his pen on the notepad. "You're telling me that our agent who was returned to us is working for Russian Intelligence? A man who spent six years in solitary confinement, interrogated and tortured every single day, and he now works for his jailers? Prove it!"

"What to prove? You once had many secrets from SVR. Karl Owen tell us. Now no more secrets. Uri Greggenkoff tell me. I now tell you. Is good information, yes?" Folozchev took another large bite of a bagel and washed it down with coffee.

"Then why, if Owen was such an asset to the SVR, why give him up now?"

Folozchev swallowed the last of the bagel and lit another cigarette. "I am standing at door to your country asking to come inside. No more spy game. Get me big SUV with driver, nice condo, good food, good clothes, good life. You give me these things, I give you secrets. I have many more."

Winchell nodded but remained skeptical. "This is all very interesting," he said, "but it's your word against his. Tell me when and how you met with Greggenkoff."

"Many times we meet. Uri likes good Starka. You know this drink?"

"I'm familiar with it, yes, but I've never drank it."

"Greggenkoff like it maybe too much. He drink and he talk. Drink more, talk more. He tell me about Karl Owen. Owen good spy for Russia, very bad for CIA. Bad like Kim Philby, I think."

The name Philby still made Winchell twitch. The damage inflicted by the MI-6 operative turned Russian counterspy was still felt across the global intelligence community. If the Russians had turned Karl Owen, then he could still do great damage. Either way, it made sense to treat this information as a credible threat and follow up. For now, at least, he would do the research on his own without sounding the alarm. Something this big could help with his career advancement. But if he blew the whistle too soon, and it was later found that Folezchev had lied and the information about Owen was wrong, it could ruin him. A cautious approach would be the rule of the day. Playing along with his defector for the time being made the most sense.

Folozchev was finally earning his keep. He pulled his phone, tapped a number from memory, and waited. "Hello, Connie. Please make me a dinner reservation for two at a local steak house for tonight. Yes, six o'clock would be fine."

Vladimir Folozchev was having his best day since entering the United States. His nemesis, Arthur Blade, would likely be dead soon. As luck would have it, the wet work might even be performed by an envious underling. He thought back to the years he'd gone head to head with Blade and was not ashamed to admit that the spy handler was the most formidable adversary he had ever faced.

He was ecstatic to have an enemy as weak and incompetent as John Winchell. If this was the new face of the CIA, he could already envision the rise and rebirth of the Soviet Union.

When he'd accepted this assignment, it was to bring closure to his own career in the most glorious way possible. It was a sweetheart of a deal. Something rarely offered to retiring members of the SVR. 'Spend your sunset years in America,' they had told him. In exchange, they gave him three tasks and warned him not to fail on any. First, he was to establish and maintain a pipeline of information by offering himself up to the CIA as a defector and informant. It was a way of providing good intel back to the motherland while feeding disinformation to his new handlers. This was important in order to fulfill the promise of item two; provide enough disinformation to discredit Uri Greggenkoff and get him loaded on a plane and shipped home. The secrets possessed by this defector could set Russian intelligence back decades. Greggenkoff was a dead man the moment his plane touched down on Russian soil. The SVR did not imprison traitors and defectors. It eliminated them.

Folozchev would enjoy hero status for inserting himself as a trusted informant within the CIA while assuring the demise of Uri Greggenkoff. But the triple crown would be won by eliminating the greatest spy handler he had ever faced, Arthur

Blade. Blade's death was Folozchev's price of admission and the most important reason for his being sent here. Greggenkoff's defection had merely expedited the plan. And what better way to prove the other spy was an imposter than by requesting sanctuary himself and insisting his counterpart was a double agent? The misleading information he'd supplied concerning a pair of nuclear warheads to be detonated in Washington, DC, brought the risk of new scrutiny upon himself. The plan was to give the CIA enough that they trusted Folozchev but not enough to find the warheads in time. He wondered if it had been Greggenkoff who helped them avert the threat.

John Winchell had no clue he was being reeled into Folozchev's ploy like a helpless fish that had swallowed the hook. He'd done research on the likely CIA operatives he would face when entering the country. John Winchell's name was at the top of the list. On paper, the man appeared more formidable. Good breeding, excellent education, even a respectable resumé. Winchell had it all. And yet, he had become the best-educated idiot Folozchev ever met.

He lit another cigarette as he thought how life in this new country would be a fitting reward for the years he had spent toiling to weaken it. Sun-drenched winters in Miami would be much kinder to his aching joints than the endless shivering nights in that tiny shack in Siberia. He smiled and redirected his thoughts to the next list of lies he would feed to this buffoon at dinner. Oh, how wonderful a good bottle of vodka was going to taste with that steak tonight!

Eleven
WHY WON'T YOU JUST DIE?

John Winchell drummed his fingers as he stared at a wall clock. The hours and days crept by, like watching mold grow when he was stuck in a room with this frustrating man.

Arthur Blade sat across from him in the meeting room of the recovery center, looking like a wrapped mummy. Every square inch of the man was concealed from view. His face and head were wrapped in gauze bandages, his hands gloved, and he wore a baggy burgundy warmup suit zipped up to his chin. There was nothing visible that distinguished him as Blade, yet Winchell knew it was him in there. That annoying, pompous attitude could only belong to one person. Even hearing him speak through a new voice did nothing to dispel the fact that this was Blade doing what he did best; evading every question.

Everything so far sounded like a press release with all the useful information redacted. Winchell pushed the pause button on the recorder that sat between them. "Arthur," he said, showing his frustration. "Forgive me, but isn't this the reason they kept you alive with that Frankenstein brain swap? Honestly, you omit more details than you include. How the hell can we move forward if you go permanently horizontal? You owe it to the company to be more forthright. Throw me a bone, man!" Winchell started the recorder again and settled into his seat, on edge, and prepared for more of the same useless dribble.

Blade's expression was impossible to read beneath the bandages, but it didn't matter. Winchell wanted to piss off the old spy. That was the point. Push him until he started giving up some useful intel. But despite his goading, Blade's eyes remained expressionless. "I'm giving you what I can, John," he said with a dry calmness. "Much of my information cannot be shared with someone at your security clearance level. My oath of office limits my responses to what I can give. Now, if you would like to put me in a soundproof room with the president or the CIA director, I'm sure I can reveal much, much more. Nothing personal, old man. Just following protocol."

"Goddamn it, Blade, we can't go forward without knowing who your deep cover field operatives are and where they're operating. Give me that much, anyway."

"Send Colson, or send the president. Until I am, as you say, horizontal, I will keep my secrets. Why don't you stop wasting both of our time and make that call now while I get a coffee and a snack."

Blade pushed his chair out and staggered, then reached for a cane and hobbled out of the room. His recovery, according to Dr. Hanspratten, was progressing well. For Blade, however, the weeks following the procedure had crawled along at a snail's pace. The physique of his new body was impressive. He longed to put it through its paces but so far could only manage the most basic of movements in frustrating slow-motion.

Blade left the room and listened as Winchell made a call to the CIA director Colson. He could be more forthcoming with his information if he chose. But with every rude comment from Winchell, he became more resolute about not offering anything useful. He had told Colson from the beginning that he was prepared to document the names and locations of his covert agents but that it must go through the proper channels. No shortcuts. There would be no release of classified intel to anyone he didn't trust. That was especially true for Winchell, who, in his opinion, was a politically appointed hack who rode in on the coattails of some flash-in-the-pan senator. There was also little doubt that Winchell would use anything he revealed in his effort to force Blade out of his job.

He concentrated on walking, further frustrated with how wobbly his legs felt. Every part of him moved like a frail, ninety-year-old man carrying a three-hundred-pound backpack. Rounding the corner into a vending area, he was seized with explosive pain in the back of his head that radiated downward. His eyesight filled with black dots, and he crumpled to the floor. An ear-bursting ringing filled his head, then faded along with the black dots. He lay there cognizant but unable to move a finger, a toe, anything. His mind felt detached from his body, as though all connections had been severed.

All around him were the sounds of shrill voices and running footsteps. Hanspratten hurried to his side, bent down, and peered into Blade's unfocused eyes. "Can you hear me, Arthur?" he asked calmly.

The only thing Blade could move were his eyelids. He blinked once.

"We've seen this before. It should pass within a few moments."

Blade hoped he was right. This was as bad as when he'd first awoken from the procedure. An unpleasant sensation crept through every limb, like the return of blood flow following the circulation being pinched off. It progressed through his entire body and, with it, the return of muscle function. He turned his head toward the doctor.

"Very good!" Hanspratten remarked. "Now, let's get you off this floor."

Blade raised the weight of his torso with his arm. It felt stronger, more assured.

"Here, let me help you," the doctor offered.

Blade waved him off. "No, let me try," he said, rolling onto his feet and standing. The increase in strength and balance surprised him. He grinned, squatted back down, and raised himself up.

"Most extraordinary," the doctor said, watching in awe. "That seizure was likely caused by accelerated neural connectivity. You are healing at an incredible rate. Let me see you walk."

Blade took a tentative step forward. It felt solid, without tremors or weakness. The numbness and tingling in his arms and legs were gone, replaced with a sense of a direct connection with every fiber of muscle in his body. Turning back, he smiled mischievously and began walking sure-footed down the hall, his gait improving with each step. At the end, he turned and attempted to quicken his step but came close to tripping over his feet. He stopped and regained his balance, staring down in frustration. With a huff, he walked the rest of the way back.

"Give it time," Hanspratten told him. "I would expect your progress from this point on to be measurable in yards rather than inches. Be careful, though. You have just seen how easy it is to get ahead of yourself. Do not exceed what your body tells you it can do. At least not yet. I would expect these brief episodes to be with you for some time to come. What did you experience just before the onset?"

"Blinding headache, ears ringing so loud I thought they would burst."

"And then the loss of motor function?"

"Yes, as though I were a marionette, and someone cut my strings."

The doctor nodded his understanding. "Remember these symptoms, Arthur. At the onset of the next episode, lay yourself down in anticipation. The last thing we need is for you to fall and hit that head of yours. There is no telling the damage you could inflict."

Hanspratten caught his attention and motioned with a tilt of his head up the hall. Blade looked to see John Winchell leaning against the doorway, watching intently. "And now," the doctor said, "others are learning your secrets."

Twelve
THE LONG KNIVES

Winchell wasted no time in sharing what he'd learned with his two assistants. "He's getting better," he muttered, doing his usual pacing from wall to wall in the tight office. "He's getting better fast. One minute, the guy is struggling to walk with a cane. The next, he's sprinting down the hall. At this pace, he'll be back in his office within weeks. Why couldn't he just do this the easy way and die?" He stopped and stared at Fossie and Mako. "Listen, you two, I need answers, and I need them now. Fossie, you've been chumming up with this dropout from Blade's team. Has he told you anything useful?"

"Duane Grady is now on our team. He's talking and says he's picking the brains of his former co-workers."

"Good," Winchell nodded, "very good. What is he telling you?"

"Well, to begin with, he shared an inside scoop about the clinic that did Blade's procedure. They're also experimenting with DNA splicing and body rejection stuff. Real pointy-headed chemistry. It sounds like they've overcome a lot of the problems connected with previous transplants."

Winchell shook his head. "I'm betting it's all still very experimental and not ready for prime time. This lab hasn't registered a single patent or produced even one double-blind study. No, my gut tells me they're not all that cutting-edge. Even if they pulled off this surgery, they would still have to play by the old rules of donor matching. That means Blade's new body can't be all that different from the old. They would need someone as close to his age, blood type, and all the other donor bullshit I know nothing about. And they would have to keep him pumped full of anti-rejection meds."

Fossie shook his head. "I'm not sure I would assume that, boss. They may have developed a few wonder drugs and are just using them for their own purpose."

"No financial viability," Winchell said, waving him off. "Nobody can afford the expense of developing these breakthroughs without going for the big payoff. No, I believe we can assume the new Arthur Blade won't differ greatly from the old Blade. Trust me on this one. Let's just say I have some insider info."

He turned to Mako. "You were supposed to be tracking down his prospective donor by digging through morgue files. Tell me you found something useful."

Mako swiped a finger across his phone. "There were thousands of older victims of major brain trauma from the last three months alone. I filtered them by age, physical characteristics, all the details you gave me to search for. That eliminated most and brought the number down to just over a hundred. The causes of death varied; motorcycle accidents, gunshots to the head, stuff like that. Most were younger or suffered massive head trauma. A few came close to being viable, but listed multiple issues on the death certificates. None of these would have been suitable donors."

"Are you looking at the national records or just local?"

"I checked both. Not a single one fits the description you had me searching for."

"Bullshit! We know they found a suitable donor. That's a fact. That means the records are there, and you missed it."

"I think what Mako is saying is you should open up the search window wider," said Fossie. "If the donor falls just outside of the parameters you're giving, you'll never find him."

Winchell shook his head. "No, I'm not wrong about this. Keep looking, damn it, but you can open the search window to six months. They might have been keeping the stiff on ice. We need this information now before Blade can come back to work. Make sure you search through any military deaths as well."

Fossie held up his hand. "That's a waste of time. The victims from six months out are not just brain dead. They're stiffs. And you're not gonna find many seventy-year-old grandpa types who just died from fresh combat wounds."

Winchell waved him away like swatting at a fly. "Just do it." He reached into his drawer and lit another cigarette without bothering to turn on the fan. "Shit! Shit, shit, shit!" He growled, pacing back and forth through his smoke cloud. "What do you do with a pest that just won't die?"

"Call an exterminator," Mako said.

"That's rather simplistic, Mako, even for you."

"Now wait," Fossie countered. "Since when is simple a bad thing? Think that through like an exterminator. You have a mouse in the house, so what do you do?"

"Set a trap and bait it," Winchell answered. But we don't.... "

"We don't what?" Fossie cut him off. "We have vermin that need to be eliminated. This is the same thing. We know he's out there, just like we would know there's a mouse in the wall even though we haven't seen him. All we have to do is set the trap, the right trap, and wait for him to expose himself."

Winchell shook his head. "It can't be that easy."

"And why not?" Fossie was on a roll now. "All you have to do is choose the right trap. Even more important is the right bait. Something he would feel driven to handle himself and be willing to step into with complete confidence. Some routine issue that was just another walk in the park for the master spy".

"Let's assume he recovers," Mako chimed in. "What if we could get him back in the field so he could try out his new hardware, so to speak? You know, he was an agent for years. I'll bet he loved doing hands-on work and would jump at the chance to do it again. Just offer him the opportunity and watch what happens."

Winchell remained unmoving as he mulled it over. A sly grin crept across his face. "That has some merit." He leaned forward and scribbled a few notes. "Let's hope he just makes it easy for us and drops dead soon. If not, we can look further into something like this."

"I met with Blade again yesterday," John Winchell said as he settled into a seat in Director Colson's office. "I spent hours, Don, hours! He didn't tell me a thing that we don't already know. Correct me if I'm wrong, but I thought the purpose of saving his life was so we could extract a little knowledge from his melon before he went to meet his maker."

"That's stating it rather coarse, but yes, that was the reasoning behind it. I also suspect he's suffering from some lapses in memory. I would hope these pass in time, and you can document more details of our field operations."

"What he's suffering from is more like selective memory, if you ask me. He has no intention of giving up what he knows. He came right out and told me my pay grade was too low to be brought in. Then he says he will only reveal his secrets to you or the president. Who the hell does he think he is?" Winchell stood and began his pacing. "I don't think he will tell even you. If you ask me, I would say he's saving the best for his Russian handlers."

Colson's eyes narrowed. "Are you going to start with your double agent diatribe again? For crying out loud, John, give it a rest."

Winchell stopped in his tracks and wagged a finger at the director. "These are questions that need to be asked. They have infiltrated us before. Think about Jim Nicholson. I read from the reports of that case that he seemed above reproach. An instructor out at the farm, no less, training our future CIA assets. Yet the SVR recruited him right under the watchful eyes of the agency. We need answers, Don. The preservation of our organization is at stake. And Arthur Blade is not above suspicion."

Colson dropped his head and squeezed the bridge of his nose. "There are questions demanding answers. And then there are the witch hunts. This feels a lot like the latter. But hey, you want to be that guy who questions everyone and everything? Go ahead. But I'll tell you this. If I was betting on the people I could trust in this building with absolute confidence, my money would be on Arthur Blade. Oh, and Don, just one more thing—"

Winchell's eyebrows raised. "Yes?"

"Do it on your own time. We have genuine issues that need to be addressed here. We're done."

John Winchell took a deep, incensed breath and headed for the door. In Colson's eyes, Arthur Blade walked on water. Every legitimate argument suggesting the Russians had turned Blade fell on deaf ears. Now the man would soon return to active service. The window of opportunity wasn't just closing. It was slamming shut. In another month, Blade would be back at the agency, and once that happened, Winchell would be trapped in his tiny office and dead-end position for years to come. His frustration reached the boiling point.

He stopped and spun toward the director. "He's lying, and I know it! My gut tells me he's withholding sensitive information that we have every right to know. I have spent years listening to liars, and I'm damned good at spotting them. I've been telling you of my suspicions about Blade for months now. If it were up to me, this entire fiasco would be shut down. We should back away and leave the man to die. We're no better off now than if he had. Only now, he represents a threat to this organization and the entire intelligence community."

Colson tried to speak, but Winchell cut him off. "Hear me out on this, Don. Somebody has to be the one who can smell a rat. If that means I make a few enemies along the way, then so be it. But I'm not fooled by what I see happening here. The big question is, how much longer do we give free rein to a man who may be a counterspy? This science experiment has been a total waste of time. He's been sitting in that clinic for weeks on end, wrapped up like a goddamned mummy, telling us only enough to make us go away."

Don Colson held up a hand to silence the tirade. "He has already resumed overseeing his field operatives, John. That means he is an asset, now and in the foreseeable future."

"Babysitting a convalescing Arthur Blade is a complete misuse of personnel and talent. It does nothing to disprove the possibility that he may be a deep-cover double agent. If this were my operation, I would..."

"You would what?" Colson sat back in his chair, folded his arms, and stared. "Go ahead. Tell me how I should be running my agency."

"I would put him in the field ASAP. Get him out of his comfort zone. He's more likely to slip up if he's out meeting with his handlers. Then we catch him in the act, and maybe we also bring in some of his network of spies."

Colson shook his head. "I still haven't seen a lick of proof that he is a double agent. Nothing. That being said, it's not a bad idea to get him out in the field. The doctors say he'll be ready to leave the clinic soon. And since you're the only one who believes he's leading a double life, I want you to show me where he can best be used. Then, maybe, Arthur can get back to work, and you will satisfy yourself that he plays only for our team. Bring me something worth his and my time. Then I'll decide if we should make it happen. You should also keep in mind that maintaining secrecy concerning his new identity is critical to any plan."

John Winchell gave a satisfied grin. His boss had taken the bait. "Right away," he said, walking to the door. "Right away."

John Winchell worked tirelessly, monitoring every bit of intel coming into Langley. The right situation could present itself at any time. He had to be ready at a moment's notice to manipulate the battlefield. Only then could his people be ready to catch Blade out from under the cover of his shadows and bandages. He also knew that he would be scrutinized by his superiors. Through it all, his confidence remained high, and his gut instincts told him the time to strike was near. Two weeks into his planning, he read an actionable bulletin and knew the moment had come.

The Cobalt car company based in North Dakota had suffered a cyber security breach. European hackers had infiltrated their computers and embedded a software bomb. If a ransom was not received within ninety-six hours, the hard drives on all the mainframe computers would be wiped clean. While this sort of hack happened with greater frequency these days, this one was a gem. Custom created for Winchell's purposes. The car company, a small but fast-growing electric manufacturer, was weeks away from the release of the first fully autonomous vehicle. Anticipation was high, and a software crash now would cost billions and destroy the company's credibility forever.

After studying the details many times over, Winchell began imagining the mechanisms needed to get Arthur Blade in the open and eliminated once and for all. Winchell spent the rest of the morning charting out the known details. He had to interweave enough fabrications that his boss, and the entire CIA, would accept it at face value. For that, he needed the two best liars on the agency payroll. He sent out a couple of urgent text messages and waited. Fossie and Mako arrived in his office a half hour later, on time for a change.

"Read this over," Winchell said, handing each of his agents a copy of the workup.

Fossie held it at arm's length. "What is it?"

Winchell gave him an annoyed stare. "If you read it, you'll know. This," he held out his own copy, "is our ticket to a future without Arthur Blade. There's a lot of work to be done in a short time, so dig in. I've documented what we already know and laid out a basic foundation of a game plan."

Mako was already on the third page. "Is this real? This isn't fabricated?"

Winchell nodded. "It almost sounds too good to be true, doesn't it? It's the real deal, and we are going to milk it for all it's worth."

Fossie stared back at Winchell. "Milk what?" he asked.

Both Mako and Winchell glared at him. "Read it!" they said in unison.

Fossie rolled his eyes and flipped open a page.

"As you can see, a lot has happened in the last few days," Winchell said. "I'm going to take this to Don Colson this afternoon. By that time, I'll need to have an air-tight plan that draws Blade out into the open. From there, I want confirmation of his death and proof that he was a double agent."

"What if we don't find proof," Fossie said, holding his hands out, "what then?"

"Then we manufacture it. Use anything and everything at our disposal. We can control this. There are parameters we have to stay within, but beyond that, we write the script. I'm still in charge of clandestine operations until Blade returns full-time. That means we use my rule book for this one. I'm going to push for Blade to be the point man so we can identify him. We have a rough idea of what he will look like and should be able to take it from there."

"You're still assuming Blade will look very similar, right?" Fossie asked, skimming through the information.

"I've not seen or heard anything that tells me otherwise. We proceed under that assumption."

"I don't see a plan in here," Fossie pointed out. "How are you going to take him out?"

"You two are going to help me write that script. That's why you're here. It's time you earned those big paychecks."

Mako had remained silent, studying the documents. He looked up and asked, "There will be an exchange on an English train, right? If we can break up the handoff, then we'll control Blade, the money, and the courier."

Winchell rubbed his hands together. "Now, this is what I'm talking about! That's right, Mako, and it's the right way of looking at it. We know the time and the location, so we can substitute the car company guy and insert Blade to do the exchange. All we have to do is stay one step ahead of the curve, then move in for the kill. Time is tight, gentlemen. Get out your laptops. Let's fill in all the blanks."

Mako opened his computer and began tapping notes. Fossie watched for a moment, then followed suit. "We can monitor overseas travel into and out of the area," he said. "We can see every agent being sent by our agency, the FBI, and maybe even our bad guys."

"That's what I was counting on, too," Winchell agreed. "I'll be the one that controls who goes over and who doesn't. Still, we should assume that extras will be sent without our knowledge."

Fossie pointed to his computer screen. "I was thinking the best place to make the tradeoff is in one of those MK2 private train carriages. Problem is their trains don't run with them anymore. They were pulled years back."

Winchell smiled. "Good observation. The Hull train is the only line that still uses them. I'm sure our hackers chose this one for the privacy of the carriages. It will work to our benefit as well. We will conduct our exchange hidden from prying eyes."

"Should we make our travel plans?" Mako asked.

"No," Winchell said. "I haven't presented this to Colson yet. And I want both of you off the radar. You will be on that train, but not in an official capacity. I need you two operating behind the scenes. As soon as I get the go-ahead, I want you to charter a private jet. Do not leave a trail, understood?

Both agents nodded.

"Good, and Mako, do you still have connections with the group we used last year for that less-than-legal search?"

Mako gave a thumbs up.

"Call them. I want the clinic raided for Blade's procedure files. We need a backup plan for this operation, just in case we don't get confirmation of a kill."

"Are you sure you want to go down that road?" Fossie cautioned. "That's one scary group. And didn't a couple of them end up in the slammer for illegal weapons the last time we used them?"

"So a couple of them are young and stupid," Winchell cut him off. "They did what they were supposed to."

"They're all young and stupid, John! This is a dangerous Asian motorcycle gang you're talking about. Trouble follows them like a foul stink. Why would we want to crawl back into bed with them?"

"Because I didn't get what I needed, did I? I wanted Blade's donor records to guarantee the success of this operation. We can't eliminate him unless we know what he looks like. This all falls into place only if Blade is the bag man doing the exchange. And since we still don't know what he looks like, then everything falls apart if he's not."

Fossie shook his head. "Listen, I still think it's a mistake limiting the donor search to someone of his age and size. This clinic may have found a way around that. He might be much younger. Hell, he might even be a woman."

Winchell gave him an annoyed look. "Stop thinking so much, Fossie. You're going to hurt yourself. Mako, make the call. If this mission fails, then we'll need the donor files from the clinic."

He thought about Folezchev and his suggestion of eliminating Blade's doctor. After he'd seen Blade's episode at the clinic, it was apparent how critically important the doctor/patient connection was for Blade to survive. Taking out the doctor was a good fail-safe. Either way, Arthur Blade would be a dead man. Winchell would wait and give the order to hit the clinic only if his team could not confirm the kill.

"And Mako," he added, "tell them it may involve some wet work."

Mako grinned and texted a message on his phone.

Thirteen
THE HACK

John Winchell met Don Colson in a soundproof meeting room at CIA headquarters. They exchanged no greetings as Winchell set his coffee down, dropped into a seat, flipped open his briefcase, and then began his presentation.

"This morning, the FBI received a call for help from the Cobalt electric car company. Ned Turner from the bureau called us in." Winchell pulled a file out and placed a short stack of documents on the table. "One week from today, Cobalt Motors will unveil the world's first fully autonomous electric vehicle. Two days ago, their computer systems locked up. All attempts to log in and troubleshoot have failed. Their IT department suspected an internal hack. They sounded the alarm and brought in experts to assess the situation and soon confirmed that a Trojan horse virus had been uploaded into the mainframe. They were attempting a backdoor entry into the software when this message appeared on the screen." Winchell passed the first document to Colson:

. . .

—We have seized control of your system. Any attempts to bypass will cause the erasure of hard drives. Further instructions to follow—

Winchell eyed Colson with a look that said, 'You know what happened next.' "Of course they tried," he said.

"And?"

"A new message appeared." Winchell passed an image of the computer display to Colson.

—Reformatting of hard drive K in progress—

"According to the in-house IT specialist, these people know the contents of this computer system well. Drive K is what they call scratch pad data. They use it for day-to-day equations and temporary storage. It was one of the few drives in the system that contained disposable data. The next time, they won't be so lucky. The following message confirmed their fears." Winchell slid another page across the table. Colson read through it, then stared back at Winchell.

—Full system reformatting begins in 96 hours.—

Winchell slid yet another sheet to his boss. "A clock appeared on the screen and began counting down. Following this, a text message came through the cell phone of the IT specialist."

. . .

—Your system is in lockdown. Our program will erase all of your files in four days. A list of demands will follow. Do not deviate from these instructions.—

Colson's expression changed to disbelief. "How did they know this IT guy's number?"

"Everyone in the building knew that number. This is the guy they've all called upon for computer issues. We traced the incoming call to a burner phone purchased six months earlier from a shop at Murmansk airport and paid for with cash. Dead end. Two hours later, they received instructions via text." Winchell slid yet a page across the table.

—-Unlock code for your system will be loaded on a self-booting portable memory device. Bring $3 million in US currency. $50 and $100 denominations, nonsequential bills, in two black duffels. Exchange instructions: Board Kings Cross to Hull 15/7 17:48 platform one, MK2, carriage compartment three. Send one courier only. Memory device with the unlock code will function after connecting to the computer system and entering the encryption key. The key will be sent after cash is received. Exchange to be made after train passes through Doncaster—.

Colson read it through, leaned back in his chair, and stared at the ceiling. "Why don't these companies use better firewalls? We've been warning everyone about just this sort of situation."

"The IT specialist over at Cobalt doesn't believe this came in through the internet. He is insistent that the system is impervious to outside attacks. He suspects someone on the inside, possibly one of the janitorial crew, may have loaded the

Trojan horse virus. This algorithm is new and very sophisticated. Our best guys are still attempting a workaround but have already said it won't be cracked in time. In four days, every file in that mainframe computer will be deleted unless this ransom is paid."

"So, who is behind this?"

"Our people pointed to the Russians. Our friends at MI5 confirmed this with related cellular chatter before and during the hack. Judging by the size of the ransom, I would assume this is a new or freelance group. That they are demanding three million in fifties and hundreds is telling. They spent time calculating the weight and volume of the cash and kept the ransom low enough for one person to carry. They also demand a face-to-face handoff on a train. We assume they will watch to see who gets on and who gets off. These guys may be new, but their MO is old school."

"Does this sound like people who know what they're doing or a bunch of high school nerds in way over their heads?"

"It may seem that way, yes, but I would caution you not to underestimate them. There is an underlying level of sophistication in every step of their plan. Take, for instance, the face-to-face meeting. They send a courier who picks up the cash for a thumb drive containing the unlock code. But that's not the end of it; the thumb drive has to be connected to the mainframe and receive an encrypted authorization code to operate. That code will not be sent if anything happens to the courier."

"What do you make of asking for cash instead of an electronic transfer?"

"Keep in mind that we have been able to crack and track most of the illicit money transfers in similar cases. These guys are showing some skill by taking a small payout and ensuring their escape before disabling their Trojan horse."

"Why can't this car company reboot their computers and start over?" Colson asked.

Winchell shook his head. "This breach has the potential to destroy their company. The integrity of their software is critical to their business model. Their entire future is at stake. If word got out that their program could be hacked, then nobody would buy a self-driving car that relies so completely on compromised company computers. It's cheaper in the long run to pay the ransom."

Don Colson thought another minute. "I take it you want to send Blade in to handle the exchange?"

Winchell nodded. "There will never be a better opportunity to get him back in the field. We can monitor his every move. And if he attempts to contact a Russian handler, we will know it."

Colson gave him a sideways glance. "I don't expect that will be the case, but this will show us what he can do. What is your plan of attack?"

"Contact MI-5 and inform them of our handoff and make sure they give us a wide berth. I'll have two agents positioned at Kings Cross and at Hull looking to identify the courier. Blade will do the exchange and aid in the courier's surveillance after the train reaches Hull station. We want the deal to be completed. We also want to go back and nail these guys once the encryption key is sent."

Colson sat for a moment, envisioning the scenario. "All right," he said, "set it up. But I want to see your entire plan of action before we put assets into play. I'll expect that on my desk by seventeen hundred tonight." He turned back to his laptop screen, signaling the meeting was over.

John Winchell packed up his notes and let himself out of the meeting room, smiling smugly as he pulled the door behind him.

Fourteen
OPERATION; NIGHT TRAIN

Garret Logan boarded the train carrying the two black canvas bags of cash.

"You're being watched, Garret," Blade warned through an earpiece. "On your six."

Logan glanced around for a glimpse of Blade or the others who were watching him. Seeing neither, he kept moving as though there was nothing unusual about his bulky baggage or the fact that someone tipped him off and was now watching the watchers.

He made his way to carriage compartment one. It would be a short, unobserved walk to take the ransom to compartment three when the time came. He slid the door shut, closed the blinds, and took a seat furthest from the door with his back to the outer window. He unsnapped the restraining strap of his shoulder holster and kept a hand near his Beretta. "I'm in the compartment," he announced into his sleeve microphone. "Anyone coming my way?"

"Negative," Blade answered. "It very well could be one of our friends from MI-5 who just couldn't stay away from the operation. He's still at the station right now and doing a rather poor job of acting discreet."

"Are you boarding soon, Arthur?"

"Right behind you. I'll be floating about." Blade never trusted that their closed-circuit communication devices weren't being monitored. He always made it a point to give as little information as was necessary. Now that he was back in the field, his old survival habits were returning. Withholding his exact whereabouts had likely saved him from being targeted at least a few times in the past. He buttoned the top flat of his overcoat, pulled a wide-brimmed fedora down over his eyes, stuffed a newspaper under his arm, then jogged to catch the train as it pulled out of the bustling station.

Blade found an open seat in the club car far enough from the door to offer a good view of anyone coming and going. A porter took his order for coffee, and he settled in for the trip.

He spotted Piper at the other end of the car but did not acknowledge him. His own team had yet to see his new appearance. He preferred to keep it that way, at least until the end of this first operation back on the job. No one could force them to give up his identity if they didn't know it themselves. Instead, he remained incognito, observing his agent observing others and doing an excellent job of it. He watched as Piper's expression changed at the sight of an Asian man entering the car. Piper had seen him before. He could tell that much. As Blade studied the man's face from a distance, he had the same vague sense of recognition. There was a memory buried somewhere deep in the folds that he could not pull to the forefront. He busied himself with the newspaper and his coffee before the man could take notice of being observed. Blade would not allow himself another glance, no matter how tempting. Such subtle giveaways were how good spies became dead spies.

The English countryside flashed by in the dimming sunlight

as his eyes focused on the paper. All the while, his other senses monitored everything around him. He picked up the scent of lemon oil from the furniture polish on the hardwood bar. Beneath that, he caught multiple variations of aftershave and cologne, all combining into one indistinguishable smudge of smell. A new fragrance emerged as a young woman walked past. Her perfume brought back a memory of Audrey Landers, and he pictured her soft features in perfect detail. The greatest error in his life had been letting her get away. Would there ever be another opportunity to see her? He dismissed the thought as he watched the woman whose scent had aroused these longings. She walked the length of the club car, exited, then kept moving through the next.

Blade glanced at his watch. Another half hour before the exchange. He did not want to signal his intentions to anyone watching by popping up five minutes before the allotted time and heading toward the carriage. Instead, he split the time and flagged the porter for a refill.

Another fifteen minutes rolled by before Blade gathered himself and headed back. He felt two sets of eyes upon him. The first was from the Asian gentleman whom he still could not place. Another less skilled man watched through a pair of cheap aviator sunglasses. Without looking up, Blade recalled his image from memory. Scraggly-haired, young, mid-height, wearing a nondescript sweatshirt with jeans and scuffed sneakers. The man snuck furtive glances about the car, then returned his attention to his phone as though engrossed in a video clip. Blade caught a whiff of body odor as he passed. This guy didn't belong. Even if this was just some working stiff on his way to the next job, it was odd that he would pick a spot in the club car and sit alone with no beverage. Blade's mind continued recording every detail of the man's face and physique. He also noticed the Asian guy never looked up. Instinct told him this man was trained to hide his interest but was aware of Blade's every motion.

Blade moved through two passenger cars before entering the MK carriage, sliding the door open in the first compartment. He glanced back the way he had come as he stepped in and pulled it shut. Logan stood inside, facing him with a pistol trained on his chest.

"Hello, Garret," Blade said with a friendly half grin. "Good to see you again."

Logan stared back. He knew the voice but not the man.

"I don't mind you keeping your weapon trained on me, but please, be a good chap and take your finger off the trigger. I won't give you any reason to shoot."

A look of relieved recognition lit Logan's face. "My God, Arthur, look at you!" He rose and took Blade in a bear hug. Both men slapped each other's backs.

Blade eyed the two duffels. "Everything ready for our exchange?"

Logan still stared at him. "Sorry, Arthur, you gotta give me another minute here. I'm a little short for words."

"Well, that's not like you at all, is it?"

"How— how does it feel? I know it's you in there, but that's not you from where I stand."

Blade nodded, patting Logan's shoulder. "It will take some time getting used to for the both of us. All I can tell you is that waking up inside someone else's body goes beyond explanation. We're still becoming acquainted, so to speak."

"Has anyone else seen you yet?"

"No, and I want to keep it that way. After l make the exchange, I'll give you the device. Then I disappear into the background and remain there. Colson has plans to use my new anonymity for more field operations."

"How do you feel about that?"

Blade gave a questioning look. "We will see where that takes us. Have you observed any foot traffic to and from compartment three?"

Logan shook his head. "Someone walked in shortly after I boarded."

"We'll find out soon enough, won't we," Blade said, lifting the satchels like they weighed nothing. "Where will you be?"

"At the front of this car, near the coupler. Piper is covering the rear. We'll monitor anyone coming in or out."

Logan slid the door open as Blade stepped through with the bags. "We're close by if you need us," he said, then gripped Blade's arm. "Watch your back, Arthur. There may be more to this one than what we see. Just a hunch."

Blade's expression turned solemn. "Then I needn't tell you to keep your guard up. Let's stay on our toes and see this through."

Blade timed his entrance so that the train was just pulling out of Doncaster station as he tapped on the door of compartment three, then slid it open. He stuck his head through and looked inside. In the seat facing him sat an attractive young brunette in a blue business suit. Her legs were crossed, hands in her lap. Blade's first observation was her forced sense of calm. She was doing everything in her power to appear in control. This was not a professional. Maybe nothing more than a hired hand. He decided to let her do all the talking.

"Have you brought something for me?" she asked. Her voice sounded rehearsed, more self-assured than her facial features suggested.

Blade nodded, held up a finger for her to wait a moment, then pulled the duffels into the compartment. He pulled the door shut and looked at her expectantly.

"Yes, right then," she said, rising from her seat. "I'm supposed to hand you this." She reached into her jacket pocket and pulled out a small, black device about half the size of a cigarette pack.

"These bags are heavy," he said. "Are you sure you can handle them?"

"What? Yes, of course, I can." She went to lift one and struggled but made a show of making it look easy. She grabbed it with both hands and moved it under her seat, then reached for the other.

"Miss, who are you?" he asked. "What are you doing here?"

"Well, I'm your bloody contact, aren't I?"

"Are you working with someone else?"

"What? No! I'm what you call a freelancer. I do this sort of thing all the time."

Blade smiled. "Well, aren't you the miscast Mata Hari?"

"What do you mean by that?"

"I mean, you are out of your element. Are you armed?"

She gave him a disgusted sneer. "Course, I'm not armed. This is bloody England, isn't it? And it's not the wild West that you Yanks are accustomed to."

"Who paid you to do this?" Blade asked. "Your life may be in danger."

"What's your problem? We made the trade, now bugger off!"

She went to slide the door open, but he grabbed her arm. "Listen to me. You are far over your head in the middle of something you don't understand."

"So says the strapping Dick from the States. Go on now, piss off!"

"I can't help you if you don't let me. Tell me, who got you into this job?"

The woman's expression changed from cocky self-confidence to one of concern. "You're serious, aren't you?"

"Deadly serious, I'm afraid. Tell me who set you up to do this, and I'll do my best to get you off the train."

"I, I'm an actress, see? I got a call from my agent for a brief part to play. He put me in touch with a guy. Hundred pounds for a few hours of simple work and a pleasant train ride."

"Tell me what he looks like."

"I don't know. We set this up in a chat room online." Her lower lip trembled. "Am I in trouble?"

"No, but you're in danger."

"They're watching, you know." She motioned with her eyes up to a tiny remote camera near the ceiling. "All I'm supposed to do is stay put until he comes to tell me I'm through."

"I think it would be best if we don't wait that long," Blade said as he let go of her arm and spoke into his sleeve microphone. "Did you hear any of that?" he asked Logan.

"All of it," Logan replied. "I'm coming to you right...." Logan broke off, and Blade could hear the sounds of a struggle. "Garret! Can you hear me, Garret?" No response. Blade eyed the woman. "We need to get you out of here now."

Before Blade could move, the door slid open. The Asian man from the club car entered, aiming a pistol with a long silencer at his center mass. Blade took a moment to study him. He had long, jet-black hair and wore a dark suit, black turtleneck, sunglasses, and a wicked grin.

"Well, what have we here?" He said, entering the compartment and pulling the door closed behind him. "Where's Blade?"

Blade said the first thing that came to mind. "Touch of the flu, I heard. They sent me to handle the exchange."

"Who the hell are you?" Mako demanded.

"Jensen, FBI," Blade answered cooly. He had known an agent Jensen years earlier and felt safe in borrowing the name. "And who might you be?"

"What the hell are you doing here, Jensen? This is a CIA operation. Do you have the encryption key?"

"I do, but as you have not identified yourself, I'm not authorized to relinquish it."

"Not authorized to relinquish!" Mako laughed. "Who

even talks like that anymore? Relinquish this!" Mako threw a punch at Blade's face that he ducked and missed by inches.

"I asked you who you are," Blade demanded. "You're interfering in an exchange. I don't appreciate... "

Mako threw another punch that Blade dodged but then felt the crack of the pistol grip across his temple. He went down hard and fast. A moment later, the door slid open, and Fossie entered.

"What about the other agent at the front of the carriage?" Mako asked.

Fossie smirked. "He fell off the train." He pointed at the woman. "Same with this one's handler. Little dirty Russian geek. Could be the same guy that wrote the Trojan horse software program. They were a small-time operation." He looked at the body on the floor. "Who the hell is that?"

"He said he was FBI. He's going to be our scapegoat."

"Shit! Where's Blade?"

Mako shook his head. "He has to be on this train. I counted only three old guys that could be him. We'll let Winchell's other team know about them at the end of the line. They can track each one down later without making a scene." He pulled the two money duffels toward the door. "Here, get these in the steamer trunk. We'll load this guy in the other and make him disappear."

Fossie nodded and pointed at the girl. "What about her?"

The woman put her hands up in defense. "I'm just an actress. Honestly, I know nothing. I won't be a problem."

Mako pulled out a Taser and jolted her in the neck. Her body convulsed, and she dropped to the floor. "You're right," he said, looking down, "you won't be a problem." He slid one of the outer windows open and looked at Fossie. "Give me a hand."

"Leave her be," he said. "She's down for the count and won't be an issue."

Mako backhanded him across the chest. "Says you. She's a witness and a loose end." Before Fossie could respond, Mako hoisted her up and pushed her still-spasming body out the window. She dropped and hit the stone bedrock of the tracks with a terrible crunch that was heard above the rumbling train. She tumbled over a few more times before rolling down into a stand of underbrush.

Fossie stared at Mako as he slid the window shut. "You are one cold son of a bitch," he mumbled.

"I'm doing my job. Do yours." He pointed to Blade. "Help me move him."

Each of them grabbed a duffel with one hand and Blade's shoulders with the other and scooted him down to compartment number four. Two large shipping trunks awaited inside. Mako held Blade up while Fossie opened a trunk and pulled out a roll of duct tape. Mako dropped Blade in as Fossie taped his legs and arms. He tore off one last piece and adhered it across Blade's mouth. Mako kneeled down so that his face was inches from Blade's and said, "I hear the English Channel is beautiful in the moonlight."

"It's done," Mako announced into his phone as he drove a utility van along the service street, leaving Hull station. "Money is aboard, along with the memory stick and the courier. It was an FBI agent named Jensen."

"What? FBI? That's just great!" Winchell said, frustrated. "One more mess to clean up. You've left me with a lot of loose ends."

"What about the three Blade look-alikes I told you about?" Mako asked.

"I've got some men on it. It's a much bigger problem than it would have been dealing with them on the train. Christ, the reason for this entire operation was to identify Blade and take him out. Now I'm paying other people to do what you failed to do. Even worse, I've got to make these look like accidents, and at least two of these three you've identified will be innocent civilian casualties. That is what's referred to as a hot mess."

"Sorry," Mako said, "we did not have the luxury of him coming to us as planned. The exchange went down, and we had to deal with other players. I suggest you go ahead with raiding the clinic that did Blade's procedure. Just to be sure."

"That's already happening," Winchell answered. "What about the contact who made the exchange in compartment three?"

"Eliminated."

"And Blade's agents?"

"One fell off the train. The other never knew what hit him. He's still sleeping off one hell of a headache."

"Tell me more about this FBI agent. Jensen, you said, right? What did he look like?"

"Tall, late twenties, athletic build, typical Quantico product. Why?"

"Because I oversaw everything on this operation, and I do not recall requesting any of J. Edgar's finest to assist."

"Maybe this guy is Arthur Blade after all," Fossie said from the passenger seat, listening to the conversation on Mako's speaker.

"Would you get off that once and for all?" Winchell hissed. "We know what we're looking for, damnit. You just let every potential suspect get off the train. Now I have to do more cleanup."

"Begging your pardon, sir," Fossie shot back with an air of sarcasm, "but we had our hands full. Another couple of guys to help would have been nice."

"And they would have stuck out like a sore thumb. No, we

had no choice but to keep this operation small." He paused, then added, "I've noted your shitty attitude. We'll talk about that when you get back. Did the empty duffels get shipped the way we discussed?"

"Exactly as planned," Mako answered. "There were tracking devices in both. They're on a truck headed back to London."

"Good, that should buy us a little time and diversion. What is your timeline?"

"We're a half hour away from the docks. A boat is waiting, fueled, and ready. We'll dump this guy about ten miles out. Then there's a private jet standing by that brings us and the money home."

"I guess that's as good as it's going to get," Winchell said. "Check in with me again before you board your plane, just in case we have to alter your plan."

"Got it," Mako replied, ending the call. He looked over and said, "I'm hungry. Are you hungry?"

Fossie shook his head. "Best to get this over and done with. We can phone ahead and tell them to have a couple of steaks ready on the plane." He chuckled and added, "Wouldn't it be funny if this guy was Arthur Blade? All this extra work we're doing, and he was right under our noses all the time."

"You can be such an asshole," Mako told him. "When are you going to learn to keep your mouth shut? You pissed Winchell off, and he's likely to take it out on both of us, so thank you very much. As if things are not bad enough already. And by the way, I hate driving on the left side of the road. I can't wait to get out of this van and on the boat."

"I thought you said you were from South Korea. Don't Asians all drive on the left side?"

Mako looked over with a snide expression. "Shows what you know. Japan drives left, Korea drives right. If you did a little research once in a while, you wouldn't sound so stupid."

"Fuck you, Mako," Fossie said, staring out the window. "Fuck you."

John Winchell set his cell on the desk and scribbled note after note about his conversation with Mako and Fossie. All the details, as fragmented and convoluted as they now sounded, needed to resemble a well-scripted field operation that had gone awry. The train track was littered with bodies soon to be discovered. Field assets were dead, injured, or missing. Three British senior citizens were about to meet their demise. Their only crime was resembling Arthur Blade. Those bodies were the least of his worries. They would fall under the heading of what was likely to become known as the 'The Great Train Murders.' And so long as one of them was Blade, then the deaths of two additional unsuspecting geezers were acceptable collateral damage. For now, he had to report to Don Colson that they recovered the memory stick but not the encryption code necessary for activation. The money trail had gone cold. So, too, had the search for Arthur Blade, who failed to check in after the operation.

He gave his notes one last look, then arranged them in the order that to be addressed. Satisfied with his handiwork, he picked up his phone and was about to dial when it buzzed in his hand. There was no caller ID. He answered and waited for the caller to speak.

"Is this line secure?" the voice asked.

"Yes," Winchell said, "go ahead."

"This is Pierce. We have eliminated all three secondary targets."

Winchell blew a sigh of relief. At least one part of this horrid operation had gone according to plan. He thought now that it would have been a good idea to have Pierce and his crew running the entire op from the beginning instead of Mako and Fossie. Those two may have become a little too comfortable with their positions and not given their full measure. They would talk later.

"One observation troubles me," Pierce continued. "Didn't you say our target underwent major brain surgery?"

"That is correct. Why?"

"None of these three had scars from such a procedure."

Winchell jumped to his feet. "Come again?" he said.

"We had a small window of time to examine each, but none had any scars visible or covered by hair."

That made no sense. Even the best plastic surgeon could not hide all signs of his handiwork. "Are you sure your men didn't miss something?"

"Negative. We were all looking for the same signs to confirm a successful kill. None of these targets had any scarring out of the ordinary. I can say with absolute certainty that your target was not among these three."

Winchell dropped the phone on the table and fell back into his seat. Blade had slipped past him, and he had just taken the lives of three innocent men. His fist beat a steady rhythm on the desktop as he stared forward, focused on nothing. The entire operation was an abysmal failure! Cleanup and damage control now seemed like an exercise in futility. He longed for a way to wash his hands of it all right now. Blame it all on outside interference. What about pointing at the Russians? No one could ever prove this entire harebrained ransom swap wasn't their doing! With a few hours and some major manipulation of the facts, he could weave a tale that would hold water. He rearranged his notes and imagined adding a few new details that could be manufactured as needed. His eyelids were already heavy from lack of sleep, but what he had to do now could not wait. He decided a large, black coffee would help get his mind churning and stood to head down to the cafeteria.

His phone buzzed before he had taken two steps. He glanced at the caller ID and stopped in his tracks. Don Colson. Of all the people in the world he did not want to talk to right now. But Colson knew he was still in the building. Ignoring the call was not an option. If he did, his boss could easily track him down. Then he risked a face-to-face meeting instead. He took a deep breath and answered.

"Don, I was just going to call you."

"John, do you have an update?"

"I'm afraid I do," Winchell started. "It's not good. The tradeoff went south. I don't know if it was Blade that spooked the messenger, but we've lost contact with him. He was supposed to hand off the memory stick to us at the Hull train station but never showed."

Colson took a pained breath. "What about his team? He had assets on the train."

"There were two that I knew of. One is missing. The other has a concussion."

"Can you think of any other reason Blade might have gone dark?"

"Negative, although he was not maintaining contact with me. I don't even know what role he played in the handoff."

"Blade was the courier," Colson revealed. "That is top secret and not to be shared with anyone, including your field assets. Blade's own team didn't even know."

Winchell's throat went desert dry, and he struggled to swallow. "The courier," he repeated. "He identified himself to my men as an Agent Jensen with the FBI. How—I mean, I thought Blade would still be an older gentleman."

"I haven't seen him myself but was told he appears much younger. He must have made up the bit about being with the FBI. Where is he now?"

Winchell stammered. "I, ah, he's—we don't know." He looked down at his notes and went with an earlier thought.

"Don, I warned you that this could happen. There was no trace of the contact that Blade was supposed to meet. The money is missing, along with the memory drive. There were signs of a struggle, meaning it's very possible that Blade did away with the contact after the exchange and fled with the money."

"That is preposterous! He had no reason to do any such thing."

"I can only tell you what my assets on-site reported to me. Right now, things do not look good for Arthur Blade. He failed us, Don. Either he was not up to this mission, or.... "

"You actually think Blade turned rogue and vanished with the money? That he traded in a lifetime of sacrifice to this agency for three million dollars?"

"It is a plausible scenario that warrants an investigation. My team is searching for any sign of him but so far have found nothing. He's vanished, and that was no accident. This plot of his involved a lot of complex planning from the start. You knew of my suspicions about Blade being turned by the Russians. We may have just supplied him with the golden opportunity he'd been waiting for."

"No," Colson said. "You're a long way from selling me on that scenario. Investigate further if you feel the need. Hold off, though, until after you find out what happened to him. You hear me, John? Find Arthur Blade."

The call ended, and Winchell's already ashen face drained of what color remained. Everything he thought he knew was wrong. Vladimir Folozchev had blindsided and misdirected him so far from the center that he didn't know where the hell he was anymore. Blade's donor had not been an older man, as Folozchev had insisted. He was young, virile, and, OH MY GOD! His crew had him right now! He hoped he still had time to catch them before it was too late! He dialed and waited. Failed call! Shit! He dialed again. Failed call! Double

Shit! He had only a rough estimate of where they would be right now and hoped it was near enough to a cell tower to receive his call. He kept dialing, failing, dialing, failing, dialing... ringing! What little remained of his composure evaporated into a sweaty cloud as he waited for the line to be answered.

Fifteen
HOW MANY TIMES MUST ONE MAN DIE?

The stiff salty ocean wind awakened Blade like a cold slap. Every muscle of his body was rigid and unresponsive, stricken by another paralyzing seizure that always came at the most inopportune time.

A low rumble vibrated through the worn, wet wood surface he lay on as it rocked fore and aft. He was on a boat. Likely, an old fishing trawler put to sea hundreds of times and forever retained the pungent odor of its catches. He shifted his eyes around to take in his surroundings. Flecks of peeling paint hung from the stern of the aged craft. Far beyond that, he could make out a shimmering line of lights from the shoreline. The boat was miles out to sea and still plowing through the dark, rolling waves.

"What's the matter with him?" Mako asked, staring back at Blade from the helm. "Looks like he's paralyzed." He walked over and kicked Blade in the back. Blade's eyes followed him, then registered the pain of the hit. Still, he lay motionless.

Fossie glanced back, then returned his attention to

piloting the craft. "You gave him quite a crack on the noggin. He might have brain damage. Who knows?"

Mako laughed. "Doesn't matter. He'll be dead within a minute of hitting the water." He cocked his foot back to kick Blade in the face, but Fossie stopped him.

"No marks, Mako. Winchell said no marks. Leave a clean corpse, man. He's done for, anyway."

Mako flashed an annoyed scowl back at Fossie. He looked at Blade, who stared back. Mako let loose with the kick but stopped with his foot inches from Blade's face. He squatted down and said, "You're toast, Jensen. I don't think swimming across the English Channel will be a skill you add to your resumé. It's a long way back to shore. I'll bet five Franklins that you don't make it a hundred yards." He looked back to Fossie. "How much further?"

Fossie checked the GPS. "We're a good way out right here. He'd have ten miles of choppy water to plow through before reaching land." He slid the throttle to neutral and turned toward Blade. "You're home, mister, ah, what was your name again? Doesn't matter, anyway. Can we walk you to the door?" He chuckled at his own joke. "Let's hurry and get him over the side. I'm cold, I'm hungry, and we don't want to be seen out here. Oh, and get this duct tape off him. It wouldn't look right when his body washes up on shore."

Blade could feel the uncomfortable tingling in his hands and feet. His body was coming back online. Thank God for small favors. But what good would it do him now? He'd heard what Fossie said. Ten miles back to land. Maybe it would be better if he just remained in this frozen state. The end might be less severe, more merciful. His lungs would fill with salt water as soon as he hit the surface. Why postpone the inevitable? He never was much at swimming. And even with this powerful new body, he could only struggle for so long. Why give himself hope only to meet the same end?

He watched as Mako ripped off the last of the tape restraints, then grabbed his shoulders as Fossie gripped both of his ankles. They hoisted him up and onto the side and held him there.

Mako leaned over him. "Any last words?" He asked, his breath smelling of rotting anchovies.

Blade looked up with an uncanny calmness, ready to accept his fate. "Checkmate," he said.

Mako chuckled. "Hope you enjoyed your brief career with the FBI," he said as he pushed him over the side.

"Wait, what did he say?" Fossie called as the man disappeared beneath the waves. "Wait, damn it, that may have been Arthur Blade! Turn the boat around!"

Mako laughed at him. "You heard what Winchell said. Blade was one of those three old guys that Winchell sent a team after. This guy was just an extra and a convenient patsy."

Fossie shook his head. "No, I'm telling you. We need to check him again. Blade was a chess expert. Doesn't it seem strange to you that the last word out of this guy's mouth is 'checkmate?'"

Mako's phone chirped. He looked at the displayed signal strength that wavered between one and no bars.

"Don't even bother," Fossie said. "I bet it's a spam call."

He ignored Fossie and put the phone to his ear. "John? I can barely hear you. What? Say again. Are you sure? That's not what... yes, understood." Mako pocketed the phone and turned to Fossie. "Winchell thinks this guy was Blade. He wants confirmation. Go back and find him now!"

"I knew it!" Fossie yelled. "You guys just wouldn't listen, but I knew!"

"Shut the hell up, will you? I saw a portable searchlight in the cuddy down below. Winchell wants a photo of this guy's face and confirmation of the kill. I'll grab the light. You take us back to where we pushed him over."

Mako climbed down the narrow stairway into the small cuddy cabin and grabbed the spotlight, plugged it into an outlet at the helm, and began running the bright beam over the rolling waves as Fossie throttled up and directed the craft to where they had last seen Blade. He ran the boat in small circles, expecting to see a bobbing head or a face-down floating torso. He saw neither.

The frigid waters of the North Sea hit Blade like icy daggers. He hit the surface face down, went under, then bobbed up and floated on his back. The waves soon began carrying him away from the boat. Moments later, he looked back and saw Mako standing aft on the trawler with a spotlight as Fossie ran the boat in a circular pattern. They were looking for him. The spotlight's beam came toward him, and he took a breath, dropping beneath the surface, listening for the sound of the prop to fade. It surprised him how long he could hold his breath, estimating he'd been down well over a minute before surfacing. The scant bit of diffused moonlight that shone behind a patch of clouds offered little help in the search. The gap between Blade and the boat continued to widen until they were over fifty yards apart. Blade watched as they scanned the waves for another few minutes before the light clicked off, and the trawler changed course and turned back toward the English coast. Mako remained standing at the stern, staring out at the vast expanse of ocean as the running lights grew dimmer and smaller.

Blade had marveled at the ease of accomplishing otherwise physically demanding tasks since he had undergone the procedure. Now, however, he was awestruck. He was treading water in four-foot swells with little effort. Perhaps his acceptance of imminent demise was premature.

Still, he was ten miles from any hope of survival. And... and he was already making for the shoreline! He moved with swiftness and efficiency that he imagined Olympic swimmers learned early in life. For him, though, this felt more like riding a dolphin to the coast. He was aware of being in control of the strokes and kicks, but only in a distant sense. It was like something he'd done his entire life, and his body was in its natural element. He stopped questioning whether he would survive and switched to making it happen. Every powerful stroke of his arms, every kick of his legs, now brought him closer to salvation, closer to walking along that shoreline, closer to payback.

Shortly into his long swim, he began noticing the drag from his clothing. Though he needed some of the layers to retain warmth, his suit jacket and shoes slowed him down. He stopped to peel off the jacket, stuffed the shoes in the sleeves, and tied it snugly around his waist. The tradeoff was being much more aware of the painfully frigid waters against his skin, but he could cut through the waves with greater ease. A moment later, he was making up for lost time.

He began replaying the last moments on the train and concluded that Langley was not just infected by a few internal conspirators. It was overrun! These two agents, Mako and Fossie, were being directed by someone internally. That meant at least one supervisor controlled their actions. But did it go even higher? Was Don Colson involved? What about his old friend, the president? Decades of developing the keen senses of an effective spy returned the answers; yes to the first, maybe on the second, and definitely not for the third. Few people could be counted on with unquestioned loyalty. Walter Lux was one of them, a rare exception. He couldn't have known of all the deception that simmered beneath the surface in Langley, but he would. Blade swore to find a way of contacting the president and bringing him up to speed as soon as possible.

He began dividing his associates into two groups; those who had earned his trust and the ones who had not. Within minutes, he envisioned a handful of people he could count on. He would find a way of contacting one or two, then rely on them to spread the word that he was still alive. He could also make use of the contacts that garnered less than absolute trust. Disinformation could be an effective tool when used correctly. By planting a few seeds of mistruth, one could watch to see who took the bait and exposed themselves.

Maintaining his anonymity now took on even more importance. Dr. Hanspratten at the clinic had referred to his new facial features as 'forgettably handsome.' He hoped it was as simple as that, and no one could identify him in a lineup or assist a sketch artist in drawing his image. Only four people had seen his face on the train; the girl, Mako, Fossie, and Garret Logan. Blade did not know the fate of the girl, but assumed she was treated as a loose end. Logan was one of the small group whom he trusted implicitly. The other two, Mako and Fossie, were the problems. Had they taken notice and studied his face? They had little reason to do so since they thought he was an FBI agent who stumbled into something much larger than expected.

The one named Fossie sensed that things were not as they seemed. He was the only one who voiced suspicions concerning Blade's true identity. Very astute observations, he thought. Too bad he was fighting for the wrong side.

Blade now realized that his parting line, 'Checkmate,' had not been helpful in maintaining his cover. But how could he know? it hadn't mattered at the time. He expected to be bobbing beneath the waves by now. But it wasn't worth beating himself down about it. Especially when he needed every ounce of energy as he made his way toward dry land.

He thought back to Langley and the internal turmoil that crippled the agency. So many of his predecessors had made finger-pointing the pinnacle of their careers as they searched for internal spies. The practice was disruptive and self-defeating, accounting for some of the least productive years of counterintelligence, not to mention lost opportunities and destroyed careers. His predecessor caused some of the most devastating breaches in the agency's history.

James Angleton, the former chief of counterintelligence, had suspected everyone except the biggest traitor of them all, his best friend, MI6 agent Kim Philby.

For now, at least, Blade had to assume the problems within the agency were deep-rooted. That meant he could not contact Colson or any of his underlings. This also meant that communication with the president was out of the question. At least until he had a better idea of who the enemy was. If just one of the president's security detail or advisors leaked that Blade and Lux were talking, the results could be catastrophic.

There would come a time when he could contact his old friend. Before that happened, he needed to discover the head of this snake and then figure out a way of communicating without alerting anyone else. In the meantime, there were plenty of details to keep him busy. Like spying on the kingdom of spies itself.

His mind returned to surviving the arduous open swim, and he realized his muscles did not feel the least bit taxed. He did not know how far he'd already traveled, but the line of twinkling lights along the shoreline seemed closer and brighter than when he had started.

∽

Don Colson had been dreading his conversation with the president. Arthur Blade was missing. So were the electronic transponders from the money bags that were tracked halfway across England before going dead. The door was open to several possibilities, including Winchell's theory of Blade going rogue and making off with the ransom. It made no sense, but the possibility had to be considered. Colson knew better than to push that scenario, especially to the man who knew Arthur Blade better than anyone.

The president reacted as expected and paced the Oval Office. "We're not talking about some rookie agent on his first field assignment," he retorted. "This is the chief of counterintelligence, for god's sake!"

"It was his first assignment since returning to active duty, sir. With all due respect, it's possible he just wasn't yet up to the task."

President Lux digested the thought for a moment, then shook his head. "No, Don, that was not the issue. This entire business went south fast, but not because Blade couldn't handle himself in the situation. No, this has all the markings of an inside leak and a double cross. How else were these people able to identify Blade? Nobody, and I mean nobody, knew what he looked like. I was even kept in the dark, and I've known the man since college. He should have been unrecognizable. Correct me if I'm wrong, but weren't his orders to take a hands-off approach unless something went wrong with the exchange?"

"Yes, Mr. President, that was the original plan. But Arthur acted as the courier because John Winchell insisted. We know now that the op was compromised."

"How many of your people were in on this? How far out did word of the operation travel?"

"We had three teams in play, sir. Blade brought in two of his agents, and I sent five operatives in two teams. I positioned three at the train stations, watching for movement by the hackers, and two traveled aboard the train. None of them were close enough to observe Blade or what happened afterward."

"So, what is the status of the exchange? Did we at least get the software key to unlock the computers for this car company?"

Colson let out a heavy sigh. "No, sir, we don't have that in our possession."

President Lux closed his eyes, massaging his temples. "Everything you set out to do has failed. Is that what you're telling me?"

"Mr. President, I...."

"Yes or no, Don, was every single part of this mission a complete and utter failure, or was it not?"

"The short answer is yes, sir. We failed our primary objective."

"I've heard there were casualties. What can you tell me about those?"

Colson slipped a data sheet out of his valise. "The woman thought to be the contact for the software hackers is missing. Garret Logan, who was on Blade's team, is in critical condition in a London hospital. The doctors give him good odds of recovery, but he has a long road ahead. It appears they threw him from the train."

Lux shook his head. "I know this man. Our wives are friends. I want up-to-date reports on his status and transportation provided to bring him home. Who else?"

"Jim Piper was also working with Blade. He suffered a concussion when he was attacked from behind. He'll be fine."

"How was it that these people could ID our field assets?"

"We are working on that right now."

"Well, work harder, Goddamnit!" The president pointed sternly at Colson. "Do not let me down on this, Don. Too much is riding on the fate of Arthur Blade to even think about stopping for a break. Get me answers and get them fast. And figure out how to fix what we just fucked up for this car company. If that was the best protection we can provide, then it's no wonder nobody trusts the government."

Sixteen
THE LONG JOURNEY HOME

Blade had lost all track of time as he swam toward the brightening shore lights. As he got closer, he could make out the dark shapes of an amusement park along the water's edge. There was no sound or movement, and he assumed it was long past closing time.

His feet made contact with the sandy shore, and he let the surf carry him the final distance. Crawling onto the beach, he collapsed, gasping for air. He lay there for most of an hour as every muscle twitched uncontrollably from the demands of the long swim in icy water. Once the pain faded, he began stretching his limbs until they moved freely and supported his weight. All the while, his mind raced through the events that had brought him here.

Blade had never seen Mako or Fossie before tonight and didn't know how they factored into what had happened on the train. Mako claimed to be CIA when he greeted Blade with the business end of a silenced Glock. But was he telling the truth? Mako also knew that Blade was supposed to be the courier. Only a handful of people were in that loop. And the biggest question of all was why he had attacked and dropped

Blade into what should have been his watery grave after he told them he was an FBI agent. Only one answer could explain all the open questions. If this guy was with the agency, it meant that someone inside was running a counter-op. He wondered what would have happened if he'd told Mako his true identity. Would he have lowered his weapon or put a couple of slugs in his chest? Another odd question popped up from the folds of his brain; was he the intended target? What could they have hoped to gain?

Colson never came across as the type of director who would eliminate his less-than-desirable employees with a one-way boat ride. A cake, a gold watch, and an early retirement party were so much cleaner. So who else could want him dead?

Stranger things had happened in the spy business, but never without a reason. Blade carried fifty years of spycraft in his head while restarting his life clock at twenty-eight. That could make him a bigger threat and a larger target for his enemies. None were supposed to know he'd survived, at least not yet, and he wondered how the news had traveled so fast.

So who else would want him eliminated? Winchell had run the operation and should have directed every agent on the train. Could Fossie and Mako be working for him? What if they were on the payroll but went rogue with the ransom? $3 million seemed like a meager reward to ruin a career and force yourself into hiding. It was more likely that they were following orders. But whose? And what was the real prize? There had to be more at stake here than anyone knew. Every other agency was out chasing leads on what they perceived was an open and shut case while the true crime may be going unnoticed. That's where his investigation would start. Cause and effect. He pondered what little he knew as the faces became permanent images in his memory. They would meet again.

Blade took an inventory of his wet pockets and fished out

a money clip with a thin fold of English pounds. He hadn't carried identification on the operation and thought it best to remain off the grid until he uncovered some answers. Right now, his needs were much more primitive; food and shelter.

He untied his suit jacket from around his waist and pulled out his shoes, slipped them on, then worked his arms into the wet sleeves. Not the most comfortable attire, he thought, but the extra layer was already helping to retain some body heat.

He spied a street sign, Lumley, and began walking toward a tall tower in the center of a roundabout. He read an inscription as he passed that told him he'd just entered the town of Skegness. Just beyond were the lights of a pub, and he headed there.

The Marine Boat Bar was bustling. The sound of the surf behind him gave way to clinking beer mugs, the dull thrum of multiple conversations, and the amplified voice of an Elvis impersonator. He found an open stool at the patio bar and pointed at the tap for Courage Best by Youngs.

The bartender filled a pint and slid it in front of Blade, raising his brows as he eyed Blade's wet attire. "Ell of a night for a dip, eh?"

"Unintended, I can assure you. Is there lodging nearby that you would recommend?"

The bartender nodded, picking up on Blade's accent. "And a Yank at that. Hope you didn't swim the entire way." He chuckled at his own line. "I believe The Number Eight still has a room or two. You may have passed it on your way up from the beach."

Blade managed a weak smile. "Might you have a phone I could use to ring ahead for a reservation?"

The bartender motioned toward a vintage red English phone booth in the corner. "Dropped our landline but didn't have the heart to let the old girl go. You can use my cell if you're quick about it."

He punched in the hotel number from memory and handed the phone to Blade.

The walk from the pub to Hotel No. 8 was a short one. Now, contently filled with a few pints and a good meal, he was recharged, yet near exhaustion. As much as his new body had overcome swimming against the currents over such a long distance, it had its limitations. It was letting him know that he'd far exceeded every one of them. He struggled to keep his eyes open long enough to sign the guest registry and pick up a room key.

Once inside the small but tidy room, he stripped out of his nearly dry clothing, then stood under a steaming shower, scrubbing the salt from his skin. Finally feeling warm, he dried off and slipped under the covers of one of the twin beds. He remained sitting, attempting to compose a few thoughts and a plan of action. There was a phone on the nightstand, but he didn't have the energy to make a call. Besides, the best course of action right now was to let everyone believe he was, in fact, dead. He did not know how deep the roots of this conspiracy ran and needed to be razor-sharp before attempting contact with anyone. One wrong call, and there would be no third chance at survival. Tomorrow, he told himself. The answers would come tomorrow.

Blade clicked off the bedside lamp, allowing himself to lie down, and was out the moment his head hit the pillow.

"Police have confirmed that they are no closer to uncovering the details connected with the bizarre and tragic events that occurred on the Hull train from Kings Cross over the weekend."

Blade's eyes scanned the pages of the morning paper as he sipped tea in a cozy corner of a bed-and-breakfast. All of his attention, however, locked on the voice coming from an old corner television.

"Two deaths and two serious injuries are under investigation," the announcer continued. "The identities have not been released. However, a confidential BBC Source has revealed that Lila Inglenook, a twenty-seven-year-old waitress and part-time actress from Heckington, was one of the victims found dead alongside the train tracks near Redford. Sources speculate she was thrown from the train but, as yet, have found no corroborating witnesses. The body of the second victim has yet to be identified. A third victim is in hospital in critical condition. Garret Logan, an American business manager, fell from the train. Authorities are eager to question him, but his injuries have made that impossible. A fourth victim was treated and released but not identified. There is speculation that all the incidents are linked, but police remain mum on the details. There's more rain in the forecast, and here's Cynthia Peck with the soggy details."

Blade let out a relieved breath. Logan would survive his injuries. It's the best he could have hoped for, considering the ambush they had all walked into. He wanted to get word to Logan, but that would have to wait. Security around the hospital would be tight, and whoever laid the trap on the train might be expecting him. It was not worth the risk. He cursed himself again for not sensing the danger beforehand.

He'd awoken in the middle of the night drenched in a cold sweat, the faces of Mako and Fossie staring back smugly as they pushed him over the side of the boat. It wasn't often that anyone outplayed him, and the big answers still proved elusive.

Another face kept materializing in the periphery of his thoughts; the scornful smirk of John Winchell. Though he couldn't yet prove anything, he sensed an unseen connection. The train exchange was Winchell's operation. No one had more insight or control over the entire fiasco. Blade wondered if it would be his fingerprints discovered at the helm of this botched mission when the truth was revealed. But what would Winchell stand to gain by staging such an elaborate sting?

There was another problem with this current line of thought. Of all the people Blade would have suspected capable of such a ruse, John Winchell's name did not even make the list. As much as he disliked the man, he never believed him talented enough to pull off anything like this. Winchell's lack of ability should have eliminated him as a suspect. But the thought would not allow itself to go down easy. It continued racing through Blade's mind, twisting and contorting until a new possibility presented itself that caused his face to flush. *What if I were his true intended target all along? What if the slimy bugger set this up to unveil my new identity and eliminate me?*

How perfectly the pieces all came together if he imagined the entire show being choreographed by Winchell. Maybe a little too well. In Blade's experience, there were always at least two possibilities in every theory; that all of this was nothing more than wild conjecture and would fall apart under closer scrutiny, or it was as it appeared. An orchestrated cover-up to get Blade out in the open, then move in for the kill.

It seemed inconceivable that the man would be so desperate for Blade's job that he would risk everything to murder his competition. But if it was Winchell behind this entire ordeal, then he had played his hand better than Blade believed him capable and come close to succeeding.

Blade wondered why his usually reliable internal alarms hadn't served him better. If only he'd felt these suspicions a few precious hours sooner. It might have saved the life of that poor girl, and Logan would not be lying in a hospital bed. He may even have avoided his own capture and long-distance late-night swim.

As Blade stood to leave, another bulletin flashed on the

television. Three elderly gentlemen had died in what authorities were calling a baffling coincidence. The three had just disembarked the Hull train and were heading to their homes when they all suffered massive heart attacks a few kilometers from the station and within minutes of each other. Autopsies were pending for at least two.

He fell back in his chair. This was no coincidence at all! He envisioned the purpose, as well as the mechanics behind the deaths. These were professional hits. The autopsies would not reveal the undetectable heart-stopping drug that was likely injected. The reason for the deaths was clear. Blade closed his eyes, shaking his head. He was being hunted, and these poor, innocent souls were killed merely because they resembled him. Because they were in the way.

Understanding an adversary's mind was crucial to anticipating their next moves. This one, however, was brazen and uncharacteristic of anyone trained to know better. Sending two CIA agents to take down one of their own was reckless and messy enough. Taking out these three innocent men, however, was the mark of a twisted mind with no bounds. The element of surprise had cloaked their actions so far. And who would expect a traitor in the ranks would be at the root of it all? Well, that card was played, and it worked—once. It would not happen again. All surprises from here on in would be of Blade's own making, and there would be many.

Now, more than ever, Blade had to maintain the appearance of his demise. At the same time, he needed someone on the inside, supplying information that he could not otherwise access. Someone who could help fill in the blanks. There would be little progress without that direct connection. It wasn't going to be easy, though. He suspected every member of his inner circle was being watched and their homes wired in anticipation of him making contact. He also assumed that whoever was calling the shots would also be attempting to infiltrate his small, tight-knit group. As much as he needed support, he had no intention of making it easy for his enemies by walking into a trap. Luckily, he knew almost every trick in the spymaster's playbook. After all, he'd written many of the pages himself.

First on his agenda was returning stateside. That required access to funds and a new identity. Every field agent is instructed on how to survive off the grid and create their own drop sites for money, weapons, and alternative identities. Blade had multiple passports available, but none would work for him now. New traveling documents were needed. That could be handled easily enough. A perfectly forged passport was available from multiple sources for the right price. Luckily, one of the best forgers in England lived just outside of London. Blade had just enough cash left to take the train into the city, collect the contents of a safe deposit box nearby, then arrange for new documents to be prepared. He could hole up for a few days and work out more details of his plan while he waited.

He had already selected his mode of transportation for the trip home. The CIA used a few overnight air freight companies, and there was one in particular known for its discretion. Again, the right price could buy almost any service without leaving a trail. When the time was right, he would hitch a night flight home as a dead-head pilot.

That still left one of the biggest decisions unanswered; whom to contact once he returned home. The list was short. Initial contact had to be limited to a maximum of one or two people. Once in the loop, they could call on the services of others. But knowing that enemies were still looking for him made the selection more difficult. He needed two people who were off the grid but had connections with others who could help. He refilled his tea cup and treated himself to a sticky sweet pastry, a rare indulgence. It reminded him of some quieter moments he'd spent with Audrey, and it brought a smile. She would be an excellent choice for first contact. If she were being watched, it would be minimal compared to everyone else on the list. And he trusted her to move about without attracting attention. He remembered more about his close friend and some secrets they shared. Audrey would have made an excellent spy.

Lightning flashed behind him, and Blade turned to watch as a light rain pattered and trickled down against the paned window. Further down the street, he caught sight of a policeman walking his beat. It sparked another memory and a choice for his second initial contact. "Azzy," he said, nodding.

Seventeen
Drinks at the Copper Tap

Arthur Blade sat at a weathered picnic table outside of a locked-up bar that overlooked a strip of marina docks on Key West. Colorful graffiti covered the steel roll-up doors, creating the illusion that this building was ripped by a hurricane from its foundation in the Bronx and dropped down here.

Blade checked his watch again and smiled. His friend obviously didn't care about opening early for the over-imbibed cruise ship crowds that encircled the other establishments just a few doors down. One got the feeling that this drinking hole catered more to the local inhabitants, who would start filtering in around lunch hour. He expected nothing less.

A few minutes later came the sound of muffled footsteps from inside, followed by the clunks of locks being removed. One of the street art-covered steel doors rolled up, and there stood his old friend. Lou eyed him curiously but returned to the task of opening for business. He rolled up the two remaining doors, then stepped behind the bar, unlocking cabinets and stacking liquor bottles onto the stacked shelves behind him.

Blade entered and sat at the bar, studying the unique decor. Inner-city meets tropical sands. His eyes followed the weathered floor planking to a back wall that could have been ripped from a New York subway. The normal row of forward-facing seats now faced each other, with tables added between. Above them hung a strip of subway hand-holds, and chrome poles ran floor to ceiling throughout. Artistic graffiti covered every inch of the walls, adding to the authentic feel. Blade studied the painting and recognized the quality of the artwork. He remembered Lou had mentored a few inner-city kids busted for spray painting their credos. Lou had recognized their talent and gotten them enrolled in art classes. It would be like his old friend to fly them down here to add the finishing touches to this Bronx outpost.

The big city decorum also helped to explain why the bar wasn't packed to the gills right now. Most of the tourists coming off the cruise ships paid thousands to escape the drudgery of city life. All they wanted now was to trade it for a temporary escape with sand between their toes, swaying palms overhead, and bottomless fruity drinks. So why would they head to a bar that made them feel like they were back north with their noses still to the grindstone? On the other hand, the locals who had relocated from the Big Apple likely appreciated a little taste of home.

Blade's eyes wandered further along the interior walls, and he could tell who made up a large part of his clientele. Arm patches of police uniforms from across the country covered one entire wall with little room for more. Blade doubted Lou would ever turn down any additional patches that were offered.

He now noticed another feature he had expected; a healthy selection of beers on tap. It's what Lou had always told him he wanted. The Copper Tap was just as he had imagined it would be.

Blade sat enjoying the light gulf breeze as the lone figure ducked into the kitchen and came back with a cart covered with more liquor bottles, then continued to place them on the empty island countertop.

Lou watched Blade watching him for a few minutes before saying, "We're not open for another half hour."

"I'm in no hurry," Blade said.

"Suit yourself," he replied, still positioning bottles. "I'll bet you could still find a seat at the Pelican just down the boardwalk."

"Do you often make it a point of deflecting your prospective clientele to other establishments? Honestly, Azzy, how do you make ends meet?"

The man stopped and stared. "How do you know that name?"

"Friend of a friend, I guess you could say. A mutual acquaintance."

"Yeah?" Lou said in a wise guy tone. "Who would that be?"

"Arthur Blade."

Lou's expression did not waver. Instead, he walked over and stood across the bar from the stranger. "Arthur Blade is dead."

"So it would seem," Blade said, folding his hands on the bar.

"No, I'd say he's a little more dead than that. I was at his funeral." Lou stared down for a moment, reliving the scene, then glanced back to his strange guest. "Care for something to drink?"

"I don't suppose in all of your selections I would find something bitter with a malty tang like, say, Courage Best by Youngs?"

Lou winked and pulled a chilled mug from a low cabinet, then filled it from the tap. "Good choice, but I'm surprised a man as young as yourself would call for this one. It's an acquired taste. I learned about it from—from Arthur." He slid a coaster in front of Blade and set the sweating mug on top. "Did you work with him?"

Blade nodded. "You might say that, yes." He took a sip and smiled.

Lou folded his arms and stared back. "Care to elaborate, or do you enjoy being vague?"

"Being vague was a tool of my profession."

Lou nodded. "So, you worked at Langley?"

"Always the detective, even in retirement, eh?"

"You seem to know a lot about me. How is that?"

"Your reputation precedes you."

Lou snorted. "Yeah, well, I'm sure that would vary depending on whether you're asking someone wearing a shield or one of the perps I put away."

Blade took another sip from the mug. "I recall a rather large case that you brought to a successful conclusion, The Steinway Street kidnapping."

Lou stopped wiping the bar and stared back. "You look a little young to know about that one."

"It was brilliant detective work, Azzy. And finding that little girl alive in the basement of a candy store, of all places. How did you figure that one out?"

Lou's expression hardened. "You're the one with all the answers here. Suppose you tell me."

"As you wish," Blade answered. "The little girl, Ginger, I believe, was her name. She was the daughter of the district attorney. As I recall, the kidnapper did some time for a crime he had always denied committing. He blamed the district attorney for the overzealous pursuit that first landed him in prison. His anger festered, and he sought vengeance by taking the little girl."

Lou stared back, stone-faced.

"You had a hunch, and you sought assistance from anyone to open the old case file on this man. I believe that was when you and Arthur first met. Am I correct? An acquaintance introduced you, and you made the case that without probable cause, you could not get a search warrant for the store. Your intuition told you there was a connection, but no one would allow you access to the file." Blade smiled. "Arthur pulled a few strings, legal and otherwise." He leaned in and whispered, "Mostly the latter." He sat back, took another swallow from the mug, and said, "Well, the file appeared on your desk the next day. You served a search warrant, saved the girl, and apprehended the bad guy. The rest, of course, is history."

Lou's eyes darted back and forth as though searching for an explanation for this strange man's presence. "Your story about the file," he said, now scanning the room for anyone else listening. "That's not public knowledge. Never has been. So how do you know this?"

Blade offered a sad smile. "Louis, I don't know of an easier way of broaching this subject.

Lou pushed back from the bar. "Nobody calls me Louis."

"Except maybe Audrey."

"Stop!" He put his hand up. "Just who the hell are you? And what subject are you—broaching? Christ, you even sound like—"

"Like Arthur Blade?"

"Tell me the game you're playing now. Tell me, or get the hell out of here."

As much as Blade had attempted to prepare for this moment, he could not find the words to explain everything that had happened in the last three months. He had to try. He needed Lou's help to help work out the next moves of his plan. So he just began with the first thing that came to mind, hoping the shock would not be too terrible for his friend.

"Do you remember what you said to Arthur the last

evening you spoke? The night before his treatments were to begin."

"How do you know?" Lou's eyes narrowed. "Yeah, yeah, I do. What about it?"

"You reminded me how much I had helped you when Karen left and when Jennie was sick. You said, 'I will always be ready to return the favor.'"

Lou stared back, shaken.

"The day you made Chief of Detectives, I was there, sitting with Jennie, watching her watching you. She was so proud of her father. She is still your biggest fan."

"And yet she won't talk to me, and—" A tear glistened in the corners of Lou's eyes. "Tell me what's going on here."

"I received my diagnosis during my brief stay in the hospital. They gave me very little time to live, even less if I agreed to a complex experimental procedure that offered the slimmest of odds at a second chance. The promise of a second life, Louis. Unfortunately, the terms of participating in this bold experiment demanded that I appear to die. There is a body buried in my grave, but it is that part of me that could no longer sustain life." He cradled his hands around the mug and stared into it.

"A partial cerebral exchange is what they call it. It's me up here." Blade tapped his head. "The rest of what you see is borrowed, so to speak, from a young warrior that deserved to live more than I. But fate was kinder to me."

Lou turned away, shaking his head. "No, no way. I don't know how you know these things, but it's a cruel joke you're playing. You can go back to the assholes at Langley who sent you here and tell them I didn't buy it." He looked past Blade and pointed to the boardwalk outside. "You need to go." He reached to take the beer mug, but Blade held it tight.

"I never questioned your loyalty and friendship, Louis. That is why I have revealed myself to you. No one, absolutely no one, knows I'm still alive and that I survived the procedure, as well as a botched murder attempt. I have managed to re-enter the country with a new identity, and I am here to ask for your help before they can finish what they started."

Lou's lips pursed as he pointed at Blade. "What was your wife's name?"

"Ginny, of course. The love of my life."

"What was her full name?"

"Very crafty, Louis, few people knew that. Giovanna Benedetta Muscedere."

"Where did we all vacation together?"

"As I recall, we did that only once and found the bungalow on Montauk Point quite cramped."

"What was my position on the force?" He said it more like a statement than a question.

A sly grin spread across Blade's face. "Ah, the force, indeed. I believe your response to anyone asking you that exact question would have gone something like, 'Do I look like Darth Vader to you?' Your position, while on the job, not the force, was Chief of Ds. And I was sorry not to be with you at McMurphy's and three hundred of your closest friends to toast you on your retirement. I was unconscious that entire night, though I remember you coming to visit in the hospital the next day."

"My god, is it really you?"

Blade nodded. "Hello again, old friend."

Lou eyed him up and down as joyful tears rolled down his cheeks. He swatted them away and said, "Sorry, but this is a lot to take in. I mean, it's great to see you still upright and all, but don't expect me to jump over the bar and hug you or anything like that."

"Of course not. I realize I've subjected you to a bit of a shock. I'm sure that...." Blade went silent as Lou leaped over the bar and took him into a tight bear hug.

"I remember standing next to your grave, thinking of all

the things I wished I had said to you. And now— now," Lou slapped Blade on the back, feeling his solid, well-defined muscles. "You have some serious traps! You were a great friend, Arthur. I always knew I could depend on you and— and—" He gripped Blade's upper arm. "And those are some big guns! What, do you live in a gym?" He shook his head. "What I meant to say is—" He mock-punched Blade in the gut, his fist thudding into the slab of a well-defined six-pack. "What I meant to say is, where can I get one of these?"

Eighteen
A TEAM OF TWO

"Welcome back to the living, Arthur." Lou clinked his beer mug off of Blade's.

"Thank you, my friend. It beats the alternative."

"And then some, I would imagine." Lou sized him up and added, "I mean, look at you! You're not just getting a second chance at life. You're living the ultimate redo. A seventy-two-year-old dying man gets to come back as a what, a twenty-something powerhouse of a warrior. Who wouldn't take that option if someone offered it?"

"Ending up with this donor was luck of the draw for me and extreme misfortune for him. Then, of course, there are complications."

"Such as?"

"I didn't come here to tell you of my difficulties."

"Humor me, Arthur."

"All right, the headaches, for example. They feel like a shrapnel explosion. There are still many normal functions that I'm not capable of performing. I can't run. I trip over my own feet. My hand-eye coordination is a mess. I was told that my donor was right-handed, and I, of course, am left. That means my brain struggles to figure out which will be the dominant hand and has not rebuilt the proper neural connections for either. Put these together, and I would be a slow-moving target in a gunfight that cannot run away or shoot back. In time, my brain will rewire these connections. Until then, I must accept my limitations."

"Did you gain anything in all of this?"

Blade took a bite of a burger that Lou had prepared. "Yes, as a matter of fact. My vision is better than it's been in thirty years, and I no longer wear glasses. My hearing seems amplified to the point of annoyance. The slightest sound can awaken me from the deepest sleep. And I've learned that this is the body of an incredible swimmer. That skill has already saved my life. This brings me to the true reason for my visit. Louis, I need your help. There has already been one attempt on my life. There will be more. I need you to use your New York connections to do some digging."

Lou straightened in his chair. "Whatever you need. But why would anyone be after you? Didn't you just say they offered you this, this rebirth, because you're so valuable to them?"

"It would seem that not everyone on my team is rooting for me. There appears to be an element that would benefit more from my demise than my survival. You, my friend, are the only one that has seen my new persona. It is imperative that this identity remains a secret. I have no confidence in anyone within the agency. In fact, there are only two other people in this world that I trust without reservation."

"Walter Lux?" Lou asked.

"Yes, I'm sure that Walter has no hand in this game."

"Then I'm thinking your other confidant is an agent in your inner circle or Audrey."

"Very astute, as usual. I expected nothing less from the former Chief of Detectives. There is only one way to combat these traitors, and that's from the inside. For that, I need to get word to my immediate team, as well as the president. Audrey can do that by contacting one of my agents. They can send word through the first lady. You can be of great service by refreshing your old connections and tapping into the database of INTERPOL. I must find out all I can about an incident that took place aboard a train a month ago outside of London. They sent me on a mission that I'm now convinced was nothing more than an attempt on my life. They came close. Such nemeses had to be operating from a position of high authority."

Lou chuckled. "I don't mean to make light of your situation. But, hearing Arthur Blade speaking through this new you is, well, sort of like watching a spaghetti western with bad overdubs."

Blade eyed Lou with a quizzical expression. "Please do elaborate."

Lou laughed out loud and slapped Blade on the back. "See? That's exactly what I'm talking about. You are upper crust, Arthur. Ivy league and proper, and you talk like an English Harvard law professor. Hearing that coming out of the guy I'm looking at now doesn't match up. If you want to stay low and keep your identity a secret, then I would suggest you scuff your shoes a little."

Blade's look told Lou that he didn't understand.

"Take it down a few notches. Pick up some slang. Kill the proper New England geek speak, and speak the way this new you should speak."

"Yes, I see your point. Or rather, I can dig that."

Lou put his head down and snorted. "Yeah, now update that by about forty years, and maybe you won't stick out like a sushi stand at a pig roast. Do some observing, my friend. It's what you've always done best. You'll figure it out."

Blade nodded as he picked up his burger with both hands, paused as he eyed Lou, then raised both pinky fingers. "Upper crust, indeed," he said with mocking snobbery, stuffing half the burger into his mouth.

Nineteen
WHAT DID YOU WEAR TO MY FUNERAAL

Audrey Landers was a creature of habit, frequenting her favorite restaurants and strolling the local neighborhoods like clockwork. Tuesdays were dinner at the Chain Bridge Inn, a quaint, converted old stone house known for great martinis and seafood. She enjoyed the short walk from her comfortable condo nearly as much as the jazz trio and the succulent stone crab.

Despite her upbeat disposition, the day weighed on her heart. Today was the three-month anniversary of her best friend Arthur Blade's funeral, and he'd been in her thoughts throughout the day. She'd toasted his memory over dinner, clinking her glass against the empty one where he should have been sitting. His loss left a void that would remain empty, and she accepted it. Arthur had been a rare friend.

There were many times when she wished their relationship had turned the corner and become more romantic rather than just a wonderful friendship. She understood his reluctance and did not press him for more. At the same time, she envied his deceased wife for the endearing and dedicated love that she and Arthur had enjoyed together.

Years earlier, she thought she had found her own soul mate. He'd turned out to be a magnificent liar with a wife in another state. She still berated herself for not seeing the signs sooner.

Every tempestuous fling in her life had been nothing more than momentary gratification. Never did the roots grow, allowing love to bloom and flourish. And each one left her feeling emptier than the one before. No one had ever even looked at her the way Arthur did. He could express a thousand words with a single lingering gaze.

She never had to question her value to him. Arthur Blade had been the nearest thing to a perfect mate she had ever come upon. She broke out of her thoughts when she realized she'd walked a block past her home.

Audrey entered the darkened condo, shook off a shiver from the brisk walk, and set the double dead bolts on the door. She hung her coat and scarf on a tall, brushed metal coat rack. A gift from Arthur and losing him filled her thoughts all over again.

She started into the great room, then spun back around. There was a hat hanging from the rack, an oatmeal-colored flat cap. The type that Arthur wore. No, it wasn't just the type; it was his hat. She wrapped her fingers around it, holding it close and inhaling. It still retained the subtle fragrance of his cologne. Arthur had worn this same hat countless times. She had even attempted to retrieve it from his home after his death but couldn't find it.

She took a startled breath and scanned the room. As her eyes adjusted to the darkness, she could make out the silhouette of a figure sitting in one of the high-backed chairs.

"Hello, Audrey," he said in a smooth, low voice.

Audrey gasped and stepped back toward the door, reaching into her purse. She pulled out a pistol and aimed it less than steadily at the unknown intruder. "Who are you? What do you want?"

"Just a few moments of your time, dear girl. Is that the hammerless .38 Ruger you're pointing at me?"

Audrey blinked in disbelief. "How—how could you know that?"

"Why, I'm the one who gave it to you. And as I recall, we loaded it with hollow points. I would ask you to direct the business end downward until you hear me out. I'm not wearing body armor, and those would do irreparable damage."

Audrey kept the weapon trained on the intruder's torso. "What sort of game are you playing? Get out. Leave right now, and I won't shoot."

"I'm going to reach over and turn on the light next to me," he said, holding his hands where she could see them. Blade reached over and clicked on the table lamp, then looked around the room. "You've done a bit of redecorating, I see. I always loved it the old way, but this is a tad brighter. It looks very nice, very nice indeed."

Audrey stared at the man, attempting to match the face, the mannerisms, and the voice, against old memories. Each seemed so contradictory to the other. This strange man looked to be less than thirty years of age yet spoke in a refined and calming voice that should have come from someone much older.

"Please, come sit beside me. We have much to discuss. You still have the pistol, and I have no intention of attempting to disarm you. By the way, your reaction to an intruder in your home was perfect. You haven't forgotten your training. I took the liberty of pouring us a spot of Tawny Port, a thirty-year-old. I didn't know whether you would be stocking one of your own, so I brought it along."

"Damn it, how do you know all these things about me? Talk! And don't keep going on with this proper Harvard rubbish. Tell me who you are and what this game is you're playing."

"That's why I'm here. Please listen to what I have to say. Then you can decide whether I pose a threat. Sit, share a drink, and give me just a few moments of your time."

"I'm not drinking that!" She said, lowering herself into the chair beside him. "What if it's drugged? Then I've made it all that much easier for you."

"Point taken. May I offer you my glass instead?"

She reached for it, then hesitated. "What if that's what you expected and drugged your own glass?"

"Clever girl. Then I would ask you to think for a moment. Is there a way of knowing with certainty? What would Arthur have told you to do?"

Audrey stared back, trying to read the intentions through his eyes. His gaze was disarming, and she fought against the false sense of security it was giving her. She remembered something Arthur had once shared with her about a similar situation he had encountered. She reached over, took his glass, and poured it into hers, then poured half the contents back. "Drink," she said.

Blade smiled, pleased with her actions. "Audrey Landers, I always said you missed your calling. You would have made an excellent spy." He reached for the glass and put it to his lips. "Cheers," he said as he took a long, satisfying sip. "I haven't had this in some time. I'm glad I waited to share it with you." He set the glass down and folded his hands in his lap. "I'm so sorry for what I've put you through, old girl. There was no way for me to tell you of what had transpired."

She stared back at him, the barrel of the pistol lowering. "What are you talking about?"

"My demise, of course."

"Who are you?" she asked. "Who are you, and why are you here?"

"This is going to be difficult to...."

"WHO ARE YOU?"

Blade fixed his eyes on hers. "I'm Arthur."

"Get out! Get out, now." She shook her head, looking away. "Don't do this to me," she pleaded. "What reason do you have to taunt an old woman?"

He offered a half smile. "You're far from old. I've always told you that. And you still look wonderful."

"This isn't fair," she said, the hand holding the pistol dropping to her lap. "There is no reason to include me in this ruse you are staging. I am of no value to you, to anyone." She paused, turning away, then added. "It's not fair. I loved him."

Now it was Blade's turn to be surprised. "Don't you think that would have been something to share back then?"

"He knew. I'm sure of that. But he lived in the memories of his wife. I never blamed him and never dreamed of taking that away. I just wanted some of him for myself. It turned out that friendship was all he could give." She turned back to Blade. "And it was a great friendship that I cherished until the day...."

"Until three months ago today, as I recall."

"You even know that." She rose from her seat and began pacing the room. "All right, if you're Arthur Blade, then tell me what happened. Why fake your death? Was your cancer diagnosis just another part of the gameplay? And how is it I am conversing with a man who insists he is my dead best friend but is very much alive and less than half his age?"

Blade nodded his acknowledgment. "Let's start near the beginning, shall we? My cancer was very real. I was coming to terms with my imminent death when a team of researchers approached me, offering a glimmer of hope."

Blade recited the details of his sickness, his staged death, and the miraculous gift of life. Audrey listened without interrupting. When he finished, she picked up her drink and downed it, then handed him the empty glass. "I'm going to need a refill," she said.

Blade returned from the kitchen with two full glasses and handed her one as he sat back down. They drank in silence for a few moments.

"Did you wear the dress I like?" he asked. "You know the one."

"What are you talking about?"

"Why, the dress you wore to my funeral, dear girl. I was not in attendance myself, you see."

Her mouth pursed as the terrible memory bloomed in painful clarity. "That was one of the worst days of my life. My dear friend was laid to rest, and you're asking me what I wore? I grieved for you for weeks. And no, I didn't wear the dress you like. I bought something more funeral appropriate. I thought you deserved that. Or should I say, the man they buried deserved it."

"It was the part of me that was dying, Audrey. The part that could no longer sustain life."

"And now you're some witch doctor's prized experiment. Just how much of you is in there?"

"From what I can tell, it is that part of the mind which contains all life experiences. All memories, thoughts, education, training, love. It is the entire existence of Arthur Blade, removed from a moribund body and implanted into a new shell. I'm still adapting to the physical changes, can assure you it is still very much me inside."

"And what of the memories of me, of us? Was there a place for those?"

Blade hung his head. "I thought of you so much more than I ever expressed. Oh, the missteps of a non-romantic man."

"You had your moments," she said. *Never enough*, is what she thought.

He turned away, staring at the floor. "That witch doctor to whom you refer was a brilliant pioneer in this field. They recently found him dead. Tortured and murdered, I suspect, by the same group of thugs who pursue me now."

"There are people after you? Why? Why would anyone want you dead?"

"State secrets, I suspect. That, plus it would have been far more convenient for certain individuals if I had died as expected. There are elements within the CIA, Audrey, who appear far more engrossed in their personal upward mobility than in keeping our nation safe. That is why I have come to you to ask for your help."

Audrey gave a disappointed look. "Is that the only reason?"

Blade thought for a moment and admitted to himself it was not. He had always felt a strong attraction toward her. But it was the memories of his wife that prohibited him from acting upon his emotions. Somehow now, having shed his old skin, all the limitations of the past seemed to have stayed behind. He was suddenly seized by a nearly uncontrollable desire to take her in his arms. She was so beautiful, one of the most attractive women he had ever seen. There were so many times in the past when he'd had this same desire but thought it ungentlemanly to act upon such urges once they had gone down the path of friendship. Audrey was as much a part of his life as Ginny had been, and he refused to spoil their relationship by giving in to physical cravings.

He extended his hand and covered hers, feeling her fingers tense and then relax. "No, Audrey, it's not the only reason. I've wanted to get word to you from the moment I regained consciousness. But I had convinced myself that you would get along better without me complicating your life. You deserved a man free of previous encumbrances. I sometimes believed that I used my memories of Ginny to ensure I would never again suffer the loss of someone I loved so much. That made me a fool, as well as a coward, for not embracing you when I had the opportunity. For that, I'm forever sorry." He offered a sad smile. "Current circumstances, however, demand immediate attention. I have to act before being acted upon. Audrey, I am here because I need your help, and... and because I have missed you so."

He stood, walked to the kitchen and, retrieved the bottle, then refilled both their glasses. He set the bottle down and stood before her. "You can help me by contacting one of my team. We should assume that all of their movements are being monitored. That is why I cannot make direct contact."

"Do they know what you look like now?" she asked.

Blade shook his head. "I don't know. They were attempting to force the doctor to reveal the identity of my donor when they killed him. It is quite possible they will now recognize me. Those files were supposed to be secure. I'm sure you know that in my business, secrets get stolen every day."

Audrey nodded. "Tell me what you need. You know I'll do all I can." She stood and started for the kitchen. "Have you eaten? Would you like something?"

Blade blocked her way and took her hands in his. "I'm reluctant to thrust you into the middle of this, but you're one of the few people who ever had my full trust. Thank you, dear girl. Thank you for being there for me yet again."

Audrey's gaze met his, and she smiled back.

Without willing his body to react, he moved toward her, wrapped his arms around her shapely frame, and kissed her passionately. Audrey did not move, did not return the gesture, but broke away from his embrace and slapped him hard across the face. They stared at each other wordlessly from a distance, the air between them crackling with electricity. He opened his mouth to speak. Before he uttered a sound, she reached out and pulled him toward her and locked her lips hungrily to his.

Tongues thrashed and probed as their bodies began a slow grind. Out of breath, she moved away and stared back at him. "Don't tease an old woman, Arthur. You're making me feel like a cradle robber. Just how old are you now?"

"I'm seventy-two, Audrey. That part cannot change. As for the rest of me? Well, consider it a hardware upgrade. Only, I'm not sure everything will function as expected."

"Arthur, you're forgetting that I'll be sixty soon with no upgrades. It's been a very long time for me. I have the same questions."

"Then it's high time we both found out." Blade scooped her up into his arms and carried her toward the bedroom.

Audrey wrapped her arms around his neck. "Are you sure this is what you want? That it's the right thing to do?"

Blade kissed her again. "I have never been more sure of anything, dear girl, never more so."

Twenty
COUNTEROFFENSIVE

Arthur Blade's phone vibrated on the nightstand of Audrey's bedroom. He retrieved it and headed for the kitchen. Looking back as he pulled the door shut, he ensured he hadn't awoken her. The display on the phone looked different, and he was surprised by the crystal clarity of the digits. His ability to focus had improved even more overnight. He recognized the number and answered. "This is rather early for you to be up and about."

"Well, I'm awake now," Lou replied. "I got a call back from an old friend who's a police inspector in London. According to him, a turf war between three municipalities hampered the investigation of your train incident. The train departed King's Cross, bound for Hull. The murdered girl's body was found alongside the tracks in Redford, and the unidentified male was found a few miles further north. All three municipalities claimed jurisdiction, so nothing got done for a while. A magistrate stepped in and settled the dispute, so everyone came together to play nice. There was another victim. An American business owner spent a month in the hospital. On his release, he headed back stateside."

"Garret Logan," Blade informed him. "He's one of mine."

"I should have guessed the CIA was knee-deep in this. What the hell happened?"

"It was a setup, and I may have been the intended target. There appears to be a group of high-level, deeply entrenched subversives that are operating outside the parameters of the organization."

"Care to repeat that in English?"

"There is a rogue element operating from within the CIA. I don't know who or why, but I have my suspicions. I walked into a trap, Azzy. It was the most elaborate ruse I have ever seen, better than anything the Russians ever attempted. I should have known better."

"Your spider senses weren't picking up on anything wrong?"

"I admit to being anxious about re-entering the field. It is very possible that my excitement clouded my better judgment."

"Don't you think they knew that and played it against you? You said this was your first field assignment. How many years has it been since you've done that?"

"Thirty."

"Arthur," Lou chortled. "Your memory and attention to detail are amazing."

"That attention to detail is what failed me. Tell me about the dead woman."

"Not much to tell. Lila Inglenook, twenty-seven years of age, an aspiring actress who entered this whole thing believing she was playing a bit part for a few pounds."

"Those were her exact words, more or less, before her death. I need a link, Azzy. Something that connects all of this to the people I suspect. I need to know who contacted her, who paid her. Do you have anyone who could help?"

Lou thought for a moment. "Yeah, yeah, I know a guy. It

might make sense to put him on retainer, just in case you need more digging. Do you have access to funding?"

"This is all on my dime, as they say, at least for the time being. Make the arrangements with your 'guy', and I'll figure a way to pay him through back channels."

"Good enough. I'll make some calls. Anything else you need for now?"

"No, nothing else just yet, but there will be. Word up."

Lou chuckled. "Oh, and Arthur?"

"Yes?"

"Ditch whatever modern slang book it is you're reading and watch a few movies. You have a lotta work to do, buddy."

The line went silent, and Blade turned to see Audrey coming from the bedroom. "My apologies. I didn't mean to wake you."

She smiled and kissed his cheek. "I'm still an early riser. Would you like some coffee?"

He took a moment to enjoy the sight of her. "That sounds very good," he said. "Tell me, do you still converse with Garret Logan and his wife?"

Audrey loaded a coffee pod into the machine. "I haven't seen Jill since the funeral, but we've spoken a few times."

"Good, could I ask you to deliver them a package today? A cake, perhaps."

She flashed an inquisitive look as she handed him a cup and prepared one for herself.

"Are we talking about a cake with a hidden message?"

"Something like that. If you have no objections, then your help would be appreciated. I must get word to the proper people that I am still very much alive."

"Arthur Blade, are you enlisting me as a spy?"

He stepped close and kissed her. "I wouldn't ask if it wasn't important. Your actions will be innocent enough so as not to attract attention. I would never ask you to do anything that might put you in harm's way."

"I know that," she said, stroking his cheek. "Tell me what you have in mind."

Audrey Landers followed Blade's instructions to the letter and purchased everything he had asked. A phone call to Garret Logan's wife, Jill, had ensured the two of them would be home.

Audrey drove the short distance to their modest but quaint bungalow on the outskirts of Arlington and knocked on the front door wearing a long white down jacket and carrying a cake box. Jill Logan greeted her in an attractive blue workout outfit, and the two made small talk over tea. "I have to speak with Garret," Audrey revealed. "I have a message."

Jill was accustomed to her husband's need for secrecy and motioned for Audrey to follow her to Garret Logan's office in the back of the house. She tapped on the door and let herself in.

Garret Logan was still recovering from his injuries suffered from being thrown off the train two months earlier. Two fractured lumbar vertebrae had caused much concern about permanent nerve damage, but he was making steady improvement. He turned in his oak office chair and rose, wearing gray sweatpants and a U of M sweatshirt.

"Don't get up on my account," Audrey said, entering the room, but he was already on his feet. "How are you feeling?"

"It's getting easier day by day," he offered, "but I'll be able to predict the weather by the aches in my bones." He gave her an affectionate hug. "How have you been, Audrey? You look terrific."

"Audrey has something to tell you," Jill Logan said. "I'll

leave you two alone." She slipped out the door and pulled it shut behind her.

"That sounded rather dubious," he said, lowering himself into his seat. He motioned to a comfortable-looking red leather high-back chair. "Please, sit."

Audrey smiled and settled into the chair. She looked about the small office and locked on the large window. "Would you mind putting on some music, please?" she asked.

Logan did not ask why but dropped a CD into the stereo. When a Mozart piece played, Audrey reached into her purse. "You're looking much better, Garret," she said. "That's good, because Arthur needs you."

Logan's smile disappeared. "Did you say Arthur? What's going on, Audrey?"

Audrey pulled out a burner cell phone, powered it up, and punched in a number. When it connected, she said, "I'm sitting with him now," and then handed the phone to Logan.

"Yes?" he said, then listened.

"Garret, thank God you're all right. I had no idea of your situation until I'd seen the news reports the next day."

Logan recognized the voice instantly. "Arthur, I'd nearly given up hope that you'd survived. We all thought that was the end of you."

"It was not for a lack of trying, I assure you." Blade gave him a summary of the attempt on his life and his ordeal afterward. "I fear your every move is being monitored, so I will make this brief. You must know by now that they set us up."

"I gathered as much but don't know who or why. The investigation within the agency is at a standstill. No one is talking."

"I believe that's because of who perpetuated this entire disaster. Garret, all the evidence I've seen points toward someone within our own ranks, someone at a high level."

"You're not thinking Colson did this, are you?"

"Not necessarily, but someone one or two steps beneath him that still has his ear, as well as his trust. None of this could have gone forward without Colson's direct authorization. There is a small group that serves beneath him. We must first identify which of them is the head of the snake, then neutralize the threat."

"Easier said than done," Logan pointed out. "I'm back on the clock at the agency, but not involved in any field ops. You're listed as MIA and presumed dead. Under these conditions, it will be difficult to get anything accomplished."

"So it would seem," Blade agreed. "But there are ways of using that situation to our advantage. Being dead has its usefulness. I would like you to start by contacting Dr. Rossenblume from the institute that performed my procedure. I'll need to establish a direct link with him once we determine whether he has been compromised. Your inquiry should not raise too much suspicion. I'll supply you with a time and a location for him to meet with me. I would also like you to document all you can about who and what you saw that day on the train. It may be possible to confirm the identities of the accomplices who were involved and trace them back to the one giving the orders."

"I already made a lot of notes," Logan said. "I'll add what I can and give them to Audrey." He paused a moment and added, "I can still see the face of the guy that sucker punched me on the train. He had a fist like a piston and a deadly roundhouse kick. I was seeing stars as he pushed me out the door between cars. I remember that face, though. Asian, maybe Korean, with long, straight hair hanging over one eye. He moved like a machine."

"That sounds very much like one of the two that threw me into the channel. I believe his name was Mako."

"I'll pass the word around to the other guys on the team and see if we can't find out who he works for."

"Proceed with the utmost caution," Blade said. "Trust only those within our immediate circle. I would expect these subversives are doing everything possible to infiltrate our ranks. Their goal was my elimination. I don't know that I would survive another attempt."

"Got it," Logan said. "Anything else?"

Blade drummed his fingers on the table. "Make sure no one is following you or Audrey. I would never forgive myself if anyone harmed either of you."

Logan offered a quick solution. "I have an old detective friend. I'll get him to keep a tail on her. We'll tell him he's being paid by a jealous husband."

"Perfect, Garret, and please share any more of your insight as soon as possible."

Logan ended the call and handed it back to Audrey. "I don't suppose you were watching for tails on the way over here?" he asked.

She grinned. "You can't be around intelligence agents without learning a few tricks of the trade. No one was tailing me, but there was a black Yukon just down the street from here. He's close enough to be listening in with a laser microphone aimed at your window."

"I thought that's why you asked for the background music," Logan said, nodding. "They rotate between the Yukon and a cable repair truck. I first assumed the agency sent them for my protection. No one at Langley knows anything about them."

Audrey craned her neck just enough to get a view of the SUV out the window. "Arthur would recommend you proceed as though it is a threat."

Logan's eyebrows arched as he suppressed a grin. "He also thought you would have made an excellent spy."

"I get that a lot these days," she said, rising from her

chair. "I look forward to some normal times in the future when this is behind us. Maybe the four of us for dinner?"

"That sounds great," Logan said as he stood to walk her to the door. "I know Jill would love it."

Audrey said her goodbyes to Jill and headed out the front door, careful not to glance toward the suspect SUV down the street. She got to her car and adjusted the rearview mirror to apply some lipstick and sneak a peek at the Yukon. She could not see through the dark tinted side windows but noticed two sets of eyes watching her through the windshield. Audrey devised a test to see whether these people thought she warranted a tail and headed out toward a shopping mall. From there, she would call Arthur from a pay phone and give him an update before heading home.

At four the next afternoon, Blade was sitting at the same table in the same bar he had occupied when first approached by Dr. Rossenblume. He watched now as the doctor entered and walked right past him. Rossenblume stopped and peered back, surprised.

"Good afternoon, Doctor," Blade greeted him.

Rossenblume stood staring another moment before sliding into the seat. "Arthur, the transformation is absolutely remarkable. I've seen your new face many times, and yet I still didn't recognize you. Curious, most curious." He sat, examining every detail of Blade's features. "Forgive me," he said, glancing about the room. "I'm just not myself since Dr. Hanspratten's murder. Is it even safe for us to be meeting like this?"

"Yes. I have people watching this building. We're protected here. And may I offer my profound apologies. I'm sure you know I am the likely cause of the good doctor's demise.

Whoever is after me thought they could identify my donor through his records."

Rossenblume hung his head, nodding. "That would explain what we saw. They ransacked Hanspratten's office. They must have gone through every square inch of his files. The computer hard drives are also missing. Thankfully, all records of our donors are stored in an off-site database. No one here has access to anything more than the printouts of information pertinent to our procedure." He eyed Blade closer. "You're doing well, I see."

Blade nodded. "All things considered, yes. There are a multitude of side effects I did not know how to deal with. I understood about the seizures. What follows each, however, was most surprising."

"Tell me about these," the doctor asked, leaning in.

"After each episode, I've noticed it is easier to perform a particular function. Some of these are abilities that were lost after the procedure and have now returned. Others are completely new to me. Skill sets that I can perform as though I've worked at them all my life."

"That is astounding," Rossenblume exclaimed. "We understand that seizures are a reaction of your brain, creating new synapses at an accelerated pace. We never anticipated your cerebrums building pathways to connect with the past abilities of your donor. I have no explanation for how this is even possible." He shook his head, struggling to comprehend the new information. "This makes our next steps even more critical and time-sensitive. I suggest we test and monitor your brain chemistry to ensure it has everything necessary to continue on this course. And—" the doctor hesitated. "We must ensure you don't suffer from any imbalances. We have seen the effects of that firsthand."

"What could I expect if that were the case?" Blade asked.

"Death, I'm afraid, and not a good one. We've witnessed it

firsthand. Rather than building the pathways as your brain appears to be doing handily, our second subject died because of the healing process spinning out of control. His convulsions began lasting longer with greater severity until he suffered a rapid succession of grand mal seizures. He did not survive. We need to document your levels and correct any imbalances as quickly as possible."

Blade grinned. "I'm impressed, doctor. You seem to be as knowledgeable about these side effects as Hanspratten himself. I thought he was the only one who knew the details so well."

"Arthur, Dr. Hanspratten was indeed the pioneer of this procedure, but it was I who perfected the process."

"How many people within your institute know this?"

Rossenblume shook his head. "It was not important for anyone else to know. Dr. Hanspratten, Rolf, and I shared our collective data together. He made the announcements of our breakthroughs. I am a humble man. being a part of such a milestone medical achievement was reward enough for me."

"Your humility may have saved your life," Blade told him. "These people were likely attempting to destroy me by eliminating the only doctor who could treat my side effects. You must put an end to any research at the institute until further notice. Allow these people to believe they ended the project by taking the founding doctor's life. In doing so, it may well save yours. Tell me, do you have the means of monitoring my condition at another facility?"

"Yes, of course, but I will need access to the solutions that were prepared for you. We can create future dosages based on the levels of what we have on hand."

"Understood," Blade said, thinking through the next moves. "The institute is likely still under surveillance by this same unsavory group. It may be dangerous for you to go there now. We'll have to be creative. I assume your imaging and chemistry monitoring equipment requires service from time to time?"

"Yes, we often have maintenance crews from at least three different companies in the facility."

"Good, very good. That's how we'll get you back into the building without being observed. My team will take you in disguised as a field service engineer." Blade fished a phone from his jacket pocket and slid it across the table. "This is how we will communicate. Just push the last number dialed to connect with me. If someone contacts you by any other means and claims to be working with us, document what they say and call me immediately."

Rossenblume nodded as he studied the phone, then stuffed it into his pocket.

"I have one last question for you, doctor, if I may."

"I would expect you to have a thousand questions, Arthur. This new life and existence are nothing short of extraordinary, and I don't recall anyone offering you an owner's manual."

"Well stated. My concern right now has to do with the age of my mind." He tapped the side of his head. "I am still seventy-two years old up here and getting older. In terms of longevity, what would be my approximate lifespan?"

"I would expect the exact opposite to be happening as we speak. Our research has shown that once the new host accepts the new brain, it replenishes and begins rebuilding it, just as it does with all of its other organs. Every cell of your body, except for the brain, is rebuilt with new cells every moment of every day. In your previous body, the aging process diminished its ability to rebuild itself. This new host body of yours, however, is at its zenith. That, along with the additional stem cells, means your brain is no longer aging as a seventy-two-year-old." Rossenblume smiled. "Our stem cell doping procedure offers the beneficial byproduct of reversing the aging process in your brain. That brilliant gray matter of yours has begun to rebuild itself and is getting younger, not older."

Blade's phone began buzzing the moment he left the tavern. He ignored it until he'd climbed back into his car, then checked the caller ID. "Azzy, I hope this means you have something for me."

"Hello to you, too," Lou said with a snarky tone. "Yeah, a couple of things. The identity of the second victim from the train is still not being released. We figured as much, right? So I asked an old friend at Scotland Yard to return a favor he owed me. He sent me the fingerprints of the decedent. I ran them through the database.... Nothin'. So I tapped another old acquaintance for another favor. I'm running out of favors here. Anyway, this guy runs the prints through the INTERPOL files and bingo, we get a hit."

"Let me guess," Blade said. "Ukranian national with a long record for computer crimes."

"Are you telling this story or me?" Lou shot back.

Blade stifled a chuckle. "By all means, please proceed."

"So the stiff is an Ukranian national with a long record for computer crimes. He's likely the point man for your botched software ransom caper."

"Indeed. Have you discovered his last known address or links to former acquaintances?"

"Slow down, Dick Tracy. Yeah, and I got more than that. The guy's cousin is here on a school visa."

"Don't tell me. He's studying computer software. Am I correct?"

"Arthur, I love you like a brother, so don't take this wrong, but it is no fun tracking down all of this for you when you already know the answers."

"My apologies, but time is of the essence. We need everything you can give us about this computer hacker. They had threatened to erase all the hard drives at this auto company, but my understanding is nothing has happened. We may have a small window to intercede."

"Fine, just act surprised once in a while when I uncover something new. I'm working my ass off here."

"As you wish, please proceed."

"So yes, the cousin is here studying software, cyber security, to be exact."

"Goodness me, that is a surprise!"

Lou blew out an exasperated breath. "A little too surprised, Arthur. Don't overdo it. Look, the kid's name is Gavriik Federov, and he's a student up in Chicago. I'm willing to bet he knows far more about this entire situation than he would lead you to believe."

"Excellent work, Louis. Do you have an address for this cousin?"

"What, you don't know that one already? I'm texting it over now."

Blade read the information displayed on his phone. "I will take care of this myself," he said. "Do you know of any retired police in the area that might be interested in lending a hand? A pair would be the best approach."

"Yeah, I have some very good friends in Chicago who retired about the same time as me. I'll send you their info. You can work out the financial details with them."

"Azzy, you are an army of one! I could accomplish none of this without your help."

"True, very true. I would warn you to watch for accomplices, but I'm sure you have that covered."

"I'll be in touch," Blade said, ending the call. He dialed up the first contact that Lou had supplied and set up a meeting for the next morning.

Blade's chartered plane touched down at Midway airport in the first light of a new dawn. Within an hour, he was driving a rental car toward his meeting with Lou's Chicago acquaintances. The three made introductions over coffee, discussed the unique situation, and formulated a game plan.

Gavriik Federov held the key to more than just the ransom demands and the botched handoff of a memory stick. Blade believed the kid could be persuaded to give up his secrets, given the proper motivation. Judging by what he'd discovered the day earlier, he held many. A call to a friend at the cyber-terror division of the FBI revealed correlations between the recent software attack and the young Russian. A file already existed in the bureau of his extracurricular activities, and his friend supplied a few of the highlights in return for some one-on-one time with the kid. Whether it required promises or threats, Blade came prepared to incorporate whatever means necessary to get Federov talking. This would go as easy or difficult as the young software hacker made it for himself.

Blade and his hired help stood outside Federov's apartment as he stepped out to attend his first class of the day. The young man caught sight of the trio and tried dashing back inside, but a foot held the door open as a hand shot out and latched around his arm with a vise-like grip.

"What do you want?" he said, struggling. "You know you're not supposed to bother me here."

"Wrong team," Blade said, pushing the young man back into the apartment. "We'd like a few words if you don't mind."

"Well, I do mind, damnit," he said, trying to break Blade's grip on his arm. He looked no different than thousands of other college-age kids. Jeans, a hooded sweatshirt, the latest tennis sneakers, and a head full of unkempt sandy brown hair.

"You're making me late for class," he argued. "Either show me your warrant or get out of my apartment."

"I'm sure that Mr. Reynolds won't mind having one less student in his class today," Blade said as he led the young man to a table and forced him down into a seat.

The two retired police officers took their places on either side. Blade made a visual inventory of the apartment's furnishings, noting everything that seemed out of place.

"You have excellent taste in entertainment equipment," Blade said. "That looks to be an eighty-five-inch display with well over a thousand watts of audio power pushing those magnificent speakers. I wish we had the time for a demonstration. But I'm afraid, Gavriik, we've come with some rather distressing news."

"Who are you guys?" Federov demanded. "You can't just push your way in here like this. I demand to see my attorney."

Blade pulled a seat up beside him. "Let's just say we represent a rather obscure division of homeland security. And I'm sorry to say it's a division that does not concern itself with the rights of non-citizens who are here under false pretenses."

"I am legal!" Federov exclaimed. "I am here on a student visa. Now leave before I call the real police."

Blade smiled, leaning in on his elbows, tenting his hands. "We'll make that call to the police for you in a moment. Before we do, let's discuss your financial means of support. I reviewed your bank account and your education stipend. Let's be honest with each other for a moment, Gavriik, shall we? Simply put, you cannot afford the lavish lifestyle you are living. At first glance, I would have to assume that you are earning unreported revenue by freelancing. I have no issue with the entrepreneurial spirit. It is the cornerstone of our free enterprise system. You, however, have chosen a profession that, although it offers immediate rewards, also comes with the unpleasant downside of significant jail time."

Blade reached into the breast pocket of his black sports coat and pulled out a stack of index cards. He laid them on the table and pointed. "Do you recognize any of these web pages and site names?"

Federov glanced at the documents and pushed them away, shaking his head. "No, I don't know what these are," struggling to downplay his recognition.

Blade picked up on it and eyed him with disappointment. "And here I was, hoping you would be more willing to offer us a little cooperation." He pulled up his phone and typed in one of the web addresses. "Let's do a little experiment, shall we?" He pushed the send button and waited. A moment later, they heard a dull ding from the next room. "Hmm," Blade said, "imagine that. I receive an email warning from what I think is my credit card company, alerting me about unauthorized charges. I click on a little box to dispute them, and I'm connected to your computer, which downloads another one of your infamous Trojan horse programs into my system. Now a message pops up demanding money, or you will erase all of my files. Quite ingenious, although very predatory. Let's try again." He selected another bogus email message supplied by his friend at the FBI. "This one tells me I purchased a new laptop online. Thank goodness there is this little button to push to dispute the charge." Blade once again pushed send on his phone and waited.

Ding.

One of the retired police officers, a man with a body built like iron and the face of a bulldog, leaned in until he was nose-to-nose with Federov. "My mother fell for that one. You took her for ten grand, you little weasel. I want it back."

"Oh Gavriik, what are we to do with you?" Blade asked. "You have broken a multitude of laws and are taking advantage of the innocent and most vulnerable. I'm sure that my friend here would love nothing more than to spend a few private moments with you to further discuss the error of your ways. After all, what you're doing is stealing. You're intelligent enough to understand that, correct? And being that your thievery is for such large amounts and your crimes cross state lines, it becomes a federal issue of grand theft. You could be prosecuted for multiple major felonies. Judges enjoy putting people like you away. So tell me, would you like us to make that call to the police now?"

Federov sat in stunned silence, attempting to keep his features unrevealing.

"You would have been wise to consider what your handlers would say if they knew you were attracting so much attention to yourself. They made a sizable investment in your education, not to mention the time spent choosing the proper candidate to enlist in the Russian SVR upon graduation. No, I don't believe they would be very pleased with you right now."

A pained expression swept over Federov's face, the first sign that Blade had hit his mark.

"You have been burning the candle at both ends, young man. Unfortunately, you've run out of wick." Blade let the young man ponder his words for a moment then folded his hands on the table. "I'm sorry to be the one to tell you this. Your cousin, Slava, is dead."

Federov's jaw tightened as he attempted to blink back tears.

Blade offered a handkerchief. "Things went badly in the exchange," he said. "Slava was found beside the train tracks. As yet, we are uncertain who is responsible. Perhaps with your help, we could bring Slava's killers to justice."

Federov looked up with mournful eyes. "He did only what I asked him to do. I couldn't be the one making the exchange. The people who pay for my education would never allow me to be involved in such things."

"Sooner than later, they will make the connection and come for you," Blade cautioned. "You are their investment. They cannot afford to have you sitting in an American prison."

"I don't want to go back. I, I can't go back, not now, never."

"You need to disappear. We can arrange that. We can also provide a much more comfortable lifestyle than you are living. You won't need to rely on these sideline hacker jobs anymore. Come work for us. We can offer employment, pay for your education, and, most importantly, keep you safe."

"You don't understand," Federov said, shaking his head. "They are everywhere. I am watched all day, every day." He threw his arms up, exasperated. "Even one of my professors is one of my handlers. I could not escape and go with you if I tried."

"Let me ask you something. Have you used your skills to peer inside the files of Russian intelligence computers?"

Federov whipped his head to face Blade, his eyes growing wide.

Blade nodded. "I thought as much. This makes you all the more valuable to us but a dangerous liability to them. What can you tell me about Vladimir Folezchev?"

Federov's face drained of color. He pushed away from the table, crossing his arms across his chest.

"Here is your opportunity to prove your value to your new benefactors. Tell me something about Vladimir that I don't already know."

"Folozchev, he is SVR."

"He *was* SVR," Blade corrected him. "Now he is in this country seeking defector status."

"NO!" Federov nearly shouted. "No, he is still SVR."

"Prove that to me, Gavriik. Prove that, and I will personally guarantee your safety with a new identity and a new life."

"And who are you that you can make such promises?"

Blade grinned. "I am a ghost, and I know a thing or two about disappearing. Give me something, and I will get you out of here right now."

Federov swallowed hard and nodded. "They sent Vladimir Folezchev as a decoy to ferret out another defector and kill him. I don't know the name, only a call sign—Benedict."

"How do you know that?" Blade asked. "SVR agents are not known to be chatty."

"You are familiar with the GRU, yes?"

Blade nodded.

"I have had three handlers since starting classes here. The GRU handles cyber warfare, hacking, all software. My first handler was GRU, and I think very bored, very lonely. He and the agent from SVR would meet in my apartment to play cards. When I went to my room, they would talk. Many times I lay awake and listened. Folezchev is well known in the SVR. Even in the GRU, they know and fear him. He is the one they send when they need a prisoner to be broken. He is an expert at extracting secrets and also at keeping them. Folezchev requested this assignment. It would make him a hero in the Motherland to ensure Benedict was either returned to Russia or killed."

The pieces began coming together as Blade thought about the identity of Benedict. He assumed the name was chosen as a slap against the United States, wondering how many Benedict Arnolds existed in Russian history.

There were hundreds of Russians seeking American asylum. So which one was Benedict? And what made him so important that Vladimir Folezchev would take it upon himself to oversee his demise? He thought of a prime candidate and understood. If he was right, then Benedict was sitting in his own safe house. Uri Greggenkoff had just become far more valuable than Blade ever would have suspected. He had to act on this information now. That meant he had to get this kid out of here with him. And it had to be done right under the watchful eyes of his Russian handlers.

One of the retired cops stood at the window and peered through a curtain, watching for activity.

"Are we clear?" Blade asked him.

"Haven't seen any activity, but that means nothing."

Blade stood and said, "Gavriik, take off your hoodie and sneakers, please."

Federov looked back, questioning, but complied. Blade offered them to the cop watching the window. "You're close to the kid's size. Here, let's swap."

The cop offered his own jacket, shoes, and hat while slipping on the one belonging to Federov.

"Do you ever wear a hat?" Blade asked.

"That ball cap by the door."

The cop took the hint and put on the hat, pulling the brim down over his eyes.

Blade looked to the other cop and said, "Cuff your partner and walk him out of here." He handed the cop's jacket, shoes, and hat to Federov. "Put these on."

Blade opened the front door and said, "Drive toward O'Hare and make sure they stay with you all the way."

The cop nodded and pushed his cuffed partner out the door.

Blade remained hidden from view and watched out the window as the cop loaded his partner into the backseat, then slid behind the wheel and drove off. Seconds later, a black Lincoln parked ten cars back, pulled from the curb, and followed. Blade waited until he was sure only one car had given chase. He and Federov then walked out the door, got into Blade's car, and drove in the opposite direction toward Midway airport.

Twenty-One
Inside the Hornet's Nest

While Arthur Blade was off dealing with the young software hacker in Chicago, Garret Logan took Blade's advice and headed back into Langley. The pretense of the trip was to visit with members of the staff he hadn't seen since the ill-fated excursion to England. The actual reason had more to do with spying on the infamous spy agency itself. Logan came to put his ear to the rail, drop a few subtle hints that he was ready to return to active duty, ask some general questions about current events, then see what bubbled up. Even in this building, constructed for the business of secrecy, people were sometimes willing to share what they knew with others. So far, though, the plan had not paid off. He had picked up on some juicy gossip but not much else.

Logan headed to Don Colson's office to ask about being reassigned and ran into him, walking the corridor with John Winchell. Winchell clammed up the moment he noticed Logan approaching, but not before Logan overheard the name Uri Gregenkoff. Colson greeted him, and Logan shook both their hands.

"Good to see you out and about, Garret. Does this mean we can put you back on the roster?"

"Yes, sir," he said, smiling. "I'm getting awful bored staring at the walls at home. If you have anything for me, then I am more than ready."

"Let's see about getting you reassigned to another division chief. I can check with Mansfield and Gilbertson to see if either of them could use you." He turned to Winchell and said, "John, how are you set for personnel on your team?"

"Can't say, as we're hurting for manpower right now. I have a good group in place. Mansfield may be the best one to start with." He eyed Logan and added, "Sorry, Garret, but my guys can handle everything I throw at them."

"Thanks, anyway, John," he said, feigning a smile.

"Now, wait a minute," Colson said. "We can use you right now. John, let's have Garret drive our friend to the airport."

Winchell's expression remained unchanged, but Logan noticed an odd eye twitch. "I already have Fossie standing by at the safe house," Winchell said, a little too defensively. "We don't need the help."

Now Logan wanted in, just to see what had caused Winchell's reaction.

"Nonsense," Colson said, waving Winchell off. "This will be a good way for Garret to ease back in." He turned to Logan. "Go down to personnel and tell them you're back on the clock. Then head to the carpool and sign out a plain brown wrapper. You'll be driving tomorrow to the Fairview safe house to pick up Uri Greggenkoff and deliver him to the airport for deportation."

"I have this covered without the help," Winchell protested.

"John, relax, would you? It's just a quick ride to the airport. Besides, I want Garret back in the saddle. With his knowledge of Arthur Blade's way of doing things, he is an underutilized asset. That changes right now."

Logan nodded and said, "I appreciate that, sir. But if I may ask, why are we cutting Greggenkoff loose? Arthur told me he received good information from him."

"Not according to Winchell," Colson said. "The battle for trustworthiness between Uri Greggenkoff and Vladimir Folozchev came down to a few tiny details that John caught before we made any big mistakes. We arranged a last-minute trade with the SVR. Greggenkoff goes back to mother Russia, and we get Pierce Washburn, an MI-6 intelligence officer. We'd nearly given up hope of ever getting him back. The Brits will owe us a big favor for returning one of their own."

All of this sounded very wrong to Logan, but he wasn't about to voice his objections now. He also noticed Winchell's previous pallor now turning red. The man was livid over Logan being allowed to drive the Russian to the airport. What reason could he have? And what had made them believe Folozchev was a credible defector and Greggenkoff a spy? He had to get word to Blade as quickly as possible.

"I'll head to personnel," Logan said to Colson. "Let me know if anything changes." He began walking toward the bank of elevators and could hear Winchell still arguing with his boss about the decision.

As soon as the elevator doors closed, he had his phone out. "Arthur! Greggenkoff is being deported. I'm being sent to pick him up at the safe house."

Blade was still in the air, flying back from Chicago. He took a few deep breaths as the news hit him. "This is a travesty!" he said. "On whose authority is this being done?"

"Colson made the call on Winchell's recommendation."

"I should have known. John Winchell cannot differentiate between a hard truth and a smooth lie. By the sound of it, he has this all buggered up." He thought another moment and said, "We cannot allow this to happen. There are questions I still have that only Greggenkoff can answer."

"I have a few more of my own," Logan added. "but according to Colson, Folozchev is the more credible of the two."

"Everything I've learned so far says he is dead wrong. Folozchev never supplied any intel that turned out to be credible or even the least bit useful. Greggenkoff has proven himself in more than one instance. Without him, we would never have found those nuclear warheads in time. They are making a prolific mistake. When are you scheduled to pick up Greggenkoff?"

"I'm on my way now to the carpool. They expect me at the safe house tomorrow morning."

Blade thought for a moment. "I can meet you along the way. There is a gas station at the corner of Byzantine and Fuller. Pick me up there."

"Are you sure you want to reveal yourself to these guys? Once they've seen you, there's no going back."

"Garret, this situation is far too important to be worried about anything but keeping Greggenkoff. I will see you tomorrow morning."

Blade pocketed the phone and stared out the window, attempting to make sense of Colson's decision to send Greggenkoff packing. What had Folozchev offered that someone deemed the least bit credible? If this new information from Federov was correct, then the old Russian's mission was to spy on the CIA from within and kill Greggenkoff.

Blade couldn't think of any information Folozchev could offer that would so cloud Winchell's judgment. He wondered for a moment if the Russian might have turned Winchell. Although it was possible, it was also unlikely. He doubted the SVR would have any use for the man. So what deceiving slice of intel did Winchell believe he possessed to make him risk everything in support of the old spy?

Folozchev knew many secrets, but he was not in the business of revealing them. He was a collector, not a salesman. It was far more likely that he had conjured up some incredible yarn that left Winchell drooling. Some deep secret that would blow the lid off the intelligence community and elevate Winchell, the maverick spy hunter, to great heights within the agency. Maybe Blade's old job wasn't the only prize that Winchell sought anymore. Maybe he was eyeing the director's office. Whatever the case, his agency was betting on the wrong horse in the defector race. The CIA was about to lose a valuable asset while holding the door open to a known enemy of the state.

He pulled out his phone and checked the GPS to see how close they were to landing. Their plane was still a few hundred miles out. Doing some quick calculations, he deduced they were about forty-five minutes from wheels down.

He looked over to Gavriik, who sat chewing his nails while staring out a window. "Are you hungry?" he asked.

"Starving."

Blade made another call. "Good evening, Audrey, I hope you don't mind, but I'm bringing a houseguest to stay for a few days if it's not too inconvenient. A new associate." He looked at Gavriik, smiled, and gave a wink. "And could I ask that you have a meal delivered to coincide with our arrival? I was thinking Chinese would do the trick... what's that? No, I think you should order a bit of everything. Shall we say ninety minutes from now? Thank you, dear. See you soon."

John Winchell kept his composure just long enough to get out of earshot of the CIA director. He rounded a corner and punched in numbers on his phone. Fossie answered, and Winchell growled, "Colson is sending one of Blade's team to pick Greggenkoff up tomorrow morning. I want you to go with them. No matter what he says, you get in that goddamn car, and you go wherever Greggenkoff goes. You understand?"

"Sure," Fossie said. "No problem."

"You see anything amiss, if you smell trouble, you text me ASAP."

"Will do."

"One more thing. If this gets out of hand, you put a bullet in the back of the Russian's neck. You got that?"

"That might be a little hard to explain, don't you think?"

"That's my job. Let me worry about explanations. I do not want Greggenkoff allowed to go free, you hear me? Either he is on that plane or he is dead, got it?"

"Got it," Fossie said, cutting the call and staring at the phone. More wet work. He believed that eliminating defectors and double agents should be a tool of last resort. Now he was being called upon again to be little more than a cold-blooded hitman. *Whatever happened to counterintelligence and outwitting, outthinking, your opponent?*

He thought about the number of times he had offered input or even an observation to his boss, and his frustration swelled until every muscle felt as tight as piano strings. He wondered again how Winchell had even gotten his present position. Or how he held it. He reasoned that whoever hired him must have been an even bigger buffoon or returning political favors. John Winchell couldn't think his way out of a paper bag. The man was one hundred percent dependent upon the ideas of others. Yet any time Fossie presented an observation or a new insight, Winchell would blast holes through it. That is until he decided to call the idea his own.

Fossie had started off at Langley with the best of intentions, being recognized early for some of his insights into difficult operations. His star was rising. That all changed when John Winchell became his supervisor. He could think of at least three key pieces of case-breaking information he had brought to Winchell. All of them made it up to the seventh floor and were presented to the director. Only it was Winchell who claimed all the credit.

So Fossie learned to keep most of his better ideas to himself. Volunteering only enough to maintain his position. Hoping like hell to be recognized by someone in the higher ranks and transferred to a new department.

He thought again of how low he had allowed himself to slither for the sake of this job. It made him sick. Life would have been so different had he been assigned to one of the other supervisors. He'd talked briefly with some of the agents working for Mansfield or Gilbertson, and they informed him that Winchell was considered the weakest link at Langley. *Great*, he thought, *all of that hard work to earn my way into the land of spies, and I get saddled with the worst boss. The Putz. How does anyone shine from behind a man who sucks away all your ideas, energy, and even the fucking air like a black hole?*

That vision made him even more desperate for a solution. A way out. But where could he go? It wasn't like he could quit this company and go work for another. The competition in this business was the enemy. And as much as he despised Winchell, and even his twisted partner, Mako, he would never turn against his own country. No, as long as he remained in this profession, he would be stuck in this rut. That meant he had to go on earning brownie points with Winchell, which also demanded some major brown-nosing.

He imagined for a moment working under Arthur Blade and felt envious of the agents on his team. No matter how good or bad Blade was as a boss, it couldn't be worse than the rut he was in.

He would never know. Blade was dead, most likely by his own hand. He remembered the last word spoken by the man that he and Mako had dropped into an ocean grave. "Checkmate." Every internal instinct told him that the man was Blade himself. Fossie tried to remember the face, but with all that had happened that day, he could not recall the image.

Winchell had been so cocksure that the revamped version of Arthur Blade would resemble some old codger. But Winchell had been wrong so many times before that he screwed up that one, too. Him and his 'Trust my gut' feelings. Winchell's defective internal compass was just one of many things that made him a lousy boss and an even worse agent. His most blaring flaw, however, was his lack of conscience. Every move he made was for the sake of one person alone, regardless of the obstacles or consequences. Fossie shook his head in disgust. How could Don Colson not see the man for what he was? A dangerous and amoral sack of shit.

God help them all if Winchell moved any further up the chain of command. He pledged to do everything he could to ensure that day never came. The notion lifted him enough that he decided not to give up all hope just yet. He would continue doing the best he could while never allowing himself to become a bottom feeder like Winchell. He also had to find a way out of assassinating Greggenkoff. Putting a bullet through the back of his neck was a traditional Russian hit tactic. Why had his boss insisted on that? Enough! It was time to refuse the most egregious of Winchell's commands. "Let him fire me. My conscience isn't dead, after all," he told himself as he took an exit off the freeway and headed home early for a change.

Twenty-Two
A Spy for a Spy

Blade had the Uber driver drop him and Federov off two blocks from Audrey Landers' condominium, and they walked along a circuitous back route. "Stay close," was all he had said.

Federov had done just that, maintaining a distance less than two steps away. "Do you think they could have followed us here?" he asked.

"One always stands a better chance of survival by assuming so."

They arrived at the back door of the condo, and Blade pulled it open. "In you go," he said, directing Federov into the kitchen. Audrey poked her head around a corner, then stepped into full view once she saw Blade. She slipped her revolver into a back pocket and waited to be introduced.

"Audrey Landers, meet Gavriik Federov," Blade said. The two shook hands, then stepped back from each other. Blade picked up on their apprehension and added, "Gavriik will be assisting us with our investigation. He, ah, needs to remain out of sight until we have neutralized the threat."

"We didn't pack any of my clothes, sir," Federov said. "If I'm going to be here for a while, I'm going to need...."

"Five foot ten, one-sixty, is that about right?" Audrey asked, sizing him up.

Federov jerked his head back toward her. "How did you know that?"

"It's a girl thing," she said, smiling. She looked at Blade and added, "I can ask Jill to pick up a few things. Boxers or briefs?"

Federov's face turned red.

"Tell me now or wear what comes."

The young Russian looked to Blade as though he'd been violated. "Briefs! Briefs!"

Audrey patted him on the shoulder. "Relax, that will be the most personal question I'll ever ask. Come and sit. There is a lot of food that needs to be eaten."

Federov noticed the multiple containers of Chinese food on the kitchen table and slid into a seat. He loaded a plate with samplings from every container and dug in.

Blade took the moment to fill Audrey in on the situation. "Young Gavriik here is a masterful computer hacker. The GRU drafted him into service. They sent him over here to be educated, and he will be expected to earn his living by breaking into American military computer systems. He was doing a bit of moonlighting and got in way over his head. That's how he came to our attention. His handlers would not have been very appreciative, so I intervened. His knowledge base could be of great value to our side." He lowered his voice and added, "Minimal flight risk. I believe he understands the danger he faces if they find him. We made him a much better offer, so to speak. I will leave him in your capable hands for a few days until we can find more suitable living arrangements." He kissed her and said, "Thank you again for all your help. I could not do this without you."

Audrey grinned. "I know." She watched as Gavriik shoveled the food into his mouth. "Did you get him to switch sides by starving him?"

"So it would seem." Blade made for the bedroom and said, "I've got an early day tomorrow."

"Don't you want to eat something first? You've been going steady all day."

He shook his head. "I'm more exhausted than hungry." He turned to Federov. "Gavriik, I brought you to stay with Audrey because I trust her judgment to keep you safe. Obey her, and she will do just that. We'll talk more in the morning."

Federov nodded as he filled his mouth with fried rice.

Blade waited at a strip mall beside the gas station he had instructed Logan to meet him. He spotted the government car from a half mile away and walked to the curb, jumping into the front seat as it pulled up.

"I wonder why they make these vehicles so obvious."

Logan worked his way back into traffic. "Once upon a time, they blended right in."

"Another issue worthy of further discussion. Tell me more about the verbal exchange between Winchell and Colson."

"More heated than necessary," Logan said, giving Blade a quick glance. "Colson thought it was a good idea to send me. Winchell fought it tooth and nail. He did not want me there."

"Strange reaction, indeed. The timing is suspect as well. Why Greggenkoff, and why now?

Logan nodded, changing lanes. "I can't imagine what information Folozchev could have passed onto Winchell to convince him that Greggenkoff was the double agent. From where I'm sitting, Folozchev is the bad guy."

Blade said nothing but stared out the windshield.

Folozchev had manipulated Winchell, that much he knew. Now it was time to find out why.

The safe house being used to hold Uri Greggenkoff was not a concrete fortress on a secluded piece of land surrounded by hundreds of yards of chain-link fence and barbed wire. It was just a normal house on a quiet street. The foot traffic in and out was minimal, and the neighbors never had a reason to get nosey or complain. Blade preferred it as his go-to house for any time he needed to ensure the safety of a low-level cooperating witness.

Logan had phoned ahead, and Greggenkoff stood waiting at the curb with Fossie, who held the left back door open as the Russian defector climbed in. Fossie took a quick look up and down the street as he walked back around and slid in on the other side.

Fossie looked to Logan, then pointed to the unknown man sitting in the front passenger seat. "Who's this?" he demanded.

Logan tilted his head toward Blade. "Astor, he's new."

Blade cocked his head but said nothing.

"How come I wasn't told you were bringing an escort?"

"Does everybody always tell you everything?" Logan asked. "Come to think of it, Colson said nothing to me about you coming along for the ride, either."

Fossie locked eyes with Logan through the mirror. "We all have our orders, don't we?" He turned to Blade, examining what little he could see of his features from behind. His black hair hung over his shirt collar, and he hadn't shaved in days. A pair of dark sunglasses obscured his eyes. "Maybe we should drop you at a barber shop along the way," he jabbed. "What did you say your name was again?"

Blade continued, staring forward, nudging his sunglasses up his nose. "Gabe Astor," he said.

"Never heard of you. And what is it you do, Gabe Astor? That is, when you're not taking up space on a ride-along?"

"Whatever I'm told."

"Ah, like a good soldier." Fossie motioned to Logan and said, "Take a right up here."

Logan continued straight through the next intersection.

"Hey," Fossie said louder, "you missed the turn for the airport."

Logan ignored him.

"I said, you missed the turn!" Fossie growled, tensing up.

"Relax, would you?" Logan gave him a sideways glance. "I go a different way. I'll catch the freeway a few miles up ahead."

Fossie sat back in the seat but remained anything but relaxed.

Greggenkoff shifted uncomfortably next to him. "I told you earlier. I demand to speak with a representative from the embassy. I refuse to board any aircraft bound for Russia."

Fossie gave the man a look like he was nothing more than a foul smell. "Did I ask you to speak?"

"Why do you need someone from the embassy?" Blade asked.

"You don't need to speak to him," Fossie cut him off.

Blade turned and faced Fossie. "My apologies. I must not have made myself clear. I was speaking to Mr. Greggenkoff, not you." He eyed Greggenkoff and said, "You were saying...."

"If I go back, I am a dead man. I risked my life to come to this country and offered thirty years' worth of secrets from working in the KGB and FSB in exchange for asylum. The CIA made promises to me. And now, I am discarded like street trash. Arthur Blade would never have allowed this to happen."

"Yeah, well, Arthur Blade is dead, isn't he?" Fossie chided. "There's a new sheriff in town, and he doesn't believe your bullshit. Now shut up and enjoy the ride." Fossie glared at Blade. "And you, a little advice because you're new. NEVER presume to have permission to question someone else's detainee. I'll overlook it this one time. But so help me, I will hang you out to dry if you pull shit like this again." He looked back at Greggenkoff and said, "I thought Mako would have convinced you it was best to keep your mouth shut."

It was him! Blade had been receiving subtle signals ever since Fossie climbed into the back seat. But they were nothing but fragmented memories that didn't connect. Then that name, Mako. It cut through the fog of his mind like a blinding spotlight. Suddenly, he was back on that dreadful night. He felt the biting, stiff wind across his face as he balanced on the gunwale of the old boat just before being pushed into the dark abyss of the North Sea. He blinked it away and stared into the mirror at the face of his would-be executioner. This man, Fossie! Who worked for — "Winchell!" Blade blurted aloud. The rest of the puzzle pieces fell into place.

Fossie stared at Blade. "That's right, you open your mouth again, and I'll start with a formal complaint to Winchell. You won't be able to find a job stocking coke machines when I'm done with you. Do you know who I am, rookie? You know who I am?"

Blade slipped off his sunglasses and glared at Fossie. "Yes. I do. You're a loud buffoon and an unscrupulous henchman. You and your corrupt supervisor caused the deaths of two innocent people on a train in England. And despite your best efforts, you failed at your attempt to kill me. Oh, yes, Mr. Fossie, I know exactly who you are. I know what you've done, and I know where you're going. The more pertinent question now would be, do you know who I am?"

Fossie still didn't recognize the face, but that voice, the way he spoke. "No," he said, disbelieving. "That can't be." His hand worked toward his shoulder holster.

"Don't," Blade cautioned. "I have my weapon pointed at your heart. And since you're not wearing a vest, these hollow points are going to make quite the unrepairable hole.

Blade elbowed Logan. "Pull to the side, please. Our friend here is leaving us." He looked at Greggenkoff and said, "Uri, please do the honors of removing Mr. Fossie's sidearm."

The old Russian gave a questioning look to Blade but did what he was told, then aimed the pistol at Fossie.

"Very good. Now, Mr. Fossie, please hand me your phone."

Fossie stared back another moment in disbelief. He and his boss had been outplayed. What surprised him was that the only emotion he felt was relief. This terrible ordeal was over. He eyed Blade with a look of calm acceptance. "Checkmate. I have a better idea," he said. "Drop me off, and I'll give you a head start before I call Winchell."

"Forgive me, but why would I allow you to do that?"

Fossie shook his head. "Look, I was following orders. You, of all people, know that we don't have to like the commands we're given. Believe me, I'm sorry for leaving you out there to die. Things would have played out differently had I known it were you. "

"Ah, but I believe you already knew. When I said...."

"Yeah," Fossie said. "When you said that, I suspected. But you went over the side a second later. This is not how I want my time at the CIA to end. Let me be on the right side for a change."

"And how would you go about accomplishing this?"

"Let me help you bring Winchell down. He's the real problem."

"Indeed," Blade said, weighing the suggestion. "What did you have in mind?"

"We'll start with your tail. Mako is following the signal of this car. Winchell instructed him to intervene if you don't make it to the airport."

Blade glanced at Logan. "He can't be too far behind us now. We'll need a diversion." He turned around and said, "Mr. Fossie, if you can be taken at your word, then I believe we could benefit from your assistance."

Fossie nodded. "Whatever you need, Arthur. Let me help."

Greggenkoff's brows went up. "Did you say, Arthur? Arthur Blade?"

Blade smiled. "Long story, Uri. I hope to share it with you soon." He turned back to Fossie, took his phone, dialed Logan's number, and let it connect. "You did not see me, nor did we have this conversation. You will ignore any incoming calls from Mr. Winchell until Logan calls and gives you instructions. Understood?"

Fossie nodded as he took the phone back, then opened the door.

"Oh, and Mr. Fossie, against my better judgment, I am taking you at your word. Do not make the mistake of crossing me again. I can assure you there is no place to hide where a ghost cannot find you."

Fossie lowered his head, contemplating the words, then locked eyes with Blade. He held the stare for a beat before nodding and stepping out of the car.

"Drive!" Blade commanded.

Logan pushed the gas pedal to the floor, spinning the tires as he shot back into traffic.

Blade turned back to Greggenkoff and held out his hand. "May I have Mr. Fossie's handgun, please?"

Greggenkoff aimed the pistol at him. "Mr. Blade, Where are you taking me?"

"Mr. Logan here is going to hide you away until we can straighten out this unfortunate series of missteps."

"You are not taking me to the airport?"

"Uri, I gave you my word some time ago. No, I will not allow you to be sent back."

Greggenkoff breathed a heavy sigh, flipped the pistol around, and handed it to Blade. "Tell me, was your procedure a full cerebral transplant or a single lobe?" he asked.

"Both left and right," Blade said. "How far along were the Russians on this technology?"

"There had been more than one hundred attempts with little success to show. Just your being here and talking to me is a remarkable achievement."

"Tell me, Uri, when did you first meet Vladimir Folozchev?"

"I have never had the misfortune of making his acquaintance."

"That's odd. I heard Folozchev on one of the debrief tapes telling how you two had met multiple times. What was that drink you two shared again? Oh yes, Starka."

"Mr. Blade, working for Soviet counterintelligence, afforded me many luxuries, but it also took its toll. I have lived with a bleeding ulcer for most of my adult life. This beverage you speak of is popular, but I could not partake without committing myself to terrible pain and a night in the hospital. I cannot drink alcohol."

Blade already knew he could check the validity of Greggenkoff's story, but it wasn't necessary. The man was telling the truth. Winchell had bought Folozchev's story of Greggenkoff's incessant drinking and passed it along as a fact without the least bit of research. He wondered now how many more of his golden nuggets of counterintelligence would be so easy to disprove.

"Uri, we will speak in much greater detail soon. For now, do as Mr. Logan instructs you, and we will keep you safe."

The Russian nodded and settled back into his seat.

They approached a strip of shops, and Blade tapped Logan on the shoulder. "Let me out here."

Logan nodded and pulled to the curb. Blade hopped out and said, "Check our friend into a hotel for a few days. Wait an hour, then call Fossie." He keyed in a message and texted it to Logan. "Tell him to pass this along to Winchell. I'll be in touch." He slapped the roof of the car, and Logan sped off.

Blade headed over to a sporting goods store, where he had seen an outdoor rack of baseball bats. He selected one, gave it a few tentative swings, left $20 on a nearby countertop, and walked back to the curb. Less than a minute later, he heard an approaching high-performance motorcycle. He watched for another moment to verify the identity of the rider; Mako. That thin frame and long, black hair were dead giveaways.

Blade kept his back to the biker, the bat tucked close to his side. Just as Mako passed him, Blade turned, took aim, and swung the bat with everything he had. He caught Mako square across the chest, stopping him dead as the bike shot out from under. Mako went down flat on the pavement and lay there, unmoving. The bike traveled another fifty feet before falling over and sliding in a shower of sparks. Blade ran to it and found the phone that Mako used to follow the GPS signal of the car. He cracked it over his knee and tossed the pieces into a nearby sewer.

Looking back at Mako, he was stunned to see him struggling to his feet. This was no time for a rematch with such a formidable opponent. Blade righted the bike and straddled it, squeezed the clutch, pushed the electric start, and dropped the transmission into first gear. The entire process astonished him. Blade never rode a motorcycle in his life and was again astonished by the new skill sets that had laid dormant in that new part of his head. He popped the clutch and shot off just as Mako reached for the bike and latched on to the back. Mako was dragged a short distance before losing his grip and rolling to the curb. Blade looked back as Mako picked up the bat, waiting to take down the next motorcycle that rode past.

With Mako out of the picture, at least for the moment, Blade familiarized himself with the motorcycle. Glancing at the gas tank and gauges, he felt something click in his brain. He knew this machine, or at least one very similar. A grin spread across his face as he thought how enraged Mako must be after losing a $17,000 Ducati 950.

Blade rode a few more miles, searching for a place to ditch the machine and blend in with foot traffic, when he caught a flash of something coming up fast from behind. His speedometer was holding steady at 85, yet an iridescent green machine approached as though he were standing still. It was Mako, he knew it, and he was ten seconds away from their second encounter of the day. This time, he had lost the element of surprise, and Mako would be looking for payback.

Blade eyed his surroundings and settled on a plan of action. He watched in the mirror as Mako zoomed closer, right hand on the throttle, the Louisville Slugger cocked and ready in his left. That meant he would be attacking from the right. Blade sped up and counted down from the expected point of impact. Just ahead, traffic had stopped for a light. He could use that to his advantage. Mako came in on the right side, just as Blade had predicted, going at least 50 mph faster. Mako twisted his torso, preparing to deliver the death blow, then released. Blade's timing was perfect, and he locked up the brakes and dropped flat on the gas tank. The bat whistled through the air just above his head as Mako realized his mistake. He had no room to stop for the traffic ahead and dropped the bat, grabbed the handlebars with both hands and nosed the bike along the white stripe between the stopped cars. He shot through the signal light, just ahead of a semi that locked up its brakes. The back end of the trailer careened left into oncoming traffic, shearing off the roofs of two hapless sedans that shot beneath.

Blade lost track of Mako, and there was nothing he could do for any of the victims here. He crossed the median, did a U-turn, and headed back the way he had come. From behind came the unmistakable high-pitched whine of Mako's green rice rocket racing toward him. There was no time to wonder how he had survived, just how to avoid another confrontation.

Blade shifted down two gears and opened the throttle. The 114-horsepower engine screamed out, spinning the rear tire in a billowing trail of smoke as the front tire raised in the air. It took off like a missile, demanding every bit of strength to hang on. In seconds he was up to 100 mph and concentrated on thinking ten car lengths ahead of the bike. Mako somehow still caught up, his front wheel coming within inches from Blade's back tire, matching him move for move as they weaved their way through morning traffic. A wall of red brake lights appeared just ahead, and Blade maneuvered the bike onto the white stripe and shot between the slower cars. A busy intersection of four lanes of two-way traffic lay just ahead. He watched the flow of vehicles, timing his approach. His mind raced hundreds of feet ahead of the motorcycle, calculating the odds of squeezing through a gap in both directions. He picked his spot and aimed for it. The narrow hole in the flow of traffic was just wide enough. He made it through the northbound side. But as he got closer, the cars traveling southbound had changed speed. His window of opportunity vanished. He locked up the brakes as the bike slid around until the front end pointed to the right, then he opened the throttle. The bike fishtailed as it caught traction on the shoulder and gained speed. Out of the corner of his eye, he spied the ominous green ninja bike. Somehow, Mako made it through both directions of traffic and ended up on the opposing southbound shoulder, riding north against the flow. He'd caught up and now raced along, separated by four lanes of snarled traffic, but matching Blade move for move, speed for speed.

Another intersection loomed ahead with an entrance ramp to the freeway just beyond. This time it was just two-way traffic that Blade had to cross, and he shot through. A quick glance at both mirrors told him Mako was not yet behind. He made the most of it and put some distance between them. He flew down the entrance ramp, merging into moderate freeway traffic, then dropped on the gas tank, twisting the throttle wide-open until he was flying along at 120 mph. Blade needed time to figure out his next move, but every ounce of his brain was busy making the calculations and corrections necessary to avoid car after car, truck after truck. Minutes later, he decided enough was enough and slowed, then blended into traffic, taking a spot ahead of an eighteen-wheeler. With his speed down below 70 mph, he could assess the situation. As much as his new skills amazed him, they were no match for Mako. Few people could handle themselves so cool under pressure. Mako was the type of agent he would much prefer to stand beside rather than cross swords against in a standoff. He didn't expect that would change soon.

This chase had to end, preferably without leaving a long, red strip of his own flesh on the freeway. He had to get back to the surface streets, where he stood a better chance of losing Mako on foot. A green flash in the corner of his eye told him that his plan would have to wait. Mako's Ninja bike shot past him on the left shoulder. Blade estimated his speed to be on the top side of 150. A panel van obstructed Mako's view to Blade's left and the semi-truck behind, and he had failed to slow as he shot past. Blade doubted he was seen but could not take the chance. He pulled right toward the shoulder and braked until he was even with the cab of the semi-truck. Angling the bike over, he got his left foot on a step below the fuel tank and grasped a handrail, pulling himself up. The bike drifted toward the wall to the right, where it scraped along and then tumbled over. Blade heaved himself up the rest of the way, pulled open the passenger door of the cab, and slid in. The driver, a large blonde woman in a sleeveless denim shirt and a Peterbilt hat, stared dumbfounded. Blade offered a disarming smile, straightened his tie, and said, "Sorry to intrude, but would you mind terribly giving me a lift?"

Blade and the lady trucker made their introductions as they rolled along the congested freeway. Dottie was her name, and once past the initial shock of someone climbing into her rig, she warmed up to Blade and made small talk for the next half hour. He conjured a story of being pursued by a gang of motorcycle thieves, which she found thrilling. As they talked, he looked up at an overpass. Mako stood at the rail, scrutinizing the traffic below, searching for him. Blade believed he hadn't been seen but knew there was no time to waste. He pulled out his phone and texted Logan. 'Lose the service car. You're being tracked. Will call back soon.'

He then made a call to Audrey. "Everything all right with you?" he asked.

"Yes, and our houseguest has made my laptop run twice as fast. He also showed me some of these internet scams to be aware of."

He has a wealth of firsthand knowledge on that subject, he thought. "Glad to hear the two of you are hitting it off. May I speak with him a moment, please?"

Audrey passed the phone to Gavriik. "Hello?" he said.

"Happy to hear you're settling in. I needn't remind you to cover your tracks, correct?"

"I use redundant virtual private networks, multiple identities, and I bounce my signal halfway around the world. No one gets my IP address."

"My apologies for inquiring. And just so that we're on the same page, you are supposed to be keeping a low profile. This is the only way I can guarantee your safety. Do not access any of your usual sites or contact any old friends or classmates. Do we understand each other?"

"Yes, I understand. How long are we going to play this game?"

"Until I can turn the tables on those who would come for you. That may take a bit of time, but I believe the rewards far outnumber the risks. Stay low and allow me to do my job. Please hand the phone back to Audrey."

"Arthur, are you all right?" she asked.

"We've kicked the hornet's nest, dear girl. The next few hours will be very telling. Stay indoors. I don't wish for any of this to arrive at your doorstep. And Audrey."

"Yes, Arthur?"

"I love you very much." He ended the call.

Blade called Logan and asked, "How are you and Greggenkoff getting on?"

"He's apprehensive, to say the least. Other than that, he's cooperating. I think he will have a lot more to share with us now that he knows we have his back."

"Speaking of which, I've kept the number of people in our little clique to a minimum. However, I'm concerned that we are spreading ourselves too thin. Let me ask you, do you have absolute confidence in Piper?"

"He has never given me a reason to doubt him."

"I thought as much. Please contact him and bring him up to speed. The two of you should be able to coordinate the security for Greggenkoff. I believe Colson will be expecting a response from you soon. After all, we kidnapped his defector."

"I've ignored several calls from Langley already."

"They may attempt to triangulate your position based on your phone. This would be a good time to go dark and shut it down. I would ask that you turn it on for three minutes before each hour in case we need to talk. And Garret, I'll need you to ask Jill to assist in the next few steps."

"Whatever you need, Arthur."

"Please ask your lovely wife to pass on a message to the first lady. It is time to bring the president into the fold. We cannot accomplish our objective without his help."

"I'll do that right now. What is the message?"

"Tell him, C3 to H8. Treat as hostile."

Garret repeated the message back, then said, "That's cryptic, don't you think?"

"Yes, it is," Blade agreed, "but Walter will understand. I'm about to crash the party at Camp David. Please ask Jill to make the phone call and deliver the message, then call me back to confirm they received it."

Blade ended the call, pocketed the phone, and then turned to the truck driver. "Dottie, do you suppose I could persuade you into dropping me off somewhere rather off the beaten track?"

Twenty-Three
Lunch and Manacles

Catoctin Mountain Park was more than a little off the beaten track. But Dottie was running ahead of schedule, and Blade promised to compensate for any additional fuel costs. He had driven to Camp David on more than one occasion, so he directed Dottie along the route he was familiar with. Just before entering the park, the phone vibrated in his jacket pocket. "Yes," he said.

"Message delivered and receipt acknowledged by POTUS," Logan informed him.

"Your timing could not have been more perfect. We should be able to sort all of this out soon. Stick with the plan we talked about earlier. I will be in touch."

"Good luck, Arthur."

Blade pointed to a side street. "You can let me off there. The park road ends up ahead, and just beyond, you'll find adequate room to turn your rig around."

Dottie nodded, slowed down, and pulled over.

He wrote a number on a piece of paper he found on the console and handed it to her. "I can't thank you enough," he said, shaking her hand. "You saved my life today. I won't forget."

Dottie said something, but Blade was already climbing down from the truck cab. He stood back and waved as she pulled forward and made the turnaround.

Blade began walking toward a nondescript log cabin. When he was near enough to see the tall electrified fences beyond the structure, he stopped, dropped to his knees, and put his hands on his head.

A voice crackled over a loudspeaker. "You have entered a restricted federal area. Get on your knees and put your...."

Another voice informed him, "He already is."

The first voice returned. "Stay where you are."

Within seconds, soldiers in camouflage uniforms surrounded him. Blade knew this drill and remained still.

"You are trespassing on federal government property," one soldier called out. "Why are you here?"

Blade eyed the soldier observing his name and rank. "First Sergeant O'Conner, I have a message for POTUS."

"Are you armed?" The sergeant demanded.

"No," Blade replied, "but you're going to search me, anyway. Do your duty."

Two other soldiers stepped forward and lifted Blade to his feet as a third did a thorough body search. He stepped back and shook his head.

"What is your name? Where is your identification?" The sergeant asked.

"Only my message is important."

"You really gonna play it that way?" The sergeant said, rolling his eyes. "Corporal, get the MPs over here and lock this joker up."

"The message, First Sergeant," Blade said, staring at the soldier. "Take my message to the president. Now!"

"You and me," the sergeant said, leveling his glare with

Blade, "we're gonna have words when this is over. What is the message?"

Blade brushed the dust off his jacket and said, "C3 to H8."

"That's it?" The sergeant asked, unimpressed. "Crackpot." He turned to the soldiers on either side of Blade. "Hold him right here." He turned and walked into the building.

Blade watched through a window as the sergeant picked up a desk phone and called in the message. The sergeant nodded, then hung up the phone and waited. A moment later, he answered the return call and listened. The man turned and eyed Blade. He spoke into the receiver, then hung up. Blade lost sight of him until he reappeared, accompanied by two military police carrying manacles and handcuffs. "Put that man in irons," he said, pointing.

Blade was pleased that the president had paid attention to the second part of the message delivered by Logan's wife, treat as hostile. It guaranteed that all other personnel would see him as nothing more than a temporary security nuisance. The downside was it would no doubt lead to some rough treatment.

President Walter Lux paced outside the detention cell. The medical team had taken blood samples and fingerprints of the prisoner and was still awaiting results. In the meantime, a pair of secret service agents had been questioning him to no avail. Lux could sense their frustration with the tight-lipped detainee. The agents both rose and filed out of the room. "What have you learned?" the president asked, "who is he?"

"We know nothing more than when we started. Honestly, sir, I would just turn him over to the FBI."

The president looked to his Secret Service Chief of Security. "I can't do that, Dennis," he said, "not yet, anyway. I received a strange message a few hours ago. Only one other person in this world would even understand what it meant. I'm just confused about a part of it. 'Treat as hostile.'"

"You think this guy sent the message?"

The president nodded. "Likely, yes."

"Then why would he send something that would ensure we would lock him away and treat him as a threat? Mr. President, may I ask, what was the rest of the message?"

Lux looked to the other secret service agent and said, "Marty, will you give us a minute, please?"

Marty nodded and left the room.

"Denis, this goes no further than right here. And I'm bringing you in on this because, because you've been chief of my security detail since I took office, and I don't know the answer to this one. The message was, C3 to H8."

Agent Denis Keller pondered this for a moment. "That sounds like a chess move."

"It is, or was, and Arthur Blade made it in a game played between the two of us. No one else would know that move." Lux snickered and added, "I had him dead to rights, and the son of a bitch countered with a queen sacrifice that—you don't suppose? Could that be Arthur Blade in there?"

Agent Keller gave the President a wary glance. "Sir, Arthur Blade died of cancer months ago. I accompanied you and your family to the funeral."

Lux shook his head. "Denis, Blade underwent a procedure that saved his life. It also altered his appearance. Transformed might be a better word. A few months later, Blade disappeared during an operation overseas. He is presumed dead."

Keller stared, dumbfounded.

"If that's Blade, then I don't know where he's been all this time or how he even made his way back here."

"He's attempting to maintain his cover," Keller said.

"What? Why? Why would he do that?"

"I don't know. Just like I don't know that it's him. You gave me what sounds like an impossible scenario. I'm telling you what I think based on his actions. Let's assume for a minute that this is him. He didn't march in here announcing the return of Arthur Blade. I'm willing to bet he had a damn good reason for that. Maybe that's where we start."

"You think I should go in there?"

"Ordinarily, sir, I would not even allow you to expose yourself to such a potential threat. But given what you just explained and how he approached, I would say it's worth the risk."

Lux pondered this for a moment, then looked toward the door. "You and I enter. We keep our distance until we see a reason to lower our guard."

Keller nodded and said, "Follow me in, then go to the far corner." He pulled his pistol, pulled back the slide, chambering a round, then pulled the door open. Lux followed him in and walked to the corner.

Keller stood a few feet from the table where Blade sat handcuffed.

Blade looked up and acknowledged the agent. "Sorry that I didn't greet you earlier, Denis, but I've never met the other agent accompanying you. How's Diane?"

Lux stepped from the corner, staring. "Arthur? Is that really you?"

Blade looked up with a pained expression. "How good it is to see you, my old friend. I apologize for all the cloak and dagger, but then again, that is the nature of our business, is it not?"

Keller cautioned the president not to step closer. "Why come forward now?" he asked. "And why like this?"

"I'm afraid we have a subversive element within our ranks at Langley. The operation in England was compromised. Our enemy attacked and left me for dead. Our true enemies came from within. Before revealing that I had survived, I needed to know whom I could trust. Only now can I share my suspicions with any certainty. As to why I maintained my anonymity? Well, it's easier to move about as a nobody. Arthur Blade should remain MIA, at least for the foreseeable future. When we conclude our meeting, you should have me remanded to the custody of the CIA. I would recommend agents Garret Logan and James Piper. Oh, and please dispose of the fingerprints and blood samples you took earlier."

Lux smiled as he walked to the table and shook Blade's cuffed hand. Keller did not stop him.

"Are you hungry?" the President asked, pulling up a chair opposite him.

"Famished, old boy. You wouldn't believe the day I've had."

Blade explained his observations and suspicions over a late lunch that the President had brought in. He insisted on remaining in chains while he ate for appearance's sake.

"It goes at least as high as Winchell," he said. "Of that much, I'm certain. I have my doubts, however, about the status of Colson. I believe we must proceed under the assumption that he may be working against us."

The disappointment on the President's face was palpable. "I've known Don Colson for a good many years, and I'm pleased with the substantial progress he made within the agency."

"Walter, he may be blameless. To be safe, we should treat him as an unknown until we can prove otherwise."

"I don't disagree," Lux said. "How was your lunch, by the way?"

Blade dabbed the corners of his mouth with a crisp white linen napkin. "This was the best prison meal I've ever eaten."

The President slapped him on the arm. "Let's hope it remains the only prison meal you ever have. Tell me, you must have come here with a plan."

Blade nodded. "I would like to set a trap and allow our enemies to incriminate themselves. Time is working against us, and we need to handpick our allies. We would be much better served with Colson working beside us, but I have seen nothing to make me believe in his trustworthiness. I suggest we do things the old-fashioned way. Get him out here and do a polygraph. If he passes, then we can proceed with his help. If not, then we've found our mole, haven't we?"

"Arthur, that's such dated technology. Why do you still put so much faith in the results? Isn't there something better by now?"

Blade shook his head. "There are certain personality types that can, in fact, defeat the polygraph. But beyond these, few can tell lies without revealing themselves. I believe Don Colson is a perfect candidate for the test. If he passes, I would put my faith in him."

"All right," President Lux agreed. "Let's get this set up. Tell me what you need."

"Let's start with one of his lieutenants, Tony Gilbertson. He can call on a couple of his agents to assist. I would also recommend an FBI presence."

"Done," the president said, heading for the door. "Will you be joining us in my office?"

Blade shook his head. "I wish to remain an unknown. If I might, I would like my phone back, as well as a double espresso. I suspect we'll be putting in a long evening."

"Leave him a key for the cuffs," the president instructed his secret service chief. "I'm sure he'll want to use the restroom at some point." He gave Blade a wisecracking grin and said, "Do lock yourself back up when you're done... old boy."

It was late, and Don Colson sat in his easy chair next to his wife, enjoying a bowl of popcorn and some mindless television. When the doorbell rang, he flinched, knocking the bowl over.

"Now, who could that be at this hour?" he huffed, getting up to answer the door. Through the front windows, he could see the glare of multiple sets of headlights in his driveway. He stopped at the door and asked, "Who is it?"

"Tony Gilbertson, sir, along with Special Agents Randolph and Winslow. The president has requested you to join him at Camp David."

Midnight had come and gone by the time Don Colson finished his polygraph exam. He exited the room, rolling his sleeves down, glowering at the group of men who waited for him.

"I expect a damn good explanation for what I just went through back there."

The president stepped forward and offered his hand. "Sorry, Don, but that was necessary. It appears we have at least one traitor in our midst."

Colson eyed all the faces gathered about him. "Where's Winchell?" When no one answered, he stared at the president. "I asked a question, where is Winchell?"

"I have not informed him of our little gathering."

"And why is that?"

"Because he is the primary focus of our investigation. We believe John is trading secrets with the Russians."

Colson scowled. "That's ridiculous! John Winchell is no more a spy than...."

"Careful," Lux cautioned. "Suspicions exist concerning your loyalty."

"By who? With all due respect, sir, but goddamn it! I demand to know the identity of anyone who questions my patriotism. Let them come here now and make their accusations to my face."

"So be it," President Lux said, "but we'll have to go to him."

President Lux, accompanied by Keller, his Secret Service Chief of Security, and CIA Director Don Colson, made their way to the holding cell.

"Grab a couple of chairs," Lux instructed. "I suspect we'll be here for a while."

The trio entered the room and set their seats down before a man sitting chained to a table. Colson eyed the President as they sat. Lux gave him a reassuring nod. The solidly built man, long-haired, with a week's growth of beard, wearing a dark suit and tie, looked back disarmingly. He sat erect with his hands on the table, fingers laced, handcuffs on his wrists. A portrait of contradictions.

"Thanks for coming, Don," the man said. "I hope Madeline will forgive the late-night intrusion."

Colson stared, open-mouthed. "Identify yourself," he demanded.

"Arthur Blade, reporting back for duty."

Colson's jaw snapped shut. "That's not possible," he murmured as he looked from Keller to the president. Both smiled back as though there was nothing unusual about this meeting. "I suddenly find myself the least knowledgeable person in the room. Please," he said, looking to Blade, "enlighten me."

Blade spent the next half hour filling in the blanks, explaining everything that had happened since he left to handle the English operation. Colson listened, asking specific questions along the way. When Blade finished, Colson broke into a smile and extended his hand. "This is extraordinary, not to mention the best news I've had in weeks. Welcome back, Arthur! How many people know you're still among the living?"

"My personal crew and just a few others. Maintaining my anonymity has kept me alive for this long. At least for now, I prefer to remain in the shadows."

Colson nodded. "I agree. I'm sure it will prove even more useful in the future. So I'm assuming you have now satisfied yourself with my loyalty?"

"Yes, and thank you for indulging us tonight. I'm sure you would have expected nothing less had the tables been turned."

"Agreed. So where do we go from here?"

"We start with what we know and suspect thus far. This latest mishandling of our two Russian defectors has been very telling."

"Winchell told me he had established that Folozchev was the more credible of the two. Based on his finding, I agreed to send Greggenkoff packing."

Blade gave Colson a quizzical stare. "Was he forthcoming with his evidence? Was his argument sound?"

Colson thought for a moment, then shook his head. "No, he didn't offer specifics, now that you mention it. Folozchev was Winchell's defector, and I trusted him to be the point man. I allowed him to operate with near impunity." He breathed a heavy sigh. "It would have been wiser to have included myself in the decision to dump Greggenkoff." He looked at Blade and added, "I can see why you would have questions regarding this. I'm assuming you have evidence to prove he was wrong."

"Indeed. None of the information supplied Folozchev had any value. He would have been smart to mix some credible intel into his misinformation, creating the appearance of cooperation. The CIA has successfully used this tactic for years. The man must think himself such a prize that we would overlook this critical flaw. Greggenkoff, on the other hand, has given us the intel that helped stop two nuclear warheads from arriving in Washington, DC. He has proven himself to be a valuable asset and the genuine defector. His loss must be so greatly feared by Russian Intelligence as to send someone as high-ranking as Folozchev to bring him down. But I still don't believe that is the entire reason for him being here."

Blade slipped out of his handcuffs and pushed his chair back, his eyes staring forward at nothing. "They could have sent just about anyone to act as a misinformant or even an assassin if need be. So why send Vladimir Folezchev? His past deeds should have precluded him from being considered for such a task. No one surrenders their most valuable people when expendable assets can handle the job. There must be some greater prize to be won. What we are seeing here is the enemy sending a battleship to sink a fishing boat." Blade looked to the President. "Why is he here, Walter? Who, or what, is his primary target?"

President Lux shook his head. "You know how his mind works better than anyone in this room, Arthur. What are you thinking?"

Blade stood, kicking his shackles into the corner.

Keller was on his feet. "You're kidding me! You could have slipped out of those any time you wanted?"

Blade gave a sly smile. "Tricks of the trade." He paced the room, scratching his chin. "What is Folozchev best at?"

"Well, we know he was the principal interrogator of most of our captured assets, correct?" the President asked.

"Yes, he has a deadly proficiency in extracting information, to the point of sadism. We also know that he directed the activities of Russian spies planted here."

"So he knows every deep cover and sleeper cell operative in this country," Colson added.

"Correct," Blade said, pointing back at him. "Now, consider the man's age. He is an old war horse, likely seeking a soft landing sometime soon."

"Maybe this is his soft landing." Lux offered.

"Very astute, Walter," Blade said. "But think about that. Folozchev is at the top of the Russian food chain, enjoying the prestige and status earned from a lifetime of service to his country. He already has access to every amenity he could desire. Does this sound like a man who would ever betray his comrades? A man desperate to leave all that behind for political asylum in the country he spent a lifetime working to destroy?" Blade shook his head. "No, I believe our dear Mr. Folozchev would be the last person in the world to give that all up. So I ask again, why is he here?"

Silence.

Then Colson shouted, "Because he is directing his agents from within!"

"I believe that to be part of their plan," Blade said. "But is it enough to send one of their greatest spymasters out to pasture? Folozchev will probably never return from this mission.

A heavy silence that hung over the room greeted his words, lingering for minutes.

The President spoke up. "Maybe we didn't just get this a

little wrong. Maybe we've underestimated the value of both men."

Blade shot him a glance. "Please continue."

"We know what Folozchev is worth to his country. We've already established that. But what about Greggenkoff? What if he knows even more than we've assumed? What if the Russians are so fearful of the secrets in his head that they would send their highest honored knight to eliminate the threat?"

Blade's brows raised, astonished. He looked away, his eyes working back and forth as though reading his own thoughts. He turned back to the president with an approving smile. "Well done, sir," he said. "Only Folozchev could oversee the assassination of Greggenkoff AND direct the actions of the embedded spy network. That's enough for us to move forward. But let us not be so full of ourselves as to think we have uncovered every reason behind their actions. This is our most formidable opponent, and they have always held back a few cards to play later. Eyes open, gentlemen. There are curves in this road ahead."

President Lux sank back into his chair. "Oh my god, we've helped to imbed the perfect double agent to spy against us!"

Blade stood staring, nodding. "I would further speculate that he is already doing just that."

"How?" Colson challenged. "He has no access to outside communications."

"I disagree," Blade said as he began pacing again. "In fact, I would bet that he began manipulating the manipulators long ago." He turned to Colson. "I remember calling the safe house and speaking to Folozchev a few times. The question is, would the old Russian be crafty enough to exploit that moment?" Blade nodded at his logic. "Of course he is. The simplest way of establishing contact with his people would be to use our own tools against us. All he needed was a phone. And although he is a master at covering his trail, there may be one to follow. We just have to know what we're searching for. Let's start with the phone records for John Winchell. Going back to the day that he began handling Folozchev. Pull the duty roster to see who was guarding the safe house and pull those phone records as well. If my theory is correct, Winchell contacted one of those guards regularly while on duty. Winchell would call in and ask to speak to Folozchev. If I were that sly old Russian, I would take that opportunity to make a second call. All that's needed is to keep talking as though still on the line with Winchell. The agent whose phone was being used would be none the wiser."

Colson blew out a pained sigh. "Right under our noses." He eyed Blade and said, "I'll get the phone records and the duty rosters."

Blade held out his hand. "Don, please accept my humble apologies for what I put you through last evening."

Colson shook it, shaking his head. "No need for that. You did your job, as I would have done mine had this situation been reversed." He stepped out of the interrogation room and began making calls.

President Lux asked, "So what now?"

"We lay a trap for our Mr. Winchell. There are multiple pieces in play on this chess board, but the most important is Vladimir Folozchev. Foremost, we must verify whether my suspicions are correct and whether he is indeed running a Russian spy network from within our safe house. If so, we must identify his agents and shut them down. We can now manipulate the actions of Mr. Winchell, as well as Mr. Fossie, to accomplish this task. The success of uncovering this deception lies in using them to convince Folezchev that his house of cards is tumbling. We must push him enough that he will take the risk of contacting his agents."

"That's a tall order, Arthur," Lux said. "Much of your plan rides on a theory."

"True enough," Blade admitted, "but it is a theory based on sound principle." He smiled, tapping his head. "To defeat your enemy, you must learn to think like him. I've learned a thing or two from Vladimir's playbook."

"It's not just a theory anymore," Colson said, stepping back into the interrogation room. "The full phone records are being sent over now, but we can already see that the connections we were looking for are there. Damn good call, Arthur, damn good!"

Blade offered an acknowledging nod. "I would have preferred to be wrong this time. We have now confirmed the existence of what may be the most damaging breach of national security in years. Vladimir Folozchev set up shop and masterminded a crafty operation in our house. We must give credit where credit is due. It was brilliant in its scope and execution. Had Mr. Winchell not come to our attention over these other issues, we may not have noticed this for years. Winchell's incompetence and over-confidence may well prove to be our saving grace. Tell me, Don, do we have the name of the guard whose phone was used for the calls?"

Colson scrolled through the information being sent to his phone. "Yes, Clarence Mackey has been on the roster since Folozchev first came to the safe house. His phone records show he received calls from Winchell nearly every day. I don't know how you figure these things out before anyone else, but you nailed it. The records show a second call being made after every call from Winchell. Each of the numbers called was utilized for a few weeks before changing to another. How would Folozchev know to switch?"

"He prearranged this prior to his arrival," Blade said. "He must have brought along a list of phone numbers and the dates of when to use each. If we are to move in on this Russian sleeper cell, we'll need to prompt Mr. Folozchev into making contact. This time, we will monitor the cell system and triangulate the receiving phone."

"I assume you have a plan in mind to accomplish that?" the president asked.

"Indeed I do, Walter. A very simple one." He looked to Colson. "Don, we need immediate taps on the phones of John Winchell and Clarence Mackey. And is there a way of monitoring the hidden safe house cameras from here?"

"That's over my head," Colson said, "but I'll get our specialists on it. They should be able to stream the signal to one of our phones." He looked at the president. "Sir, you will need to grant executive authority for these wiretaps without waiting for a judge to issue the usual warrants."

President Lux nodded. "Done. In the interest of national security, you have my authority."

"One more thing, Don," Blade interrupted. "I would also like taps on the phones of agents Fossie and Mako."

Colson gave him a thumbs up, then dialed a number at Langley to allow his network team to tap and monitor the phone lines. He listened for a moment, checked his watch, then ended the call. "The taps will be in place soon. I'll get a confirmation call when everything is ready."

Blade tented his fingers, his mind assembling a sequential list of everything that had to be done and ready before they could achieve their objective. When he was satisfied that everything had been considered with nothing left to chance, he said, "We are just a few moments from putting our plan into motion. For now, the most difficult task will be to sit and wait for the phone to ring."

Twenty-Four
ENTRAPPING THE TRAITOR

Fossie asked for a second cup of coffee as he glanced about the crowded and hastily set up command post. Every set of eyes stared at him. He counted three FBI agents, four CIA, and two state police troopers. He thought again of his last confrontation with Arthur Blade. Despite his fight-or-flight instincts screaming at him to run like hell, he knew he was doing the right thing. After doing the dirty work of John Winchell for years, that was a major change. He wondered if he could ever be a good agent again. The path to absolution was a bit more jagged than he expected, but he was ready to walk the walk.

They had come for him in the pre-dawn hours that morning, demanding his phone, weapon, and credentials. It sure felt like being arrested, although no one had cuffed him as they directed him into the backseat of the State Police cruiser. That was the point of this show of power. 'You're this close to going down. Cooperate or fall the rest of the way.'

He was thankful that Blade had somehow survived his ordeal at sea. It meant he had no blood on his hands. Hopefully, that would make it easier to find forgiveness.

"You and I met yesterday," Logan said, handing him his coffee. "When you were transporting our defector to the airport. Tell me, why was it so important to get Greggenkoff out of the country?"

"Winchell didn't believe him," Fossie said, then took a tentative sip. "Could I get some sugar?"

"No. Why didn't Winchell believe him?"

"He spent very little time explaining himself. All I know is that he trusted Folozchev and thought Greggenkoff was a liar." Fossie closed his eyes, shaking his head. "Winchell and his gut feelings. God, what a crock of shit." A thought burst into his mind, and his brows raised, amused. "He kept saying the new Arthur Blade would look like the old one. He insisted on it." Fossie shook his head. "I wonder if he got that from Folozchev. You guys might want to check into that."

Logan nodded. "You can ask him yourself at the safe house."

Fossie's expression darkened. "Hey, wait, I thought I was going to do my part over the phone. Nobody said anything about going there."

"We all have a part to play. Today, you're the star of the show. Or we can just hand you back to the FBI over there and let them arrest you as a spy. I'm sure that would make their day."

Fossie waved him off. "Fine, I already agreed to do whatever you need me to do. Just cover my back, okay? I'm trying to do the right thing here."

"You have nothing to fear from any of those people over there or the ones at that safe house." He leaned in and whispered, "I'm the only one that wants you dead, and I promised to keep you alive. Just as long as you're cooperating."

"I said fine! I'm cooperating already, damn it."

Logan smiled. "Good, it's important that we understand each other. You tried to kill my boss. Your asshole partner threw me off a moving train. That hurt. A lot." He pointed to a stack of notes on the table and asked, "Did you memorize your script?"

"Yeah, I'm good to go."

Logan nodded and tapped a number on his phone. "Arthur, it's Logan. I have Fossie prepped, and all the equipment is ready and standing by." Logan nodded as he listened, then passed the phone to Fossie. "Someone wants to speak with you," he said.

Fossie eyed Logan as he put the phone to his ear. "Yes?" he said.

"Mr. Fossie, do you have a first name?" Blade asked.

"Bartholomew," he said, nodding "Ah, Bart, sir."

"Well, Bart, as I recall, you offered your services. Your words were, and correct me if I'm wrong, 'Anything you need, let me help.' I hate to see good talent squandered, as I believe Mr. Winchell did in your case. We will offer you the latitude to redeem yourself today. Stick to the script and work as one of my team, and we may offer you the opportunity to become part of it. I won't bother reminding you of the consequences of betraying me and this operation. I believe you understand what that would entail, correct?"

"Yes sir," he said, "I understand."

"Good, then let's get to it, shall we? Please put Mr. Logan back on."

Fossie handed the phone to Logan.

"Yes, Arthur?"

"We are awaiting implementation of the phone taps, which should—hold on—" Blade covered the mouthpiece and spoke with someone, then returned. "Garret, the taps are in place. Give it a minute or two after we disconnect, and then make the call."

"Got it," Logan said, ending the call and pocketing the phone. He looked at his watch, then handed Fossie back his own phone. "We are on in two minutes," he announced to the rest of the room.

There was a flurry of activity as people hurried over to tape recorders and donned headphones. One by one, everyone in the room gave a thumbs up. Logan pointed to Fossie, who keyed in Winchell's number. He picked it up on the first ring.

"Fossie, where the hell have you been? Where's Greggenkoff?"

"We had a glitch," Fossie read from the first page of his script. "Greggenkoff is dead."

"What? How?"

"There was a new guy with Logan. He pulls a gun on me and says he's taking Greggenkoff. I grabbed his pistol, and we fought. The Russian took a slug in the belly before I could disarm the guy. Logan's dead from a bullet to the brain. The new guy got away. I stuffed both bodies in the trunk and left the car in a seedy neighborhood with the engine running. It's likely stripped and torched by now."

"Why didn't you call in before now?"

"Are you kidding? I just killed Blade's right-hand man, not to mention Greggenkoff. And here's the other thing. That new guy? I'm pretty sure it was the same guy we dumped in the North Sea. John, That was Arthur Blade. Somehow he survived, and here he was, aiming a gun at me."

"Was he an old man?" he asked.

"No, younger than me."

"It's a wonder he survived. According to Colson, that was Blade. I still have my doubts."

"John, the last thing this guy said as he went over the side that night was, 'Checkmate.' That sure sounded like something Blade would have said. Honestly, you need to check your source. I'm sure they were wrong about the age thing. Arthur Blade is alive, and he's out there."

"No," Winchell insisted, "I'm not convinced, although

this man may still be the one who attacked Mako and knocked him off his motorcycle. You knew he was trailing you, right? Mako chased this guy, but he got away. Very few people have ever gone up against Mako and lived to tell about it."

"What do you want me to do?" Fossie asked.

"Sit tight wherever you are. I'll make some calls and get back to you."

The call ended, and Fossie looked at Logan. "So now what?"

"We have planted a seed. Now we let it grow."

John Winchell sat stunned, hands covering his face, eyes squeezed shut. How could such a simple task have gone so far south so fast? Every single step of his well-conceived plan had failed. It wasn't a bad thing that Greggenkoff was dead. But a federal agent had been killed. Fossie had once again proven himself incapable of following the simplest directions. He outlived his usefulness the moment he pulled that trigger. Now the agent's reckless actions would rain back down on Winchell unless he could ensure Fossie took the fall for everything. Better yet, his silent corpse would take the fall. The man could still be useful for something, after all.

And speaking of useless, Mako wasn't doing him any favors, either. What he did on the train was reckless and unscripted. True, sometimes his improvising had made him a valuable asset, but not this time. He had ignored all of his instructions and written his own rules. So much for keeping a low profile and doing away with Arthur Blade.

Eliminating both of his agents now seemed like the only option left on the table. A thought came to mind of how to make that happen that was both simple and clean; what if he could pit them against each other? If both perished, it would be all for the better. If one or the other survived, then blame could shift to the unlucky stiff. That could work. He scribbled some notes, then moved on to the next problem. What to do about this new guy who witnessed everything that happened to Logan and Greggenkoff? How much time would pass before he began talking? Even worse, what if Fossie was correct, and this was Arthur Blade? Winchell shook his head, still disbelieving anyone could have survived being dumped in the middle of the English Channel.

But he was getting ahead of himself. If he could take it one piece of the puzzle at a time, everything could still work out in the end. First, he needed to plan and rehearse the part he would play when calling Colson to report all of this. He imagined the conversation, surprising himself with the new lies that rolled so smoothly off his tongue.

"That was Arthur Blade on the train in England? Oh my goodness! The agents must not have known who he was and mistook him for an enemy combatant. Me? No, I would never authorize my men to eliminate anyone. They acted on their own. Tell me, did Arthur survive? Thank God! But it seems odd, doesn't it? If Fossie had attempted to eliminate Arthur Blade on the train, why didn't they recognize each other while transporting Greggenkoff? Odder still is that the ransom is still missing, and Arthur shows up alive and well."

Winchell listened to himself repeating the lines and conceded that even he didn't find this story credible. You could only feign ignorance for so long. He was in deep shit. Maybe it was time to seek another exit. He thought of Folozchev and their talk the night he had taken him to a private dinner. The Russian had not come right out and offered to help Winchell defect, but he'd implied it.

"Russia welcome you as hero," the old spy had told him as

he washed down a mouthful of rare prime steak with the most expensive bottle of vodka in the place.

Those words stuck with him, gnawing at the back of his brain. He was out of options and knew that shifting the blame was not a viable exit strategy. Besides, the CIA would lock him up on sight for suspicion of treason. There was no other way out. He burned all the bridges behind him. His thoughts switched from denial to scorched earth. If he couldn't lie his way out, he could leave a wake of chaos and destruction to cover his trail. At least it would at least buy him some time. He picked up his phone and dialed.

"Outgoing call from John Winchell," one of the FBI agents announced from his recording console at the command post. He started a recorder and put the call on speaker for everyone to hear.

"Hello, this is Mackey."

"Winchell here. How are things with Folozchev today?"

"Same as ever," Clarence Mackey replied. "He reads, he watches tv, he eats. He's about as exciting as a slow day of CSPAN."

"Good, put him on, will you?"

Mackey passed his phone to Folozchev. "Yes?" the old Russian replied.

"Vladimir, there are some problems."

"I am listening."

"I am going to need an exit strategy."

"Why for?"

"Well, for starters, all your information about Arthur Blade was inaccurate. His new suit is much newer than you led me to believe."

"I told you of Russian technology. Maybe this change. How for I know? I have no one to tells me."

"I made major assumptions and put plans into motion based on what you told me. And you were wrong. Dead wrong."

"So sue me. You know what they say about assume? Never do this. It make ass of you and me."

"Now listen to me! Greggenkoff is dead, and Blade is somewhere out there putting the pieces together. I think it's about time you and I had that talk about my defection. Can you set it up?"

"I don't know," he replied. "You have secrets to sell?"

"You know the answer to that. Hell, yes, I have secrets to sell. Now, I got rid of your problem with Greggenkoff. You need to help me with mine."

Folozchev went quiet a moment, then keeping his voice low, he said, "You need to drop off message."

"Now would not seem the greatest time to be doing another drop for you. I only helped those other times for you to contact your family."

"Yes, and now you carry message to say you go to Russia. I write introduction. You come get message."

As everyone in the command center listened, Folozchev ended the call. Within seconds, another outgoing call connected. A female voice with no discernible accent answered.

"Service desk."

Folozchev continued to carry on the conversation as though still on the line with Winchell. Clarence Mackey, his handler, sat with his face glued to the television, engrossed in a home remodeling program and paying no attention.

"Yes, Mr. Winchell," Folozchev said, "I can help you. What is term, 'tit for tat?'" He waited for Mackey's television program to gain in volume, then whispered, "Winchell comes to you with message in book. Same place. Follow instructions." He finished the exchange by raising his voice, saying, "Yes, I understand. I am waiting." Folozchev handed the phone back to Mackey. "Your boss coming," he said.

Mackey gave a sideways glance without taking his eyes off the TV.

～

Back at the command center, Logan was on his phone in an instant. "Arthur, did you hear that?"

"Every word," Blade said. Don Colson's phone was routed into the phone tap, and Arthur Blade, the president, and Colson had listened to the exchange from inside the holding cell at Camp David. "Our Mr. Winchell has just shown his true colors by requesting asylum on the red side. Was the FBI able to triangulate the phone that Folozchev called?"

Logan asked for a progress report from the agent working on the triangulation data. The man looked over, shaking his head. "No, Arthur, the call was too short."

"Then we have no other choice than to let Mr. Winchell's plan play out and catch him in the act. I'll call you back."

Blade looked to Don Colson. "Let's build on what we know. Winchell is on his way to the safe house to retrieve and deliver a message for Folozchev. He's putting that message in a book that will also act as a letter of introduction for the people who will smuggle Winchell out of the country. We need to know the contents of that message. We also need agents on the ground watching Winchell when he meets with Folozchev's Russian network. Don, I need a GPS tracker installed in Winchell's car when he arrives at the safe house. Let's also have three mobile teams standing by to track his movements."

"Done," Colson said, tapping numbers into his phone.

Blade checked his phone display. The video feed from the security cameras in the safe house was missing crucial information. "I don't see the signal from the bedroom camera," he called out. "Folozchev just went in there." He dialed Logan back at the command center. "Garret, we need eyes inside the bedroom to see this message he is getting ready to send."

"Give me a minute," Logan said, then conferred with a CIA agent at another table who was watching all the camera feeds from within the safe house. "You're right," Logan confirmed. "The output signal from that bedroom camera is dead." The agent checked a list of all the installed cameras in the house. "There are two in that room. We know Folozchev found one of them and turned it, so the viewing angle is useless. Let me try to send a refresh code to the other. Give me a few minutes."

"We don't have a few minutes," Blade said. "We need that message now!"

"Sorry, but watching Folozchev sleep wasn't a top priority until now. It should be another minute."

Tense moments ticked away as everyone at both locations awaited the missing video signal.

"Got it," the agent announced. "I'm linking you to the signal feed now."

A new image appeared from a camera positioned over Folozchev's shoulder as he sat at a desk, writing on a yellow legal pad. His index finger scrolled down a page of a book.

Blade studied the writing on the pad as Folozchev worked. "It's encoded," he said. "Does anyone at the command center have the means of decrypting this?"

Some of the CIA and FBI agents took a stab at the message and shook their heads. "No," Logan answered. "This doesn't appear to be based on any simple decrypt key that we use."

"It should not be that difficult," Blade pointed out.

"Folozchev didn't have any encryption tools with him when he came over. Gentlemen, stay on this." He thought a moment, then replayed the message, capturing a screenshot. "I have one other source that may help," he said, then dialed Audrey Landers.

"Arthur, good to hear from you," she answered.

"And very good to hear your voice, Audrey. But right now, I have an urgent need to speak to our young houseguest."

Audrey passed the phone to Gavriik Federov.

"Hello again, Mr. Blade. I hope we can...."

"Gavriik, I just sent an image of an encoded message," Blade interrupted. "Are you familiar with this format?"

Federov studied the image. "Give me a few minutes to run it through a few programs. I'll call you back." He disconnected and turned to Audrey. "Okay if I borrow your laptop?" She nodded as he flipped it open and began typing. "I have a hunch," he said. "It could be as simple as, as, damn! Could you call Mr. Blade back, please?"

Audrey hit redial and handed him the phone.

"Mr. Blade, the first characters of the first line are missing. Did you get those?"

"Not yet," Blade said.

"Did he write this while reading a book?"

"He had a book next to him as he composed it. Why?"

As soon as Blade said the words, he understood the answer. "The book is the key!"

"Likely, yes," Federov agreed. "I've seen this type of encryption many times before. It is simple but effective. The problem is the missing first line would have listed the page and paragraph number being used to encrypt the message. We also need the title of the book he used."

"Excellent work, Mr. Federov," Blade said. "I believe we can figure the rest out from here. Thank you."

Blade ended the call and dialed Logan. "The book being

used to transport the message is the decryption device. We need to see that missing top line and the book title."

Logan relayed the information to the CIA agent monitoring the video surveillance. The agent began zooming in on other angles of other cameras throughout the safe house to see either the encrypted page or the spine of the book itself. One of the camera angles offered some hope. He magnified the image, squinting. "I have part of the first line," he called out. "Page 221."

"Arthur, did you hear that?" Logan asked.

"Yes, page 221. Now all we need is the name of that book and the paragraph number, and we need them now."

Colson was listening to the exchange and said, "Arthur, I have a thought."

"You have my undivided attention, sir."

"Can we ask our agent inside the house to look and let us know without appearing too inquisitive?"

Blade nodded. "I would expect so. I also suggest you make the call to Mr. Mackey so this sounds like a routine check-in. I'm going to call Logan and let him know what we're doing." He dialed and instructed Logan to put the call on speaker, linking both the Camp David interrogation room and the command center.

Colson fished his phone from a jacket pocket and made the call. "Agent Mackey, this is Director Colson. I have an interest in the book that Folozchev is reading. Find out the title without letting on and call me back."

Agent Mackey got up, went to the bathroom, and returned with two bottles of water, offering one to Folozchev, who had now come from the bedroom and sat at the table with both arms over the book. The Russian reached out to take the bottle, uncovering just enough of the title for Mackey to see.

"You hungry?" Mackey asked, heading to the kitchen.

Folozchev rolled his eyes as he unscrewed the water bottle. "You have metabolism like hummingbird. Always moving, always hungry." He shook his head and covered up the book again.

Mackey opened the refrigerator and held his phone inside as he texted the name of the book to Colson: 'Hemingway, Old Man, And The Sea.'

Folozchev watched him. "You always send message from inside ice box?"

Mackey waved him off. "Grocery list, Vlad. They bring nothing good to eat here." Shutting the door, he continued his search through the pantry, finding a bag of chips. He brought them back to his chair, then grabbed the tv remote.

The Russian watched him in disbelief. "You are eating machine."

Mackey looked back unfazed and said, "There's a home remodeling show coming on you might like. It's called, 'This Old Dacha.'"

"Funny man," Folozchev quipped. "Don't quit day job."

"Our book is The Old Man And The Sea, by Hemingway," Colson announced to the room as the message appeared on his screen.

"Did you hear that?" Blade repeated into his phone. "Old Man And The Sea, page 221. Get that message broken down."

"Arthur," Logan responded, "we don't know which paragraph. How can we.... "

"It doesn't matter. Start searching each paragraph on the page. One of them will yield a message. Let me know when you've uncovered it."

The front door to the safe house opened, and Winchell

stepped in carrying the usual tray of coffee and donuts. Back at the command center and the interrogation room, all eyes followed every movement of Folozchev, Winchell, and Mackey.

"We are not receiving any audio," Blade called out. "Is there something you can do on your end?"

Logan eyed the CIA agent controlling the video signals from the safe house. The man held up a finger as his other hand pushed a mouse around, clicking and scrolling, then turned to Logan and nodded.

"The audio signal should be coming through soon."

A scratchy crackle emitted from all the computers and phone speakers, followed by the low, boomy voice of Folozchev.

"Ah," the Russian observed, "you stop at place with good coffee and not-so-good donuts."

"You told me you like the stuff from this place," Winchell said as he pulled the coffee cups from the holder, irritated by the lack of appreciation for his offering.

"No, is okay," Folozchev countered, pulling the lid off a steamy cup. "Place with good donuts have bad coffee. Right now, I like good coffee." He took a long, satisfying sip and looked up at Winchell with his half-open Basset Hound eyes. "Sit, relax. You look stressful. Blood pressure must be terrible. Have donut."

Winchell's glare narrowed. "You and I have things to discuss," he said, lowering himself into a chair. He leaned forward, keeping his voice low. "You know what I mean."

Folozchev pushed back from the table, waving his hand dismissively. "Always you want secrets, John Winchell. I don't know good one to give today. I think maybe you work too hard, not so healthy. Day off would be good. Go home, drink fancy cocktail, read good book." He pushed the book he was holding across the table. "Maybe you read this. Is good story about big fish." Folozchev gave a slight nod, breaking eye contact as he glanced down at the book.

Winchell reached for it, but Folozchev held on another moment. He eyed agent Mackey, then in a muffled voice, added, "Go now. We talk again another day."

Winchell flashed an expression that said he'd expected more but accepted the book.

Folozchev reached into the bag, sampled a donut, and washed it down with coffee, then stared back at Winchell. "Why you still here?" he asked with a note of annoyance.

Winchell's brows furrowed as he grabbed his own cup in one hand, the book in the other, and headed for the door.

John Winchell made it to his car, then sat staring out the windshield. There were so many thoughts whirring inside his head that he struggled to focus on just one alone. What seemed like a few speed bumps just a few weeks ago now towered over him like mountain peaks. This wasn't the time to fall apart, and he chastised himself for not being the one in control. But then, it was difficult to sit day after day with a master manipulator such as Folozchev and still think you controlled even your own breathing. He knew he had failed and admitted to being exploited by the very spy he was sent to dominate.

The old Russian had just given him the bum's rush, and he didn't appreciate it. On the flip side, he had a book to pass along that was his passport to the people who would get him out of the country. He picked up the novel from the passenger seat and spied the note inside. Slipping it out, he glanced it over without a clue of its contents. It was the same as the last two messages he'd delivered. Rather odd, he thought, that the man had encrypted a letter addressed to his daughter. What was there to hide in such an innocent communication? It was a little late to ask questions after he agreed to drop off the first messages. He had trusted an untrustworthy man and now depended on this former enemy.

Somewhere, a clock was ticking, counting down the seconds until his arrest. He would be labeled a counter-spy and charged with a grocery list of broken laws and breaches of moral codes. It amazed him how far and fast he had fallen over a failed but simple goal. Eliminating Arthur Blade and assuming his role had become an obsessive quest. But he was still sure the man was a double agent. No doubt about it. It remained baffling beyond words how no one else possessed the common sense to see the connection. Maybe he would offer a parting shot. An evidence trail that would leave Blade's name mired in the mud. He added that to a growing list of tasks to be finished before he disappeared.

With those thoughts at least partially sorted out, he moved on to the details of his exit. He had $2 million of the ransom money from the failed software key exchange in England. The other million had been split between Fossie and Mako. That could make his new life much more comfortable, so long as his new handlers didn't see fit to confiscate it as part of the deal. He felt at least partially confident that a few bribes here and there would ensure he kept the bulk of the money. Either way, it wasn't like he had much choice in the matter.

Fossie and Mako were another story. It appeared each was becoming an even greater liability with every passing minute. He didn't trust either to keep their mouths shut. So long as the two of them were drawing breath, they posed a risk to his exit strategy. He still needed to pit them against each other. That would silence them once and for all. He envisioned a cage fight with the opponents punching and kicking to the death.

What a great thought!

There was enough animosity between them to guarantee the desired outcome. His pulse quickened with the vision of crushed knuckles and faces beaten to a bloody pulp. The confrontation might not devolve into a knockdown fistfight, but the bloodshed? Yes, he could make that happen! A good, old-fashioned shootout. That was the simplest solution. And if done correctly, it could eliminate a few other outstanding issues. He took in a deep breath, feeling his confidence return, then pulled his phone out and hit speed dial.

"Incoming call to Fossie from John Winchell," an FBI agent announced. He waited until everyone else in the command post had donned headphones, then gave Logan a thumbs up.

Logan sat down next to Fossie and nodded. Fossie took a breath and answered his phone. Before he could announce a greeting, Winchell's voice cut through harsh and direct.

"Where are you?" he demanded.

"I'm sitting in a diner eating breakfast."

Logan nodded back at Fossie for his quick response, then spun his finger in a circle. Keep it going.

"Listen carefully," Winchell continued, his voice rising, "I believe Mako has been conspiring with Folozchev. Mako may be the counter-spy after all. I need you to go to the safe house and put a bullet in them both."

"You can't be serious!" Fossie blurted out before catching himself. Logan shot him a disapproving look.

"What, I don't sound serious to you? Shit, Fossie! Mako has likely been passing on secrets with Folozchev right under our noses. If this gets out, we all go down, understand?"

Fossie hesitated.

"I asked you if you understood, damnit!"

"Yeah, I understand. But you're asking me to put a hit on a fellow agent and a defector in a government safe house! How would you ever explain that one away?"

"I wasn't asking for your input. Dead men tell no tales. And both of them are far more dangerous to us alive than dead. Go there and provoke something. Piss Mako off. That's easy for you to do. Get him to draw on you. Take him out, and Folozchev goes down in the crossfire."

"What about the other agents guarding Folozchev?" Fossie asked.

"Mackey will be on duty today. Send him out for a break. Tell him you and Mako will watch over the old rat bastard for a while. I'm sending Mako there now. Get this done, and both of them will be the fall guys for everything we've done. We come out on top, they go down in shame, and you get Mako's share of the ransom cash. Not a bad haul for half a day's work."

"John, do you realize what you're asking me to do?"

"Like I said, I'm not asking!" Winchell corrected him. "Now grow a pair and go do your duty!" Winchell disconnected.

"Now that was interesting," Arthur Blade commented over Logan's speakerphone.

Colson asked, "Did we get that recorded?"

Logan looked to the agent monitoring the recording equipment, who gave him a nod. "Yeah, we got it all."

"Well, Mr. Fossie," Blade continued, "I believe you have a date with destiny."

"Wait, you don't expect me to still go there, do you? What if Winchell is telling Mako the same thing about me? This will be a shoot out at the not-so-OK corral."

As he said this, an FBI agent announced, "Outgoing call from Winchell to agent Mako."

"I believe your question is about to be answered," Blade said.

∼

"Mako," I need you at the safe house ASAP." Winchell's voice was once again confident and commanding.

"I can be there within the hour," Mako answered. "What do you need me to do?"

"Fossie has gone off the grid. He killed Greggenkoff and one of Blade's agents. I suspect he is taking orders from Folozchev. I need you to eliminate Fossie and Folozchev and make it look like he was there to kill you. Can you do that?"

There was a brief pause. "Yes."

"I'm depending on you. Call me when it's done."

Mako ended the call without responding.

∼

"What did I tell you?" Fossie said. "Mako is a cold-blooded bastard. If he says he's going to kill me, then that's what he'll do."

"We have no intention of letting that happen," Blade reassured him. "We will set you up with a vest, a wire, and adequate backup." Blade turned to Colson. "We'll need a combat team standing by out of sight. Reposition them outside the doors once both Fossie and Mako enter."

Colson nodded as he walked out of the interrogation room, then dialed up Langley to make the arrangements.

"Garret," Blade said into his phone, "please lend Fossie your car and get him on his way to the safe house. We need to let this play out."

Logan handed his keys to Fossie. "You know what to do," he said. "You know where to go. All eyes are on you now."

Fossie took the keys and rose from his chair. He turned and walked toward the door with the look of a death-row prisoner on his way to execution.

"Oh, and Fossie," Logan called after him.

Fossie stopped and turned.

"First round is on me when you get back."

Fossie flashed a half-hearted grin and headed out the door.

"How is the decryption process coming along over there?" Blade asked.

Fossie checked with the FBI agent tasked with identifying the correct paragraph. The man shook his head. "Still working on it," Logan answered. "He hasn't broken it yet."

"Get another agent to work the page from the bottom up," Blade commanded. "We are losing valuable time."

Logan asked if anyone was available to assist, and another agent volunteered. Logan explained what they needed, and the agent jumped in. Within moments, he had downloaded the encrypted message and located an electronic copy of the book. He checked with the first agent to confirm he was working with the same page from the novel, then began searching for the hidden message, starting from the last paragraph and working up. "We'll have this cracked soon, Arthur," Logan offered.

Colson returned to the interrogation room at Camp David. "I've got two snipers and four rangers on their way to the safe house," he announced. "ETA is half an hour."

"Good, very good," Blade said. "Now we need message cracked before we lose Winchell. I would love to know what he is doing right...."

"Outgoing call from John Winchell to Don Colson," the FBI agent announced from his recording console.

Blade eyed Colson and gave him the nod to answer.

"Don, it's Winchell. We have a problem. One of my guys may have gone rogue and is not communicating. I don't know if Greggenkoff ever made it to the airport. The tracer on the car they were driving went dead shortly after they left the safe house. Have you heard anything on your end?"

"John, we have some problems," Colson said to him. "Where are you?"

Winchell ignored the question. "Agent Mako was tailing the car when someone jumped out and attacked him. Was he one of yours?"

"That was Arthur Blade, John. Your agent tried to kill him. If we add this to what happened in the English operation, that would make twice. I think it's time to come clean, don't you?"

There was a long, palpable silence before Winchell spoke again. "Neither of them told me about that part. This must mean they've both gone off the reservation."

"Where are you, John? We need to talk."

Winchell again ignored him again. "We can't trust either of them. They're both headed to the safe house but won't be there for another hour. They're out of control, Don. We have to stop them."

"I'll send some extra men out. Hopefully, they can arrive close to when your agents get there."

"Like I said, about an hour," Winchell repeated. "Don't take any chances. Shoot to kill."

"Why don't you come in, John? We can talk about it."

"Arthur is alive?"

"Yes, John, Arthur Blade is alive. I'll make sure he's here when you come in."

The call ended

"Do we have Winchell's GPS coordinates?" Blade asked Logan.

An agent in the command center overheard the request on Logan's speakerphone and answered. "He's coming up on Glen Echo Park Aquarium off of MacArthur Boulevard."

Blade listened, then turned to Colson. "Don, can we get something in the air to monitor his movements? Judging by your last conversation, he won't be coming in anytime soon."

"I don't think so, either," Colson said as he made a call. "Hello, Colson here. Do we have any aerial assets near Maclean, Virginia? Yes? How soon could you arrange this? Good, I'll send over the coordinates." He turned back to Blade. "We'll have a copter available within the half hour."

Blade shook his head. "That won't be soon enough. I'm afraid that our friend is planning to leave without saying goodbye. We need eyes on him now." He spoke into his phone, which was still connected to Logan in the interrogation room. "Garret, please ask the gentlemen from the FBI and State Police if they have any vehicles near Glen Echo Park Aquarium."

Logan called out the request to everyone in the room. A Maryland State Police captain nodded and came forward. "We can help you with that, sir. What type of vehicle are we looking for?"

Colson spoke up. "John Winchell is driving a white, late model Malibu, Virginia license plate XXG-3399."

The trooper jotted the information down and sent out the request on his radio.

"Any further progress on our message?" Blade asked.

There was a pause as Logan checked with the agents working to decrypt the message. "We are making progress, Arthur. They scanned the page from top to bottom and came up with something, but it wasn't clear. I looked and picked up a few words. It's written in something between English and Russian. We now believe that we've isolated the message. There's an agent fluent in the language breaking it down as we speak." The line went silent for another moment before Logan came back on. "Arthur, they've cracked the code. And according to what I've read, we have less time than we thought. I'm texting it over right now."

Blade waited for the message. His phone beeped, and he stared at the screen, reading the message through twice. "There's no time to be lost," he announced. "Mr. Winchell appears to be seeking asylum with the Russians. But according to this message, Vladimir Folozchev has an ulterior objective."

Don Colson and President Lux were both on their feet in an instant. "What does it say?" Colson asked.

Blade turned to them and recited the message from memory. "John Winchell seeks asylum. Low trust. Take him. Expect to be followed. Disappear. Extract information. Dispose. Will contact via 9099."

John Winchell stood beside his car, processing everything that had taken place and all that was yet to come. His plan was sound, with a high potential for success. All he had to do was ensure everyone involved stuck to his script. That meant keeping them in motion while they chased after the crumbs he offered. Hours from now, his primary adversaries would be nothing more than bad memories.

He'd come so close to taking down Arthur Blade, who, by rights, should have been dead months ago. And to think, it all could have ended with the simple slip of a surgeon's scalpel during that ridiculous procedure.

It gnawed at his very fiber that nobody believed Blade was a double agent. While his gut instincts were mostly accurate, he could not understand how others with less developed gifts wouldn't trust and depend upon those with superior senses.

The unenlightened and meek followers of this world were now leading the parades.

Ignorance and a twisted sense of righteousness had robbed the intelligence community of the tools and mindset necessary to battle their enemies. These watered-down tactics and useless interrogation tools couldn't crack an egg! For a moment, he envisioned himself in Folozchev's position. That man's success at interrogation resulted from unbridled freedom to use any and every tool he deemed necessary. In such an environment, Winchell would have risen to god-like status.

He thought again of the months of interrogating Folozchev that had yielded next to nothing. The old Russian had played them well. And despite Folozchev's assurances of a good life on the other side, Winchell didn't expect good treatment. That would change once these embedded Russian spies realized their master manipulator was dead. With Folozchev out of the picture, his own value would increase tenfold.

He would remain an asset to them so long as he played the game as Folozchev had by divulging just enough information to goad them along another day. By pacing the interviews, he could ensure they would never open the more invasive toolbox. He knew only too well what was inside: A car battery wired to his testicles. A good old-fashioned water boarding. And of course, the classic tried-and-true method of extracting one's fingernails. Just the sight of a pair of needle-nosed pliers gave Winchell a frosty jolt down his spine.

He had a list of information to offer his new captors, starting with the identities of key field agents, that were likely already compromised. A few bombshell revelations would establish his worth. After that, he could turn the spigot down to a steady drip. In time, he hoped to work his way up the ranks to a position more commensurate with his talents. Yes, with Folozchev out of the picture, he might even work himself into that vacant slot.

He would need certainty that Folozchev was dead before giving himself over to the Russians. A wicked grin curled the corners of his mouth as another splendid vision filled his mind. More guns! An uncontrolled hale of cross-firing weapons could offer the closure he required. He pulled his phone from a pocket and hit a number in memory.

"Outgoing call from John Winchell to Don Colson," announced the FBI agent.

There was a quick check of the recording equipment. "They're all set over here, sir," Logan said.

Colson answered the call. "Hello, John. Are you on your way in?"

"I'm sure you know the answer to that, Don. I'm calling to tell you that Folozchev has found a way to direct the actions of a sleeper cell of agents. He needs to be stopped at all costs."

"What do you propose?" Colson asked.

"Kill him now before he can cause any more damage."

Blade stepped over and spoke into the phone. "John, what have you gotten yourself into, old man?"

Winchell inhaled. The tone of voice was foreign, but the inflection could only emanate from one man. "Arthur, is that you?"

"You've boxed yourself into a corner, John. There's no good way for this to play out. Be a good sport and come in to face your accusers. It's the least you could do."

"I can't do that. Not until you know all the facts. For now, you need to get to Folozchev and stop him cold. I don't know all the details of how he's communicated with his people on the outside, but I've seen enough to know the threat he poses. Eliminate him now."

"Just curious, John, why didn't you deal with him yourself?"

Silence. "I'll be watching from a safe distance," he said. "There's one more thing you should know. I have strong suspicions that Agent Mako is a North Korean plant. Maybe you should let him shoot Folozchev for you, then take him down."

Twenty-Five
SHOOTOUT

Agent Mackey sat planted in his usual chair in front of the television as Mako entered the safe house. Mackey threw an uninterested glance his way and returned his attention to a program. Mako figured Folozchev was in his room or in the can. His main business was with Fossie, so he took a seat at the table and waited. "Hey, Mackey," he called out.

Mackey half turned his head.

"Take a break. Me and Fossie will babysit for a while."

"Yeah?" Mackey said, working himself out of the chair. "Where is your partner in crime?"

As if in answer to his question, the front door opened, and in stepped Fossie. "Well, isn't this cozy?" he said, scanning the room. "Where's Vlad?"

Folozchev emerged from the bathroom, adjusting his belt. "Son of bitch. Is Grand Central Station here," he huffed. "How many Americans it take to guard one Russian going shit?"

"Ah, come on, Vladimir," Fossie said, "doesn't it make you feel special?"

"Fuck to you," he said, with an indignant sneer, dropping

into a seat opposite of Mako. "Give me day of no questions. Take break."

"Okay with me," Fossie answered with disinterest. "Okay with you, Mako?"

Mako pursed his lips and stared back.

"Well then, I, for one, will take a break," Mackey said, walking to the front door. "I could use a nice meal on the company dime." He pulled the door closed behind him, and an uneasy silence fell over the room.

Fossie and Mako locked eyes on each other.

"Why did Winchell send you here?" Mako asked.

"Same reason he sent you, I'm sure." Fossie crossed his arms low, keeping a hand near his holster. "So what now?"

Mako stood, took off his sports coat, and hung it on a chair back, revealing his Sig Sauer in a belt holster.

Fossie glanced at it. Even with the Kevlar vest he was wearing, those nine-millimeter hollow points would do some damage. That was if he was lucky enough to take a hit in the torso and not the face. He hoped Mako would aim for center mass. "Lot of unanswered questions," he said. "Sort of like Winchell is directing his loose ends to eliminate themselves. Ever feel like you've been played?"

Mako shrugged. "It's a job."

"All of this is just a job to you?" Fossie gave him a disbelieving glare.

"Well, maybe a bit more than a job. After all, I do get to shoot people."

Folozchev picked up on the tension between the two and stood. "You cowboys have problem? Go outside, have good time."

"Can it, old man," Mako commanded, keeping his eyes on Fossie.

He started walking toward his room. "Keep me out of family feud. Call me when done."

"Sit your ass down, you fat bastard."

"I am no taking orders from little North Korean shit," he said over his shoulder. "Call your boss. Maybe is time to talk."

Mako shook his head. "Anyone ever tell you that you talk too much?" With lightning quickness, he reached for his pistol and shot Folozchev twice in the back. The Russian let out a guttural moan and crumpled to the floor.

Fossie sprang from his seat, pulling his Kimber 1911 from a shoulder holster and letting loose a rapid volley of shots at Mako. At least one found its mark. Mako, looking unfazed, turned sideways to his attacker, making himself a smaller target. He took careful aim and squeezed off three rounds. Two of the slugs slammed into Fosse's vest, flattening against the bullet-proof material. The force of impact cracked his rib cage with like being hit by a home run slugger's bat. The excruciating pain emptied the air from his lungs. Breathless, he fell back and dove for the cover of a stone coffee table, knocking it over and shielding himself behind while wheezing for breath. He peered over the top and watched as Mako did the same with the kitchen table. He took aim and was ready to pull the trigger when a new pain flared from his left thigh. It was covered in blood. Mako's third shot. No chance of a clean in-out wound with the hollow points. These things made a mess and stayed in. He pulled off his belt and wrapped it around his leg, just above the wound. He was only delaying the inevitable and could bleed out soon if help didn't arrive. "I'm hit," he whispered, hoping someone was listening to the signal from the wire taped to his chest. "I'm hit bad. Folozchev is down."

"Shots fired inside the safe house!" All eyes in the command center watched a monitor as Folozchev was gunned down from behind. A second later, both Mako and Fossie squared off and began firing at each other. Each dove for cover, and a tense, temporary silence gripped the room.

"Fossie's hit," called the agent monitoring his wire. "He's not doing good."

"Send everyone you have in there now!" Blade commanded.

Colson gave a quick nod, reached for a radio handset, and pushed the send button. "Shots fired in the safe house," he announced to the soldiers outside. "All assets, take the building, now!"

Fossie managed a quick glance from behind the table and saw that Folozchev was still breathing. He lay face down, a pool of blood growing around him. He didn't give the man much chance to survive. Most of the bleeding had stopped in his own wound, but he could feel the numbness setting in. The bullet likely missed a major artery, but it was still just a matter of time before he lost consciousness. He took in a breath, wincing in pain. The bullets had also cracked a few ribs. There was no waiting for help. He had to bring this to an end now. Dialogue was always the preferred method of defusing a hostile situation, but no one could talk Mako off this ledge. He breathed in as deeply as he could before the pain of three cracked ribs stopped him. "Did I hear Folozchev call you North Korean? I was only joking when I said the same thing. Is it true?"

Mako responded by shooting three slugs into the stone tabletop he was crouching behind. Fossie ducked lower and did some quick math. That was eight shots. Mako used a stock Sig Sauer P229 pistol with a fifteen-round magazine. He had seven more shots before reloading. Catching him when he ran out seemed like his only chance. Mako was deadly accurate. The three hits he'd taken already were proof enough of that. What were the odds that at least one of his remaining slugs wouldn't find his head? He hoped a better option would offer itself while he could still act on it. In the meantime, he was thankful for the slab of granite tabletop that was shielding him. Three direct hits had not even caused a crack.

"Did I hit a nerve with that one?" Fossie asked. "I mean, Kim Jong Un? Why would anyone follow that chunky manchild with the bad haircut? But maybe you could clear up a question I've had. Is it true that he is nobly born and never requires the use of a commode?"

A glass light fixture hung over Fossie's head. Mako aimed and put two rounds into it, showering glass fragments. Fossie pulled his jacket up over his head just in time to shield from the bigger pieces. Many smaller shards still found their mark, stabbing him in the arms and back. He pulled at the tiny spears within his reach, wincing in pain. Five rounds remaining.

"Is that any way to treat your old partner?" He called out. "I thought we worked well together."

"You are a foolish man with a big mouth. Could you hurry up and die? I have places to be."

Folozchev moaned and moved. "Why you do this?" he asked of his executioner. "Your cover was safe."

Mako sneered and said, "Time to clean up the mess and go home."

"So it's true," Fossie said.

"I was talking to the fat Russian, you idiot." Mako took careful aim and shot anywhere he noticed Fossie was exposed. The tip of a shoe, a tuft of hair sticking above the makeshift shield. The shoe shot grazed a few toes while the indirect headshot cut into his scalp. Fossie ducked lower as blood dripped down his ear. Two shots left.

The sound of rapid footfalls coming from outside suddenly echoed throughout the building as the team of Army Rangers prepared to break down the door. Mako aimed low at the entryway and fired.

Folozchev struggled to take a deep breath, his lungs making a sound like rustling leaves. "Our countries fight side by side," he said, making one last appeal to Mako. "We take down United States. We become superpowers of world."

Mako laughed at him. "You are a useless old man from an old, dead country. Meet your new masters." He pointed the pistol at the back of the Russian's head and pulled the trigger.

Nothing. He was out!

Fossie had expected him to reload after shooting at the door but now remembered Mako had taken his jacket off and hung it on a chair. That's where he kept his spare magazines. It now sat far out of reach.

Mako rose and started for the jacket. Fossie stood and laid down three shots of suppressing fire to stop him. Mako turned toward him, seething with anger, and did the only thing left to do; he threw his pistol at Fossie, who had to duck or take it in the forehead. By the time he raised his head back, Mako had run through another doorway into Folozchev's bedroom.

The front door exploded in a loud, bright flash, blinding Fossie, and pelting him with wood and metal debris. Four armed rangers rushed through with their weapons trained on him. "Freeze!" A voice shouted. "Hands on your head!"

Fossie dropped his sidearm and complied. "He went into the bedroom," he called out, pointing as he choked on the thick dust.

A ranger stood over him. "Identify yourself," he demanded.

"Fossie," he croaked, "Mako is the one you want. He shot our defector and ran into the back bedroom."

The ranger pointed to the other three soldiers. He flashed

two fingers and pointed toward the bedroom, then held up one finger and directed the third back out the front door and around. He held Fossie at gunpoint and spoke into his radio. "I have one occupant, Fossie, wounded. The other, Mako, is in a back room."

The radio crackled with static. "Fossie is the friendly. Repeat, Fossie is with us."

The ranger lowered his weapon and examined Fossie's leg. He keyed up his radio again and said, "We need a medic in here, stat."

The other two rangers rushed from the back room. "He got away through a window. We're going to see if we can pick up his trail." Both headed out the front door.

Fossie slumped to his knees, grateful to have lived through the ordeal and hopeful he had earned his place on Blade's team. He pointed to Folozchev. "I don't know if he's going to make it."

The ranger knelt beside the Russian, took his glove off, and checked for a pulse.

"Not so dead yet," Folozchev mumbled in a near whisper.

The ranger flinched at the sound of the unexpected voice. "Make that a medevac copter for two," he radioed as he pulled Folozchev's shirt up and examined the wounds. Time would tell if the old man survived, but he'd seen people live through worse.

His radio crackled again. "We picked up Mako's trail," one of the other rangers reported. "Looks like he had his escape plan worked out. He was on foot and squeezed under a fence about two clicks from the house. We found motorcycle tracks where his footprints ended."

"Copy that. I'll relay the info."

Before the ranger could make the call himself, Fossie spoke into the wire taped to his gut. "Did you hear that?" he said.

"Mako jumped on a motorcycle about a mile and a half from the safe house."

There was no response, but everyone heard him.

Don Colson was listening to the signal from Fossie's wire when he heard of Mako's escape. He turned to Blade and asked, "What bike was Mako riding when you two tangled?" "A lime green Kawasaki Ninja, as I recall. He may have ditched that one and stolen another. Still, we have to start somewhere." He picked up his phone and said, "Garret, can you find out if we have eyes in the sky?"

Logan called out the request to everyone in the command center.

"I believe we've got eyes on him," a state trooper called out. "One of our patrol units just clocked a green motorcycle at a hundred and sixty mph traveling north on I-95."

"That was a lucky break," Blade said. "Can you continue to track his movements without giving chase? We need to bring him in."

The trooper spoke the instructions into his radio, listened, then nodded to Logan. "We've alerted all units further north to stand down and observe only."

A State Police captain had called in a request for air surveillance. "We have two birds available," he said. "The first is already in the vicinity of Glen Echo Park. They confirmed eyes on your agent's car outside the aquarium. I redirected the other to follow the subject on the motorcycle. He should be coming up on him."

"Excellent," Blade exclaimed, then turned to Colson. "We need our people ready to move in on Winchell the moment he contacts Folozchev's handlers. What assets do we have available?"

"Already on it, I sent in two teams. We also have agents at either end of MacArthur Boulevard. All movement in or out is being monitored."

Blade thought a moment. "We should take this opportunity to do a little investigative work," he said. "I'm assuming you have an address where Mako lived. Let's dispatch a spycraft detection team and rendezvous with them there. There are secrets waiting to be discovered."

"Good plan," Colson agreed. "Will you be joining us on this expedition?"

"Wouldn't miss it for the world," Blade said, then cracked a grin. "And if you wouldn't mind..." He held out the handcuffs and leg shackles. "Let's keep up appearances, shall we? At least until we've left Camp David."

Colson obliged and slapped on the cuffs but left the shackles on the table. "I think we can do without these, don't you?"

President Lux looked on, grinning. "Arthur, I do believe you're enjoying this."

Blade offered a sly wink as he exited the room with Colson.

Twenty-Six
THE PREDATOR'S LAIR

Arthur Blade and Don Colson had just entered Mako's rented townhouse when Blade's phone rang. "Arthur, it's Logan. I'm at the Glen Echo Aquarium. Winchell is gone."

Blade froze in his tracks. "How is this possible."

"We had aerial surveillance and assets on the ground. The road leading in was monitored. When our people entered the main building, they found no one. I did a foot search of the immediate area. There's a tree-covered bike trail running behind the building that could have been used to get Winchell over to the Barton Parkway without being seen from overhead. They must have had a passkey or a lock pick to make their way through the employee areas and out the back exit. We can't triangulate his phone because he left it in the car. We've lost him."

"Don't give up so easy. Locate every traffic monitoring camera in the area and start watching tapes. If they made it to the parkway, a car must have stopped to pick them up. The trail may be cold, but we are not out. Call me when you have something." Blade looked to Colson. "Let's hope this expedition proves more fruitful than the last."

"The search team is still twenty minutes out," Colson told him. "The search warrants are approved and on the way, just in case you wanted to start without them."

Blade was already working the lock with a pick tool. Within seconds, he had it open, then paused before opening the door. "Our friend, Mr. Mako, is likely the type that would booby-trap his place of residence. Let us keep our movements slow and methodical until we locate any of his 'welcoming' devices."

He stepped off the porch, walked around to a side window, and examined the inside of the front door. "There is an alarm system panel next to the door that does not appear to be armed. Mako either left in a hurry or assumed his secondary devices would take care of any uninvited visitors." He scanned the area further and noticed a thin cable running from a rug at the door. "Ah," he said, "deterrent number one." He walked back around to the front door and said, "There is a welcome mat just inside the door that appears quite unwelcoming. Be sure to step clear of it."

Blade pushed the door open a crack, further examining the frame and peering inside. Once confident he had identified the only threat, he let the door swing the rest of the way inside. He stepped over the mat and traced the wire to a wooden box against the wall. "Clever," he said, inspecting it from all sides. "I've only seen this type of device once before. It shoots an array of darts into the intruder's leg. Quiet and quite deadly." He turned the box so that the darts would shoot into the wall. "I've disabled it, but steer clear of that rug."

Both men worked their way through the townhouse, room by room. The entire dwelling had a cold and sterile feeling about it. The walls and ceilings were all white, without a single picture hanging. The furniture was sparse and appeared little used. Every surface, every table, corner, and counter top was spotless, confirming that Mako spent little here. It could have been all for show, and he might reside at another location that was off the grid. Blade was leaning toward that conclusion until he examined the bedroom. There were clothes and extra linens in a single Ikea dresser, as well as a few suits and shirts hanging in a small walk-in closet. The master bath showed signs of use but kept meticulously clean. This was a man who did not want to leave any trace of his having lived here. That alone suggested there were secrets here yet to be discovered.

"Find anything interesting?" Colson asked.

Blade put his finger to his lips as his eyes scanned the bedroom from left to right. "Let's proceed for a moment under the presumption that Mr. Mako was, in fact, a North Korean plant, and this was his principal residence. With that being the case, we are not seeing things that should be here. Where is the primary source of communication?"

"Are you talking about a satellite phone?" Colson said.

Blade's brows furrowed. "I would expect to see radio equipment."

"Sort of old-fashioned, don't you think? Most of our agents rely on sat phones or the internet in the field these days."

"For most fieldwork, yes, they are effective. However, their calls, as well as every computer keystroke, are traceable. For an embedded agent, the old-fashioned ways are sometimes still the best. If you ran the records on every communications satellite searching for transmissions from this location, I believe you would come up empty-handed. If this were my operation, I would have directed the agent to send and receive encrypted signals via the numbers stations on the shortwave radio. So long as Mr. Mako uses his book of numbers, the information passes under the noses of anyone who attempts to monitor it. I would expect the numbers book would remain in his possession. The equipment, however, must be here." Blade looked around the room. "We are searching for a false wall, possibly an appliance that doesn't quite look right. I'll start in the bedroom. I would suggest you begin with the kitchen and work your way out."

Colson nodded and headed for the kitchen.

Blade worked his way through the master bath, re-examining every cabinet and grout seam, finding nothing out of the ordinary. He went next to the dresser, pulling it away from the wall, then sliding each drawer all the way out. He felt along the bottoms of each. When he got to the lowest drawer, he heard a slight shift. Pulling it out, he probed along the back and found a box attached to the underside. One end was open, and he worked his fingers in, pulling out a small book. He opened it and flipped through a few pages, not believing his luck. Mako's numbers book! Mako must have intended to come back here before exiting the country, hoping his position within the CIA was still secure. Well, if the book was here, then there had to be—

"Arthur, there's something here you should see here," Colson called from the kitchen.

Blade slid the numbers book into his suit coat pocket and hurried to the kitchen.

Colson was standing next to the refrigerator, staring at the floor. He pointed down and said, "I'm seeing multiple scuff marks over here. I'm assuming it's from one of those dining chairs in the next room, but why? There's nothing else here but the microwave."

Blade worked his way around the scuff marks and made his own examination. "Very astute," he said. "Not bad for a pencil pusher, as we would say." He went into the dining room and confirmed it was the feet of one of these chairs that had made the marks. So what was the reason? Was he accessing something on a top shelf? He estimated Mako's height at a few inches short of six feet. He grabbed the closest chair and slid it into the same position on the kitchen floor, then stood on it, looking into the cabinets above. Aside from a few boxes of cereal, there was nothing. He felt around inside, searching for a hidden panel, again coming up empty.

He was about to climb down when he noticed something odd about the power cord coming out of the countertop microwave. It was much thicker than any he had seen before. It appeared to be at least a five-conductor cord instead of the normal three. Blade stepped down and pushed the chair away, staring at the wall outlet and giving Colson a sly look. With both hands, he carefully worked the cable out of the connector. He was right! The receptacle and microwave power cord both had five connections. Next, he rummaged through the kitchen drawers until he found a knife and used it to unscrew the plastic outlet cover. Inside the junction box was the reason for the two additional connections. A coaxial signal cable with an outer ground wire snaked from the receptacle and up the wall. A radio antenna!

"I believe you have discovered Mr. Mako's source of communications," he said, patting Colson on the shoulder. "And now, let's see the rest."

Blade sat in the chair and pulled the microwave before him. He noticed now that the door was opaque, with no view of the contents that would be cooking inside. His fingers worked around the body of the box. He felt along the seam, then began pushing on the number pad, finally working his way to the door's open button. It would not push in like a normal door mechanism. He studied the number keypad and now noticed the stop button had more wear than the others. He pushed on it harder and heard a click. But rather than swinging open like a normal microwave, the front panel dropped forward, revealing the control panel of a short-wave radio. All the exposed writing was in Chinese.

"Well, I'll be damned," Colson said, astonished. "Excellent work, Arthur!"

"I have you to thank for pointing the way, old man," Blade said. "Let us ensure we don't touch any of the controls. I'm sure the evidence team will want to dust for fingerprints."

There was a knock on the door. "CIA evidence team, we have a search warrant."

Blade shot out of the kitchen toward the front door. "Director Colson is in the building," he shouted. "Do not enter until I...."

His words were cut off as the evidence tech stepped through the door and onto the 'unwelcome' mat triggering a small explosion from the box that Blade had aimed at the wall. Everyone dropped to the floor with guns drawn.

"I was hoping to avoid that," Blade said, standing and dusting himself off. "The danger has passed." He walked over to the box and moved it away from the wall, exposing a smoking hole with four short stainless steel arrows sticking out.

"I thought you said that thing shot little poison darts," Colson said, examining the damage. "That thing would have cut you off at the ankles!"

Blade shrugged. "This appears to be a variation in the original design. An upgrade, if you will." Unfazed, he waved the evidence team in. "This way, gentlemen," he said, leading them to the radio. He extracted the book from his pocket and handed it to one of them. "This is a North Korean numbers book. I believe he marked the last line used to encrypt a message. Let's see if we can't use this to decipher some of the other radio traffic out there."

The evidence technician's eyes lit up as he accepted the

book. Rather than touch it himself, he had Blade slip it into a plastic bag, which he labeled and slipped into a metal case.

Colson's phone chirped. He answered, listened a moment, then turned to Blade. "A bit of good news, Arthur. We pinged Mako's phone. He is still traveling along north on I-95. A Maryland State Police copter kept an eye on him through Delaware and broke off when he entered Pennsylvania. We're still attempting to get another eye in the sky, but no luck so far."

"Eventually, he will dispose of the phone, Don. We're running on borrowed time now. What about a satellite feed?"

Colson nodded and began punching numbers on his keypad.

One of the evidence techs came out of the bedroom and approached Blade. "We found a hidden panel in the clothes closet."

"Anything of interest inside?" Blade asked.

The tech nodded with pride. "A safe."

"Show me," Blade said and followed the tech into the bedroom. A section of floor carpeting had been pulled up from inside the closet, and Blade peered into the hole at a small safe bolted to the floor joists.

"Excellent work! Get your best people over here. We need this opened ASAP."

"On it," the tech said, unclipping a handheld radio from his belt.

Blade wandered back into the kitchen just as Colson was wrapping up a call. "Arthur, we'll have access to satellite imagery within fifteen minutes. In the meantime, we've gained more eyes on the ground. Pennsylvania State Troopers have spotted Mako near Philadelphia. I have advised them to let him pass. Do you think he's headed for the airport?"

"That's always a possibility, though I doubt he would be so brazen as to believe he could board a commercial flight without being detained. There are few places one could run if cornered at a major airport. Chartering a private plane from a small airfield would be the wiser move. Mr. Mako likely had a number of exit strategies, though I believe we caught him unprepared. His options are now limited. Perhaps his phone records and the contents of the safe will reveal his intentions."

"Are you sure he wouldn't just hole up somewhere and await new instructions from his handlers?"

"Good question, Don, but no. I believe he exceeded his usefulness. His cover is blown, and I would expect him to be called home for retooling, so to speak. He is an effective counter-agent. His handlers would anticipate his return and debriefing. A few rounds of plastic surgery, a new identity, and he's back on the street."

Colson's phone buzzed again. He listened, then ended the call. "Mako must have gotten rid of the phone. The triangulation signal stopped."

"What of our other sources of surveillance?"

"Pennsylvania police tracked him into New Jersey. We have nothing since."

"And our satellite?"

"Still waiting. We should have that any minute."

Blade laced his fingers behind his back and paced. "So, at this very moment, we are blind." He looked to Colson and added, "Now is the time to imagine ourselves in his shoes. Most likely, he is making for home. So how would he get there? I believe we can assume he had a doomsday plan to fall back on if all else failed." He stopped, his eyes scanning left and right as though reading his thoughts as they appeared outside of his head. He began walking again at a quickened pace. "His current direction of travel toward the coastline offers us yet another clue." He pointed at Colson. "The next best way out of the country would take the longest. But it would also provide the best cover. A cargo ship. That is how I would expect him to make his escape."

Colson's phone vibrated again. He listened, nodding, asked a few questions, then waited. "Stay on the line a moment," he said, then turned to Blade. "The satellite feed is coming in. They have him in view, zipping up the freeway just past Brunswick. Estimated speed now one-twenty."

"Very good," Blade said. "With every mile he travels, more is revealed about his final destination. At his current speed, we shall know with certainty within a few minutes."

Colson gave a few more instructions before ending the call, then he and Blade walked back through the townhouse, observing the work being done by the evidence-gathering team. A master locksmith sat working on picking the safe. He finally leaned back, wiped his sweat-soaked brow, and announced, "It's open." He pulled the door back, examining for booby traps and finding none. "It's all yours," he said, stepping away with a satisfied grin.

The evidence tech extracted the contents and placed them on a nearby nightstand. Blade watched as he extracted three passports, a stack of American and Euro currency, along with two additional cell phones. "Please dust those for prints and trace the call activity," he said.

The tech lifted each by the edges with gloved fingers and handed them to a fingerprint specialist standing by.

Colson answered his buzzing phone yet again, a wide grin appearing as he listened. "We'll need assets on the ground," he replied. "Send whatever you have." He pointed to Blade, nodding. "Very astute call, Arthur. Mako is heading into Port Jersey. We confirmed it just before the satellite passed out of range."

"Then there's no time to lose. We need to go there as soon as possible."

Colson dialed and made the arrangements. "Let's go," he

said, heading for the door. "They're prepping the chopper at Langley."

Blade called Logan as they walked toward the car. "Garret, where are you now?"

"Just headed back to the office. We've wrapped up the search for Winchell at the aquarium. We can do nothing more from here."

"Agreed. Tell me, is Kim Chapman still working at the information retrieval desk?"

"Yes, she was promoted and now heads the department."

"Even better. Please contact her now and redirect her team's efforts to pull every ship manifest scheduled to disembark Port Jersey within the next few days. We'll narrow it down once we gather more information."

"Got it," Logan said.

"And Garret, have you heard anything about the condition of Fossie?"

He nodded. "I was just on the phone with him, yes. He'll be out of commission for a few days, but he's going to be fine. Couple of broken ribs and some bullet fragments in his thigh."

"I'm relieved that we did not send him to his death. And what of our Mr. Folozchev?"

"Touch and go. They tell me he is critical but stable. Another surgery is planned for once he gets stronger."

Blade and Colson climbed into the car and drove toward Langley, both still on phone calls.

"Do you know what security measures we have in place at the hospital?" Blade asked Logan.

Logan laughed. "Yeah, I have a pretty good idea. Fossie said there were feds coming out of his ass. I assume that means both of them are secure."

"Excellent. We will deal with Folozchev in due time. For now, let's stick to tracing the steps of Mr. Mako. Please report back just as soon as those manifests become available." He pocketed his phone just as Colson turned into the Langley parking lot and headed toward the helipad.

They pulled up nearby, and Colson gave the spin-up sign as they climbed out. The turbine engine began whining as it spooled up. They scrambled in and were off the ground before they could buckle their seat belts.

Twenty-Seven
Turnabout is Fair Play

Twenty minutes later, the CIA helicopter touched down just inside the security gates of Port Jersey. Jim Piper stood waiting with a group of customs inspectors as Colson and Blade climbed out and hurried toward them. Piper stepped forward and held out his hand. Blade shook it and winked as Piper worked to conceal a sly smile, happy to see his boss alive yet showing no signs of recognition. "How can we help?" he asked.

"Let's start with the ship manifests I requested," Blade said. "I also need a couple of customs uniforms for the two of us. Let's be ready to board a ship if and when we identify Mako's location."

Piper was holding a large tablet. He tapped the screen and held it up for Blade and Colson to see. "There are three ships being loaded that are bound for either South Korea or Japan."

Blade took the pad and scrolled through the details. He pointed to one manifest and said, "Let's begin with this one. It's leaving the soonest and heading to South Korea. I also see that the cargo is aircraft parts. Our Mr. Mako might have an interest in procuring some of the confidential technology aboard." He turned to Colson. "Don, we need for Piper and myself to get aboard that ship as customs inspectors. We should also maintain eyes on all three vessels as we try to get a visual on our target."

Colson nodded and walked away to make more calls.

"Tell me what else we know about Mako," Blade asked Piper.

"He left the bike in the parking lot right over there, then went on foot. We're assuming he went directly to the ship."

Blade shook his head. "Let's not make any more assumptions than necessary." He eyed the area and the flurry of activity surrounding them. "I count three security cameras monitoring this area alone. Let's start by monitoring their signals and see where he went. Can you locate the security building?" "Already got it. Come with me."

Piper and Blade walked the short distance to the security building, and Piper flashed his identification at the door. They entered a darkened room with a wall of video monitors displaying the entire port from multiple angles. Blade explained what they were looking for, and a technician pointed them to a section of monitors with a view of the area they had just come from. He instructed them how to rewind up to one hour of video and single step through the frames.

Piper reversed the feed until he caught sight of Mako entering the frame, then ran it forward in slow motion.

Rather than making a beeline directly for the ship, Mako chose a circuitous path, stopping multiple times to blend in with workers, at one point even pausing to flip his windbreaker jacket inside out. He stopped near a Japanese freighter before making his way to the Korean cargo ship, the Chong Gen. They watched as he flashed his credentials to a worker at the gangplank and then boarded the ship.

Blade had his phone out in an instant. "Don, we have verification that Mako has boarded the Chong Gen. It would appear he plans to take the voyage to South Korea. We need to set up our own surveillance to monitor the ship from all angles. Let's hedge our bets as well. I want sonobuoys placed along the starboard side. I would also feel more confident if we brought in a team of Navy SEALs to patrol the area. We can decide how to take him into custody once we've eliminated all possibility of escape."

"I'll set that up now," Colson said. "We're already monitoring cell phone chatter from the ship, and it appears he has contacted someone on board. There was an outgoing call just a few minutes ago announcing that the 'traveler' had arrived. Stay where you can maintain a visual on that ship until we can get the rest of our surveillance and backup teams in place."

The head of security delivered a pair of customs uniforms, and Piper and Blade suited up.

"You and I will rotate shifts," Blade explained. "I'm going to get a closer look while you watch those monitors."

He changed into the uniform, then headed out to where he met another customs inspector near the freighter. Together, they came up with an improvised game plan. The pair headed up the gangplank to speak with the officer in charge of the crew and passengers. The customs inspector accompanying Blade, a man named Brody, was pleasant but professional in requesting the ship's manifest. They followed him to the bridge to retrieve it. Blade made mental notes of every face they passed along the way. As expected, Mako was not listed on either the passenger or crew manifest. The crew officer handed over a clipboard, explaining that twenty-seven crew and six passengers would make the journey. One of those passengers, Mr. Quon, was a recent addition and had just checked in.

Blade's phone rang as they were finishing up. It was Colson. "More cellphone traffic from onboard, Arthur. They have taken notice of the customs inspectors. It's time to divert some attention away."

"Agreed. We will head over to the other two freighters and repeat our process to make them think it's all routine." He ended the call and dialed Piper. "Pay close attention, Jim. We have already spooked our passenger. Let's see if he changes his plan."

Piper concentrated on the video feed showing the Chong Gen and figured out the playback controls to enlarge the image. A moment later, a face appeared in a porthole of the crew quarters. Piper zoomed in and took a screenshot with his phone, then sent it to Blade. It only took a glance to make a positive identification. He texted back to Piper and Colson; identity confirmed. Mako is aboard.

The two newly installed security cameras began transmitting within minutes, giving them eyes on every angle of the rusty freighter.

A Navy SEAL team entered the mouth of the harbor aboard a twin-engine center console, posing as typical boaters. Once out of sight from the target, they dropped two divers over the side. The SEALs swam beneath the surface undetected and came up alongside the Chong Gen. Each placed several sonobuoys along the length of the ship, tested them for functionality, then disappeared again under the waves. Mako could not exit the ship now, either by land or sea, without being detected.

Arthur Blade and the customs inspector finished checking the documents from all three freighters. As they walked toward the massive warehouse, Blade's phone buzzed yet again with another call from Colson. "Mako must be a precious asset to his handlers," Colson explained. "They've decided not to risk his staying aboard the ship. A rescue team is being sent tonight by sea. We have triangulation of the phone used to call in the details."

"Excellent, Don! Tell me, how many South Koreans do we have working at Langley headquarters?"

Colson thought for a moment. "Six that I know of. Why?"

"Let's arrange a crew swap. If we can track this phone to the boat they're going to use tonight, then we can capture their personnel and substitute them for ours. A few drones in the air monitoring the local marinas would give us an even bigger edge."

"I'll get back to you," Colson said, ending the call.

Mako's liberators gathered at midnight on a marina dock within Great Kills Harbor, a few miles south of the busy Jersey seaport. The crew of two Koreans and an American boat captain loaded gear and supplies into a thirty-four-foot center console, then paused near their car to take a cigarette break before casting off. One of them made another call to the phone aboard the Chong Gen, confirming the arrival time of 2:00 a.m. The plan was set.

Arthur Blade waited in a nearby utility van, along with most of the South Koreans who worked at Langley. The rescue boat head count was not available ahead of time, so they all came, ready to play whatever part needed to assist. Blade played back portions of the cell phone conversations between the North Koreans as they plotted Mako's escape. Each of the passengers in the van took a stab at imitating the voice of the man on the rescue team. Matching his inflections and timbre was the most critical part of the plan. One voice soon was proving to be the best candidate. Dak Ho, an employee from the surveillance department, rehearsed his lines as they waited.

The center console boat captain went back to his car to retrieve an extra handheld GPS unit. A pair of black-clad

SEALs appeared out of the darkness and attacked him from behind. Within seconds, the captain lay gagged and cuffed on the ground. The two North Korean crewmen crushed out their cigarettes and headed for the dock. A team of ten SEALs surrounded them, illuminating the men with the red laser sights on their weapons. With no possibility of escape, they raised their hands above their heads.

"What the hell is this?" one of them demanded in perfect English. "We've done nothing wrong."

The lieutenant stepped forward and pulled the man's cell phone from his pocket. "I'm sure you're right," he reassured them. "We're just following orders. Please come with us. It shouldn't take long." He tapped another soldier on the shoulder. "Go let the people in the van know that the boat crew is two, plus the captain."

The soldier nodded and jogged to the utility van, and knocked on the sliding door. "Two plus the American captain. We're ready to go."

Blade climbed out first. "Where is the captain now?" he asked.

The SEAL pointed to where the man was being held, and Blade walked over, eyeing the man's appearance. He took a quick photo with his phone and borrowed the man's cap. "I'll return this soon," he said, then headed over to the other two crewmen. Again, he sized them up, took photos, then walked back to the van. He opened a large case containing clothes, then displayed the photos. "Dak Ho," he said, "this is you." He pulled up the next photo and pointed to another of the van passengers. "I believe you would be the best choice." He showed them both the pictures and said, "Try to find something to wear in here that resembles your target."

They both rummaged through and picked appropriate pieces. Blade did the same to match the clothing of the boat captain. When finished, they made their way along the dock and out to the center console.

The SEAL team leader approached Blade and introduced himself. "I'm Lieutenant Kaiser," he said, handing Blade the confiscated cell phone along with an earpiece. "This is a two-way device," he said. "We'll be in contact all the way in and out. Give this phone to your crewman who is doing the talking. We'll be staying back out of sight but watching and listening." He pointed to the fiberglass top of the center console. "We also have mics and a camera up there."

Blade pushed the earpiece into his right ear and passed the phone to Dak Ho. The three of them then climbed aboard the boat. Blade gave it a once over, opening the door to the small head located forward of the helm. He looked back to the SEAL commander and said, "It will be best if we can convince Mr. Mako to stay inside here. The less contact we have with him during our short ride, the better. Please request that the Coast Guard stop us to do a routine inspection after we pick him up. He must believe he needs to remain hiding and that we are his only chance for freedom."

The commander nodded and pulled his radio to make the request.

Blade familiarized himself with the helm controls and started the twin three-hundred horsepower outboard engines, then switched on the running lights. His two-man crew stood waiting for orders. "Speak only when spoken to by either myself or Mako. The less information he garners, the better." He put his hand on both their shoulders and added, "Thank you for offering to assist this evening. There are at least fifty people watching and doing everything necessary to keep you safe." He eyed the dock lines and said, "Let's cast off."

∽

Blade directed the center console up the New Jersey coastline and into the mouth of the shipping harbor. He dropped his speed and checked the large GPS display on the helm console that was overlaid with radar data. The Chong Gen was just up ahead to the port side. Blade turned to Dak Ho and whispered, "Do not greet Mako as he comes aboard. Just tell him the Coast Guard saw us come into the channel with only three people aboard. He must remain silent and out of sight." Dak Ho nodded, then moved to the bow to watch for Mako.

Blade checked his watch. They were three minutes early as he killed the running lights and closed in on the freighter. Just ahead, he could make out its silhouette outlined by the bright spotlights of the busy shipping port.

His earpiece crackled. "Sonobuoys are picking up activity on the starboard side of the ship. Mako is in the water and swimming your way."

Blade eyed both of his crew and held his finger up to his mouth. He pulled back on the controls and slipped the engines in neutral, then let the boat drift toward the freighter. A moment later, a hand appeared on the port gunwale. A backpack was tossed up and landed in the boat. Then another hand gripped the side. Blade gave his crew members a nod, and they hefted him up and in. Mako stood, eyeing each of them. "Ammyeong, Kwang Sun," Mako said.

Dak Ho knew this was his cue, and Kwang Sun must be the name of the man he was here to impersonate. "Ammyeong, Mako," he answered in Korean, imitating the voice inflections he had heard earlier on the taped phone conversations. "Greetings can wait," he said with authority. "You must remain out of sight. The Coast Guard has already seen that there were only three of us." Dak Ho opened the door to the head and pointed. "Stay in here until we reach open water."

Mako held his glare on Dak Ho, looking for any sign of fear, a twitch, a trembling hand. There was none, as Dad Ho played his part admirably. satisfied with the man's identity, Mako bent down and opened his backpack, extracting a plastic-wrapped box and holding it out for Dak Ho. "A gift for our glorious Air Force. This is the control computer to the latest American remote-controlled drone."

Dak Ho offered a bow as he accepted the box. "I will ensure our leaders receive it soon."

Mako climbed into the small compartment and pulled the door closed behind him.

Blade turned on the running lights, slipped the engines into gear, and turned the boat back the way they had come.

They had just reached the mouth of the harbor when a Coast Guard patrol boat appeared from the darkness and sounded a blip on its siren. A moment later, flashing blue and white strobing lights lit up the night sky. Blade slid the control back to neutral and shut down the engines, waiting to be boarded. It was all for show, but critical that Mako believed every bit. Two of the officers threw lines to Blade and Dak Ho that they secured to the forward and aft cleats. A third officer asked for identification and questioned why they were cruising an active seaport in the dead of night.

"My fault," Blade said, playing along. "New boat, trying to show it off to my friends. I hope we didn't break any laws."

"Observe the no-wake law until you reach the outer buoy," the officer instructed as they let go of the lines. They drifted apart until they were a safe distance away, then the Coast Guard boat opened up its engines and sped away.

Everyone remained silent as they idled the boat past the outer buoy, then turned east to open water and went full throttle. The sleek center console jumped up on top of the surface and cut through the three-foot swells at 50 mph. Blade kept the boat on a straight course out to sea. Fifteen minutes later, he cut the engines, instructed his other two passengers to sit at the bow, then knocked on the door to the head. Mako cautiously opened the door and peered out.

"Why have we stopped?" he asked. "Is there another boat coming out to meet us here?"

"No boat. But I'm afraid this is where we part company," Blade said, stepping forward, the stainless steel slide of his Kimber 1911 pistol glistening in the moonlight.

Mako's jaw dropped. "You! Now I remember. It was you that night that went over the side into the English Channel." He stared a moment, connecting the mental dots. A slight grin appeared as he understood. "Then it's true. Arthur Blade, version two, and one hell of a swimmer!"

Blade grinned. "And now I can return the favor."

Mako shook his head, the grin turning to a full smile. "I would love to see Winchell's face when he realizes how wrong he was about you." He imitated Winchell, saying, "Trust me on this, I have a gut feeling." Mako laughed out loud. "The man is a fool. And now look at you, Mr. Blade, all that knowledge and experience repackaged into a body less than half your age. I can only imagine the perks that come with that combination."

"I want an answer," Blade demanded. "Why did the girl have to die on the train? She was not important enough to warrant a death sentence. What sort of sadistic animal kills for pleasure?"

Mako shook his head, wagging a finger. "You, of all people, should understand, Mr. Blade. A watertight plan requires a ship free of holes. She would have been a leak."

"And Winchell approved of such draconian measures?"

Mako crossed his arms and flashed a grin. "Let's just say I'm very good at following orders."

"What was the actual target that day?" Blade asked. "We both know the computer hacking exchange was just a ruse."

Mako took a step forward, nodding. "You must have suspected. The target was you. Winchell wanted you out of the way. Only, you just couldn't die like a normal, sick old man, could you? People still want you gone, Blade. I don't think there's a street you can walk down without someone watching you through a rifle scope. Other countries want you dead. Your own country wants you dead. You should just hand me your weapon and climb over the side. That way, you die on your own terms."

"Another time, perhaps. This night is about you."

Mako started taking another step toward him, but Blade fired, grazing his shoulder.

"Now there will be blood in the water," Blade said. "That's an open invitation to unwelcome company. I don't know how fast you can move in the water, but I've never heard of anyone out-swimming a hungry shark." He motioned toward the open ocean. "I'm giving you the same send-off that you gave me. Land is about thirteen miles away. Just head toward the lights. I believe I covered the same distance in about six hours."

Mako shook his head. "You can't do this. I refuse to get off this boat."

"You're right. I can't force you to climb over the side. But you're going in either of your own volition or with a few holes in your abdomen. I don't care, but it is time to choose." Blade held the pistol outstretched, the barrel fixed on the man's midsection. "Goodbye, Mr. Mako. I seem to have caught you at a loss for words. Might I suggest one? Checkmate—"

Mako prided himself on reading people's intentions through their eyes. He wanted to believe that Blade was bluffing. Everything he knew of the man told him his actions tonight were out of character. He couldn't possibly follow through with such a threat, could he? But the man standing before him was not the same elderly, frail spymaster he had heard about. There was contempt in these eyes. A sort of purposeful pleading for Mako to challenge him. To stand his ground and give Blade the excuse he needed to pull that trigger. That shooting him here and now was what he preferred. He stared into those eyes again, looking for any sign of wavering. There was none. This man was going to kill him. With that realization, he stopped looking for the logic of the moment and jumped into action. He leaped over the side milliseconds before Blade again pulled the trigger, the bullet missing him by mere inches.

Mako heard the roaring boom of the pistol as he flew over the side and plunged deep beneath the waves. A moment later, he listened as the engines fired up. The boat surged forward and made a big loop around him before heading back toward land. Mako bobbed back to the surface and watched as the running lights grew smaller. He still could not believe what had just happened. None of this should have been possible. Blade was supposed to be dead. He should never have made it to shore that night. And now Mako was in the same position he'd left Blade those few months ago. He wondered about his chances of survival. His confidence felt like it was being chipped away each time the man's last word echoed back through his head: checkmate.

The ocean swells had grown taller, and he calculated his rise and fall at five feet. One moment, the glimmering shoreline was in sight. The next, a rolling wall of black water obscured it. No matter, he knew what he had to do. He fixed his bearings on the line of light and began swimming in that direction. After all, he'd been an alternate on the North Korean Olympic swim team. He could do this, couldn't he? Couldn't he?

The boat traveled a few miles further toward land before Blade backed off the throttles and held it at a steady idle. "Kaiser," he called out.

"Kaiser here," came the response in Blade's earpiece.

"He's all yours," Blade told him. "Use our last position as the drop-off spot. Oh, and I recommend you let him work off some of his energy with a nice long swim. He'll be much easier to handle afterward."

"Copy that," Kaiser acknowledged, "standing by."

"Thank you for your help, Lieutenant. Heading back to port. Over and out."

Twenty-Eight
A Second Beginning

Arthur Blade and Audrey Landers sat huddled together before a fire pit on the back deck of Audrey's condominium. A new dawn was just breaking over the horizon, turning the entire sky a glowing warm orange.

Two days had passed since the capture of Mako, and they spent the previous evening celebrating their victory with the small group of people who helped make it happen. The last of their guests had headed home at eleven, and Blade silenced his phone at midnight. They toasted the moment, then nestled close to each other, watching as the flames flickered in the peaceful silence.

"I don't know whether to start the new day or end the last one," Audrey said, shifting a blanket over her shoulder.

Blade kissed her forehead. "I suspect someone will make that decision for us, and all too soon."

"You had a long phone conversation with the president. What did Walter have to say?"

"To offer his congratulations, of course. But he also asked some important questions."

"Such as?"

"He asked me if I still believed Don Colson to be the best choice for CIA director. Nothing shapes a man's mettle more than fighting back from the throes of failure. I believe that some of life's most valuable lessons come from our mistakes. Colson is a good man, and he will be even more vigilant in his duties because of the setbacks we faced and overcame."

"I could see the respect you have for Colson," she said, snuggling closer. "I'm glad he could visit last night. The two of you didn't seem to talk much business."

"Audrey, your talents of observation are as keen as the best of spies. We talked briefly about these latest operations. He showed me a message that Vladimir Folozchev attempted to send from the hospital. He conned a nurse into lending him her phone. She was one of ours, of course. We were hoping he would contact his people and get us back on the trail of his deep-cover cell. Hopefully, that would lead us to the whereabouts of Winchell. All we had from him was that last phone number, 9099, and were waiting for it to be used." Blade pulled out his phone and showed Audrey Folozchev's intercepted message: "It is your father. I am in hospital, but well. Please send regards to Uncle John. Look forward to speak soon. I hope you still read book I send you. I most like page 324."

"Just what does that mean?" she asked.

"We don't know all of it yet. Uncle John would be John Winchell, which would indicate he is being kept alive after all. Folozchev used book pages to encrypt his messages. We hope he sends more."

"Colson also informed me that Mako is now being held at Kings Bay, Georgia. It's doubtful we will extract any useful intelligence from him. I hate to see it, but his true value will be in exchanging him for one of our captured assets in North Korea."

"That means you may face him again, doesn't it?"

Blade nodded. "Mako is a formidable opponent. But as with Colson, I've learned from my mistakes. If the day comes and we square off again, he will not get the better of me."

"Logan and Piper seemed happy to be back working together again. Jill tells me that Garret's physical therapy is coming along great. They expect he'll be able to jog soon."

"I've never worked with a finer team," Blade admitted. "I'm looking forward to better days ahead for us all. And speaking of a great team, Gavriik Federov is already proving his worth. I was told that he pointed out an unseen vulnerability in our own system. We had a crack in our firewall, and the Russians had been chipping away. It was just a matter of time before they gained full access. Our young friend is teaching the teachers. In time, he will give us an edge we have never enjoyed."

"He's a good kid," Audrey added. "He just needed to be set on the right course. I think you've done that for him."

"I agree. He has a brilliant career awaiting him."

"What else did the President have to say?"

"He wanted me to think about accepting a new role. Now that I'm invisible, so to speak, he thinks I would be more valuable back in the field. I told him I would give it some thought."

She rested her head on his chest. "Everything has been coming so fast. We've had no time to question what we're doing. Now that we can catch our breath, I am mentally and emotionally exhausted." She looked up into his eyes. "Arthur, are you and I doing the right thing? With all that's happened, we must ask ourselves if we are meant to be together. Is this best for both of us?"

Blade stroked her hair. "I let you slip away from me once before and regretted it for years. You stood by me, waiting to see if I would come to my senses. I was reluctant because you had so much more life ahead of you than I. It would have been unfair to chain you to that old shell of a man I had become. That's all changed now."

"Yes, it's changed. But the tables have turned, not equalized. Now we have the exact opposite situation. The gap between our ages has grown even wider. Arthur, you're now the young man, and I'm an old woman."

Blade smiled, shaking his head. "I am not a day younger. But it has given me a second chance to spend my life with the most beautiful, the most wonderful woman I have ever met. Only a fool would allow you to slip away again."

"Are you sure that you won't feel differently in a few years? Arthur, I must know that you will still want me after time deepens the wrinkles and takes away the image of me you see today."

Blade pushed a strand of hair from her cheek and kissed her lips. "I'm not asking you to trust me, dear girl. I'm asking you to let me show you. And I will do so every day you allow me to be part of your life. Give me two years, give me twenty, but allow me to be by your side. I love you, Audrey. I have for years. Only now can I pledge myself to you. Now that I have something to offer that is equal to what you have always given me. I've been fortunate to be endowed with this upgrade. It has allowed me to have that which I've desired all along."

Audrey smiled slyly. "Endowed is a rather subtle way of putting it. I can think of many more descriptive terms for your new equipment."

"Why, Audrey Landers, you're making an old man blush."

Audrey stood and took Blade's hand. "Come, let me show what else I can do, old man...."

Epilogue
THREE MONTHS LATER

John Winchell crept through the shadows of the dark, tree-lined street toward the safety of his townhouse, glancing back every few steps to ensure he wasn't leaving a blood trail for his former captors to follow.

Not much further, he reassured himself, before he could tend to the wounds that pulsated with unimagined pain. He crouched behind a tall oak to catch his breath and examine his hands, blotting them on his blood-stained shirt. He once debriefed an agent who endured the same torture of having every fingernail extracted by enemy interrogators. Winchell had discounted the man's description of the excruciating pain, thinking that nothing could be as bad as he claimed. Now he knew.

A few blocks up ahead, he spied the front door of his destination, and he fought the urge to break out in a run. The comfort he found there would be temporary. Right now, that's all he required. Inside his home was everything he needed to regroup, recharge, and continue his exodus; weapons, cash, and meds, all hidden beneath the floor panels.

He would require less than an hour to clean up, medicate, bandage his hands, and be out the door.

Pausing across the street less than a block away, he scanned the area for activity. He'd escaped from his Russian captors just two hours earlier. Could they already be here waiting for him? He examined the line of parked cars to ensure that no one was sitting inside any of them. It didn't mean they weren't here. He grimaced from another jolt of pain as he forced himself to wait and watch a few moments longer. He took a deep breath and looked down, noticing his shoes and pant legs covered in red droplets.

There was no motion anywhere on the quiet residential DC street.

He continued toward his destination, flitting behind trees and parked vehicles. Two doors from his unit, he stopped to pick up the spare key he had secured beneath a flower pot at a neighbor's house. He remained in the shadows another moment before stepping out and climbing his steps, struggling to appear composed.

He unlocked the door and slipped inside, setting the deadbolt while watching for motion through the spyglass. Once satisfied that no one followed him, he turned and headed for the master bath with thoughts of a hot shower and a quick meal already warming him.

The living room lights suddenly lit like blinding spotlights. He froze in place, shielding his eyes with his hand as he squinted to adjust to the harsh brightness. As his pupils contracted, the silhouette of a man sitting in his favorite chair resolved into focus.

"You've looked better, John," a smooth, controlled voice called out. "I guess this means your new relationship with the SVR didn't go as planned."

All hope that had been building for the last two hours since escaping his captors was dashed as he recognized the voice, not so much by its tone but by the refined inflections and mannerisms of the CIA spymaster. How he reviled this man!

"Arthur Blade. I was so hoping I'd seen the last of you."

"It wasn't for lack of trying. You gave it your best effort to have me killed more than once."

Winchell scoffed. "That's a lie. You have no proof."

"I should have expected nothing less from you, John. But under the circumstances, I thought you'd have learned a lesson or two and been more willing to cooperate." Blade looked about the room. "Not much of a decorator, are you? Even white-walled rooms can appear warm and lived-in with a few wall hangings. You share your lack of taste with your former agent, Mako. Both of your residences display all the life of a sterile petri dish."

"I heard you returned the favor to him for taking you on that one-way boat ride. You dropped him at sea and let him drown. Has his body washed up on shore yet?"

Blade's brows raised. "One shouldn't believe everything one hears. Who knows? Maybe you'll run into each other in some prison yard."

"In that case, I hope he's dead. He wouldn't hesitate to kill me."

"Speaking of killing, did you know you were mere hours from being rescued? Your heroic escape, although impressive, was unnecessary. We've had that building under surveillance for the last three days. You just beat us to the quick by a few minutes. But good for you. It's rewarding to work toward a goal, isn't it?"

"You son of a bitch!" Winchell took a step toward Blade. "You knew I was being held against my will and tortured by the Russians, and you allowed it to happen? That was sadistic, even by your twisted standards."

Arthur Blade shook his head, folding his arms into his lap.

"Seriously, John, you seem to have developed a short-term memory issue. After all, it was you who attempted to defect to the other side with every intelligence secret you could lay your hands on. I must admit, it took some time to pick up the trail and locate their base of operations once you disappeared. But we've been able to monitor their motions and extract some very useful intel."

"Monitor them how?"

"John! You *did* work for the CIA, remember? We've been monitoring all communications going in and out and, of course."

Winchell stiffened. "And?"

Blade smiled. "It was commendable of you to keep your most valuable secrets until they extracted the last few of your fingernails. But let's be fair. The information you withheld the longest was what you hoped would make you an asset to the enemy. It was interesting to listen to your reasoning as you struggled to make a deal even as they pulled out the last nail. Quite a painful business, I'm told. In the end, you had nothing left to offer them and had become just another liability requiring disposal."

Blade crossed his legs and flattened a wrinkle on his trousers. "I know we've had our rows and disagreements, but it still surprised me how willingly you gave up all the information concerning our agents in the field and the details of my medical procedure."

Winchell gave a disgusted sneer. "You mean your brain transplant and rise from the dead? You should have been thrown in a hole and buried last year. What new identity have you slithered into now? I guess it makes sense you can't keep going by the name of a dead man, especially one twice the age you now appear. You were old, Arthur. Old and sick. It would be best if you let nature take its course. What you are now is... an abomination. Your Seventy-two-year-old brain in the body of a dead Navy SEAL is some sick doctor's idea of playing God. You are now living proof that just because science can make something possible does not mean they should pursue it."

Blade nodded. "In truth, John, I would not have disagreed with you. I was ready to accept my fate. One would think that forty-plus years in the CIA, twenty of them as field director, would have been enough. I was tired and had always given everything asked of me. However, the president's request that I undergo the procedure to extend my life was strongly worded. They kept me alive for the volumes of details that only I knew and for what I could yet offer my country. Under those circumstances, I felt compelled to comply. And unlike you, John, I will always give everything to defend the country I love."

Blade rose from his chair, his imposing six-foot muscled warrior's body filling Winchell's periphery. "Well, I think that's enough small talk for now, don't you? I would be most appreciative if you would set your knife and the pistol you took from the interrogator you killed on the floor and step away."

John Winchell pulled the pistol from his waistband in the small of his back and aimed it at Blade, his fingers smearing the weapon with blood. "I think it's time to kill that old brain of yours once and for all."

Blade closed his eyes, shaking his head. "I gave you the benefit of the doubt, John. I want you to remember that."

A powerful force crashed down upon Winchell's arm, nearly breaking his bones. The pistol flew from his hand and slid across the floor. Blade bent down to pick it up as Winchell then felt the cold steel of a gun muzzle pressed against the side of his neck. Someone pulled his arms from behind and shackled his wrists.

"Sorry, old boy, but you did bring this on yourself," Blade

said, walking toward him. "I don't believe you have any secrets left to offer us, so it's off to prison for you. You're guilty of espionage, treason, and murder of two people on that botched mission in England."

"That wasn't my doing. Now you're just throwing spit wads at the wall to see what will stick."

"I don't know why I continue to think you're smarter than this, John, because you just keep proving me wrong. Director Colson assigned you that mission, and every miscalculated detail of it was yours from start to finish. You had other plans and used the software hacking of a car company as the cover to get me out in the open and take me down. The ransom exchange was all your handiwork. The place, the time, all you doing. And then you sent your subordinates in with orders to kill the software hacker and an innocent actress making the exchange. But what do you know? One of your agents grew a conscience. Remember your man, Fossie? He's back on the home team and is working with us to fill in the missing gaps."

Winchell's scowl deepened.

"We know your entire plan and that it was you who ordered me dropped off in the middle of the English Channel. Who would have expected I could survive a twelve-mile swim in frigid water? Not me. But then, how could I know that this new body of mine was built to be a marathon swimmer? Quite the stroke of luck, wouldn't you say?"

"You're a freak, Blade," Winchell seethed. "A freak of nature that shouldn't be drawing breath."

"So says the man who conspired against his country and co-workers for monetary gain and an office with a view. Now, let's see. Have I forgotten anything? Oh yes, the ransom money that you divided between yourself and your crew? We've recovered it all. Including what you had hidden beneath the floor under your bed. Clever, but not clever enough. Oh, and John..."

Winchell looked back with scalding eyes as he was being led away.

"Normally, when the CIA incarcerates an adversary, there is some tit for tat. An exchange of secrets in exchange for a lighter sentence, privileges, that sort of thing. In your case, old man, you have nothing to offer. Therefore, neither have we. Your time behind bars will be long and brutal. My advice? Take a good long look at the sunrise this morning. It's likely the last one you'll see for some time."

END

Acknowledgments

I've been very fortunate to find a group of discerning readers willing to invest their time in proofreading the works of a new author. My beta team members have offered input, editing advice, and, most importantly, their support.

Thanks to; Marjorie Allen Britt, Cindy Allen, Tim Apel, Scott Goemmel, Mark Giersch, Jesse Roberts, and, of course, my wife and first reader, Johanne.

This marks the first time I've incorporated the experiences of a friend into a story character. The life adventures of Lou Azzilonna of the New York Police Department gave me the inspiration to create 'Azzy' for this and future Arthur Blade novels. It was a great experience picking his brain.

Thanks again to all the members in Michigan of the Grand Blanc Writer's Group, who have been a sounding board for many of my projects.

Since relocating to Southwest Florida, I've now connected with the Gulf Coast Writers Association and the Florida Writers Association. I'm grateful for their support.

Sometimes, just sometimes, we are rewarded for our curiosity when listening to a new artist or picking up a new book. I hope this is one of those moments for everyone who invested the time to read this book and that the story entertained you enough to consider spending more time with me.

Thank you for reading and joining me on this great journey, and until next time... Richard

About the Author

Richard Drummer is a lifelong musician and songwriter who has now transitioned into a successful novelist. He spent many years traveling across the country performing one-night shows but eventually found himself drawn to writing as a means of fulfilling his creative aspirations. He now writes full-time with the support of his wife and first reader, Johanne, and the welcome distractions from his furry companion, Caticus Maximus. When he's not busy crafting his next storyline he can sometimes be found entertaining audiences near his new residence in Naples, Florida. Just keep an eye out for the long-haired, left-handed, barefoot drummer.

THE SECOND LIFE OF ARTHUR BLADE is Richard's third novel, and he has begun the sequel, as well as penning multiple short stories, some of which appear on his website at; RichardDrummerAuthor.com

Made in the USA
Columbia, SC
31 March 2024